The Sky Ranch Flying Society

A Novel
Written and Illustrated
by

DAN KRAUSHAAR

Although parts of this book are based on real events, this is a work of fiction. Characters, companies, and organizations in the novel are either the product of the author's imagination or, if real, used fictiously with out any intent to describe their actual conduct.

For information contact:
RW Books, 6007 Crisp Lane, Knoxville TN 37920
SkyRanchFlyingSociety.com

ISBN 0-89826-104-x

R W BOOKS • KNOXVILLE TN

PRINTED IN THE UNITED STATES OF AMERICA

Thanks:

To the many friends who have encouraged me to keep at this labor, my heartfelt thanks. To Gran Rose who, at ninety plus, continues to teach everyone *reading is the basic skill*. You continue to amaze us all with your energy and dedication. To Sharon who has believed in me for over forty years and who made many large contributions to the book, I love you. If there are grammatical errors here and there in the book it is probably because I made changes after she corrected the original mistakes.

Born into a large southern West Virginia family of master story tellers, Dan Kraushaar wrapped his first two stints at the University of Tennessee around a three-year tour of duty in the U.S. Army. The second stint got him his Bachelor's degree and a South Knoxville girl born and bred. Kraushaar later earned a Master's degree, because teaching school paid better with more education. It also allowed him to move to the Knoxville City Schools central office which paid even more (but still not much). He's now retired from the world of public education and enjoying the pursuit of varied interests including, but not limited to, flying, playing the piano, and doing a little writing — all on his own time.

THE GREAT POOL POLLUTION CAPER

There was a pretty good crowd sitting on the clubhouse porch taking some sun and coffee in about equal doses, when I rolled into the parking lot. Big Charley was in his usual spot by the door along with Big Bill Henry, the Wanger, Father Gene, and several others.

I had just settled into an open chair with a cup of coffee when C. Grover Cleveland came walking up from his hangar and said to me in a tone as if he were interrogating a prisoner of war, "Where were you last Wednesday night"?

"Miss Shay and I were in Charleston doing some shopping. Why? Do you want to make a donation to help offset some of the cost of my trip?" Cleveland replied, "No, I just wanted to know where the hell you were." "Grover, Grover, Grover, Charleston is in South Carolina, not in hell, you are mixed up in your geography. Here read this motel bill for the night in question in Charleston SC. If you read it out loud to the group here, it will help you remember." Cleveland handed the invoice back to me and headed for his Bentley and left in a cloud of dust.

Most of the folks on the porch went out to inspect an airplane that had just arrived and Big Bill Henry and I sat down at the big table in the clubhouse. I asked Bill, "What's wrong with the Warthog? That was even lower than his usual standard of behavior." Bill said, "You were on his list as someone to blame for 'the great pool pollution caper'. He hasn't been able to find many of the likely suspects, so he thought maybe you did it." I asked, "What in the world is the great pool pollution caper?" So Bill tells me the tale.

It seems that some person, or possibly persons, borrowed a big loaded honey wagon off of Buford Bailey's lot and drove it out to Shang High Hills on Wednesday night and put the whole load into the Warthog's swimming pool.

I had a good chuckle and asked, "Do we know if the Warthog went for his usual swim on Thursday morning?" Bill said, "Yes we have absolute proof that he did." "Proof?" I asked. "Yes, it turns out that Billy Bob Wanger had set up his video camera for a good look at Willow's diving practice scheduled for a little later in the day but he screwed up the program scheduler so the camera came on two hours early. It's just a damn shame we don't have sound."

"Bill," I asked, "do you know who drove the truck over there and made a deposit in the pool?" Bill said, "No, but someone had to drive the damn thing because they don't put auto pilots on honey wagons. I hope we can find out who it was so we can give the son of a bitch a goddamn medal; but, to answer your question, no I don't have a clue."

Later in the day Small Sam looked in on me and asked, "Dapper do you have time for some coffee?"

I said that I needed a break because I had been working for at least twenty minutes and that was my new limit. Sam said, "Sounds like a union man to me."

I asked Sam if he had seen the video tape of the Warthog going into the pool. He said that he had not seen the video but that he had talked to some of Captain Tom's students who had been in the clubhouse about ten o'clock when the Warthog came running in wanting to know where Wanger, Coyote, Henry, Long, or Kurlee were.

"He asked Swifty's boy, Sandy Flynn, and Sandy said that he didn't know all of those folks, but he had seen Mr. Kurlee the other day. The kid said that he asked Mr. Cleveland what had happened to his skin because it looked very red. The Warthog told him that he had been exposed to some dangerous chemicals and he was getting a reaction to some of the medicated lotion that he was using."

DADDY AND WARTHOG

C. Grover "Warthog" Cleveland is the only son of the late C. G. "Pretty Boy" Cleveland who made his fortune bootlegging whiskey into the city back before Knoxville went wet. Pretty Boy had drive-through whiskey stores long before the fad hit the hamburger market. He also had a delivery service long before the pizza folks figured it out. His City Service Cab Company invented the term "full service". They delivered all kinds of whiskey, ladies of the evening or afternoon, took bets, and on a slow day would even haul ordinary folks from place to place.

Pretty Boy, as his moniker suggests, was a dandy. He dressed sharply, drove the latest model Chrysler and, according to everyone who knew him, was fun to be around. The real old time Sky Ranchers all knew him because he flew in special orders of booze in an old Piper airplane. I haven't heard anyone mention anything about his wife.

C.G. Cleveland, the son, did not receive the genes that allow you to keep all your hair after age thirty, although he tries mightily to hide the fact by combing what little he has left over the top of his dome and using copious amounts of hair spray. He is short in stature, but, as Big Bill Henry says, he makes up for it by having a poor personality.

Part of the guy's problem is that he has always had a lot of money and there are folks out there who try to take advantage of him. Most of them find out that he is not short in the art of making and keeping a buck even if he does not have all the social skills that they do. As soon as he found out that I truly didn't want to try to take advantage of our relationship to get at his money, we have gotten along pretty well. Money has not been one of my major goals and that is fortunate considering my chosen profession.

A DAY AT THE OFFICE

I unlocked the gate, drove around the edge of the airstrip, opened the clubhouse, started the coffee pot, and the Sky Ranch Flying Society was open for business.

The road into the island is a pretty tough obstacle course with a 180 degree turn to get off the main highway, and then a 90 degree turn down the hill passing over a grade crossing of the main line of the CSX railroad. Then, if you didn't hang anything on the tracks, you cross a culvert, pass through a steel gate and you are on the Sky Ranch, the "Promised Land" of the pilots of the Sky Ranch Flying Society. The gravel road takes a turn and follows the runway up the island, and around the end of the strip to the parking lot at the clubhouse.

There are two plate glass windows in the front wall flanking the door and one window on each side wall of our 15x30 concrete block building. Some of the window panes have a large diagonal scratch from corner to corner left there by a member who did not want to leave anything of value for the city when they were planning to close the airport and turn it into a water treatment plant in the early 70's.

In the spring we have to keep the door open so the flying ants can get out to bother someone else. We have a bug service man who comes around to spray the place and so far the roof hasn't fallen in, but I think we are most likely living on borrowed time.

In the summer the porch is one of the favorite places for the faithful to gather to spin yarns and offer opinions about almost any topic you can name. We all have our opinions and it is not unusual to have three Sky Ranchers and four opinions.

I'm Dapper Kurlee, retired educator, working musician, proud owner of Cessna 02U and keeper of the books. My office in the clubhouse is in a converted closet which is about 8' by 5', and most of the space is taken up by a built-in table held up by two-drawer filing cabinets with a computer and a printer on the top.

The club books are kept with the help and hindrance of an ancient computer program which was written by a company who went out of business several generations back. We don't have the source code, so changes in the program are not going to happen. Since I retired from the school system and supposedly have more time, I may get around to writing a new program, but so far I have managed not to.

Many of us belong to a number of organizations for reasons that we may not have a good grip on all of the time. Some of the groups that I have belonged to over the years were professional organizations in crafts, education and music. I also belonged to some quasi-civic outfits.

Some of the civic groups should be called sales representative clubs as all of the members seem to be salesmen trying to sell each other something. My wise buddy Jerry use to say that some of the companies encourage their men to wear a company badge so they won't waste time trying to sell to each other. The social club I belong to however, has a much higher purpose.

At one time I belonged to the National Education Association, the Tennessee Education Association, and the Knox County Education Association in the misguided belief that if I needed help fighting the guys in the black hats they would be there to protect and serve the down-trodden. Boy was that a joke. The thing that they were best at was writing press releases about how overworked they were.

The only efficient part of their operation turns out to be the section that collects dues. The combined take for the three groups was over $500 per year. After I found out what they were really good for, I decided I would spend that little pile on wine, women, and song, and if there was anything left over I'd just waste it.

The Sky Ranch Flying Society that I keep the books for is dedicated to promoting grass roots aviation, providing an island sanctuary from the world of trivia, and enjoying good company.

This group of about two hundred and thirty souls gets together on an irregular basis and argues about the best way to operate the organization. I have some problem using the word organization, but we do try. The club owns five airplanes, an island in the Tennessee River known as the Sky Ranch, various hangars, and an antique tractor collection with which to mow a whole lot of grass.

There are several not entirely distinct divisions of the club. First there are the renters who depend on the club to provide them with a choice of three different types of planes to rent and fly. If asked by either the Tennessee Department of Sales Tax or their wives, the members will tell you that the flying that they are doing is required by the FAA (Federal Aviation Authority) to meet training and proficiency requirements. Uncle FAA keeps telling us that he is here to help us and sometimes, due to the vast array of impedimenta which the agency calls regulation, they may actually have helped a little, although it would be accidental.

The owners group has either a whole airplane or a portion depending on whether they have partners or not. They fly anything from Cubs to twins and prefer to be at the Sky Ranch because they can enjoy a little more freedom for owner maintenance and the general atmosphere. There are also the porch pilots and the Knife and Ford divisions, but I'll get to them as we go along. We also have a few folks who just hang around because they like the company

OWNERS DIVISION

The owners division provides a yin to the renters yang. The owners group is as rich in diversity as the renters. One owner has four birds to pick from on any given day, whereas another owner may be part of a partnership where as many as four guys have a plane. The planes vary in age, complexity, speed, and type - just as their owners do. If you infer from this that some of our owners are not too swift, just remember they own and fly their very own *airplane*, do you?

Big Bill Henry owns one-third of a 1948 model Navion painted a bright canary yellow. The other partners in the airplane are Small Sam Long and Sgt. Oskar Yenderushak, aka "the Mad Flaming Russian". The big yellow bird enjoyed a short production run after the war when all of the aircraft manufacturers were predicting an airplane in everyone's future.

A couple of other groups tried to keep production going but could not do so despite the fact that it had some mustang-like qualities. Bill is the immediate past chief mechanic for the club and an FAA licensed tech inspector. Now he just works on his own birds and for a few of his close friends and coconspirators.

One room in Bill's house is set aside for a different kind of bird. He has about a dozen assorted talking, squawking, feathered friends. His wife Beulah says it's like being in a zoo when the sun comes up.

Bill must like the color yellow. He built himself an experimental biplane at the Sky Ranch. The resulting beauty, a bright yellow biplane, was featured on the TV show "The Heartland Series." Shortly after his TV work, he had engine failure on take-off one day and had to put it in the lake at the south end of our island. The airplane was destroyed and Big Bill got some bad back injuries out of the crash. Big Bill also owns a 1948 Champ, N574, which in years past belonged to me. It was also yellow.

There is an interesting group of folks who are in partnership on another old Champ. Some of them actually fly the bird but others in the group just come out occasionally to have their picture made with some friend of theirs standing next to the airplane. According to conversations I have heard there is always something wrong with the either the pilot's health or the mechanical health of the airplane. The other partners are happy to keep them on the books because in the world of high and advanced mathematics, the larger the number you divide by, the smaller the answer.

In this group there are members of the Protestant, Catholic, Greek Orthodox, and Jewish faiths, and one I'm not sure about. There is a bricklayer, a used car salesman, a university professor, an orthopedic surgeon, a lawyer, and a security guard from Oak Ridge in the group. They must have some interesting airplane meetings.

Like most other groups a couple of them do all the work and the rest complain about the way it was done. One of the worker bees was sitting on the porch resting the other day and mentioned that he was tired of people who would not put their shoulder to the wheel but always want to dictate how it turned. Big Charley added, "The one that shovels the coal in the engine is the only one who should get to blow the whistle, but it very seldom works out that way."

Big Bill Henry came wandering up to the clubhouse and asked if we had heard that the Red-tailed Hawk clan was breaking up. Now the Red-tail Hawk clan is a group of four guys who are partners in a C-172 of about the same vintage as 02U. I once wrote a newsletter item about this bunch and the name has stuck ever since.

THE SKY RANCH AIR MAIL
AIRCRAFT ANNUAL INSPECTION TIME (dapper)

The Red-tailed Hawk People, Rex, Joe, Bill, and Paul, are at that happy time of year for airplane owners when the big aircraft annual inspection is taking place. You may think that those of us who have airplanes actually own them, NOT.

Regardless of what the registration says, we only made a down payment on the bird and each year at the annual we get to make another payment. This is in addition to the insurance premium which, if you are careful, falls at another time in the year.

The Hawk People were well into the inspection, sometimes called reverse roulette, when I arrived to watch the proceedings. There were the usual small things which you always find like stuck pulley wheels, dirty belly, and so forth, but the real sweaty part starts when you see the head croupier or mechanic pull out the compression gauge. You know that is where a bad spin on the wheel of luck can spell valve job or top overhaul, either of which can translate into a high dollar day.

The compression wheel was pretty tough on the Red-tailed Hawk Clan this year, so if you see any of them walking with a list to one side, it's because their wallet is suddenly so light on one side that their back won't stay straight.

In case this epistle should fall into the hands of a personal money manager, spell that spouse, all of the above is written in jest. Airplanes are a wonderful investment which will only appreciate over the long term and our resident SHRINK assures me that the achievement of good mental health can be traced directly to being a pilot and a member of the Sky Ranch Flying Society.

The best advice I can give you about flying and airplane expenses is to pay cash when you can so you can forget it as soon as possible; and never, under any circumstance, get out your trusty #2 pencil and calculate how much per hour it cost you to fly. You really don't want to know. What you want to do is stay healthy and keep ego and id and all of those parts in the proper place.

Next week I get to spin the wheel, 02U is due for her annual.

CHEAPSKATE

There was a note on the door to call Big Bill and I thought I knew what it was about. I had mailed the Sky Ranch Air Mail, the club newsletter, just before we left town. It contained a story about him.

THE SKY RANCH AIR MAIL
12/94
CHEAPSKATE (dapper)

Big Bill Henry wanted to fly ever since he saw his first airplane up close and personal as they say. Bill learned early on that flying is an expensive habit and started looking for ways to cut down on the expense.

He first got his A&P, an aircraft mechanics license, so he wouldn't have to pay someone else to work on his and Beulah's airplanes. Later when he wanted a biplane that had more zip, rather than fork over the cold cash Bill built one from scratch from a set of plans that he probably traded from some poor unsuspecting soul.

Bill's yellow experimental biplane that he built himself on the Sky Ranch was always a featured performer at all regional fly ins.

Bill got to counting up how much money he was spending on gasoline and depreciation on his truck driving back and forth to the airport and decided to he would just buy a house trailer and park it next to the hangar at the Club. He once admitted it also saved him money because he could walk home for lunch and not need to go out to the Duck Inn or some other well known high dollar restaurant.

Bill must figure that he doesn't have too much time left now because he started hanging around over where his wife Beulah works, talking poor mouth and looking pitiful until they finally offered him a job. He has always wanted to do everything for himself and it will be real interesting to see how this turns out because Beulah works at the largest and oldest establishment of its kind in South Knoxville, the Beaty Funeral Home.

I'm not real sure what he does around there, but I figure it's more like fetching flowers, toting chairs, and carrying coffins rather than holding the grieving rich young widow's hand during her time of need.

There's a couple of things that I'm sure that you can't do, be your own grandpa and conduct your own funeral, but maybe Beulah will at least get an employee discount when the time comes.

I gave Bill a call and he had seen the document in question and wanted to know if I had any ideas on how to impress the management at the funeral home so that he could do some of the rich young widow hand-holding that was talked about in print.

He said he had a big parrot with the dribbling runs and needed something to put in the bottom of the cage so my newsletter would not go to waste, but that it might be covered with waste. He also said he would be by later and we could go to lunch at the Duck Inn at around 12:30.

THE FIFTY FIVE FORD

Willy Clyde Coyote and Billy Bob Wanger have been after each other for years. No one remembers how the contest got started but there have been some great chapters in that book. The most recent bout is about a pickup truck.

The Coyote's loving accolades for his restored '55 model Ford pickup truck, including endless references to his log of gas purchased versus miles driven, finally drove Billy Bob to a scheme which included making a wager that he could improve the mileage figures.

The $100 bet was if the Coyote would start using a secret additive, supplied by Billy Bob, the miles per hour number would rise by at least five miles per gallon. The participants shook hands and the bet was on. They agreed that they would meet on Saturday at the clubhouse to start the test.

Billy Bob showed up at the air strip the next Saturday with five plain pint bottles with some kind of deep blue liquid in them. One of the bottles was emptied into the tank and the tank was topped off from a five gallon can that was in the back of the truck.

This bunch always has a gas can in the truck to use in gas engines of one sort or another. If there is a machine that moves by any means or just sits there and makes noise, there is someone in this club that has one or at least has access to one.

They parked the truck in Billy Bob's hangar and rolled out his pride and joy, a 1948 Aeronca Chief. The boys did a quick preflight and headed down to Athens to see a man who had an antique gas engine that had once been used to run a threshing machine.

The porch pilots then started to discuss the probability of the success of the fuel additive and very soon after that the idea of further wagers became a reality. Oskar Yenderushak, a retired regular army type, announced he would make book and cover all bets as usual. It was soon apparent that most of the money was with Billy Bob that the miles per hour would increase by more that five miles per gallon.

The results of the first two tanks of gas were posted at the club and the additive was indeed making a difference of right around the five mile figure. Interest was running high and Oskar had some more action on the bookmaking front and started to complain that the odds had to be changed or he would lose his shirt. Through an agreement of all the parties involved, the results of the last three tanks would be posted at the last fill-up of the truck's tank.

The appointed day finally arrived and the tank in the '55 was duly topped off and the final figures tallied. The results showed that there had been an increase for the first four tanks, but the final tank was lower than the norm before the whole thing started. The Coyote started cussing a blue streak claiming that the @#$%^ additive had ruined his freshly rebuilt engine and there would be hell to pay.

Billy Bob paid off the $100 bet to the Coyote and, due to the press of urgent business in other quadrants, left the area posthaste. Oskar collected from all the folks present who had lost on the betting operation, rented a Charley One Seven Deuce, and took off for parts unknown.

After the commotion settled down some I closed the office, grabbed Big Bill Henry, and we went down to my hangar and fired up 02U, a '64 model Cessna 172.

The engine run-up at 1700 rpm showed a magneto drop of less than 100 left and right and the carb heat was doing its thing, so I dropped two notches of flaps and taxied to the north end of the strip. After a quick look around the pattern for aircraft traffic, deer and geese, I took off and turned to a heading of 090 for Gatlinburg where we planned to have a quick country ham sandwich and cup of coffee at the airport grill.

When we got there, I gave them a call on 123.0, entered downwind for runway 10, and landed. We taxied back behind the maintenance hangar so

2U would be in the shade and walked through the hangar into the back door of the Pilot's Grill.

Sitting in the last booth were our fellow club members, Oskar and the Coyote, deeply involved in a discussion over a sheet of paper on the table between them.

Big Bill looked at them for a minute and said, "I knew there was something rotten in Denmark, or maybe Kiev, when this thing started. I don't want any of the action, I just want to know how you did it."

They looked at each other for a minute and then the story came out. The Coyote opened by saying, "The additive was nothing but white gas with a little STP fuel treatment for color. I adjusted the mileage numbers by either adding or taking gas from the tank of the '55 while it set in the driveway at the Wang's house."

Big Bill said, "I knew you wouldn't be able to make any adjustments to the fuel tank at the club because there were too many people with bets on one side or the other, but that still leaves that big dog Billy Bob has at his house. He don't bite much but he does love to bark."

Oskar jumped in with "Come on Bill! Don't you remember where that dog came from? He came out of the same litter as Coyote's dog, so all the Coyote did was take his old dog with him to Wang's place and let the dogs get together while he adjusted the contents of the fuel tank on the '55."

Big Bill then pointed out that just as we were taking off from the Ranch we could see in the Wanger's hangar where he was pulling the hood off the '55 so he could lift the engine out for a major rebuild. Bill said, "Billy Bob told us he was really worried what that additive had done to his engine.

"The Coyote told us he would buy a new gasket set and replace any parts that were bad in the engine and for us to tell Billy Bob as soon as we got back what the deal was."

Big Bill Henry came in the clubhouse, poured himself a cup of coffee, fished out a card of nicotine pills, cut the foil off of one and speared it with his pocket knife. Putting the pill in his mouth Bill said, "These damn things just ain't near as much fun as a cigar," and let out a long sigh and I knew he had something to tell me. After a sip of coffee Bill told me, "You remember the other day when we got back from Gatlinburg, and I went over to the Wang's hangar to tell him that the Coyote would pay for his gasket set?" I said, "Sure I remember."

Bill continued, "Well I told him what the Coyote said and he didn't seem mad at all and I couldn't figure out what the hell was going on until Billy Bob confessed that he had a brand new three-quarter-race cam and had planned to take the engine down anyway. What he had been looking for was a way to get the Coyote to help him out with expenses." Bill looked up at me and said, "You know, me and you don't need to watch them TV soaps as long as we have this crowd here to watch."

OSKAR FALLS OFF THE WAGON

Swifty Swanson came lumbering into the clubhouse, picked up a cup of coffee and settled into a chair at the big table. Swifty is about three hundred pounds, with at least half of that being made of his good heart. No one is quite sure how he stays on the police force with all that he carries around. Some say that he also carries around some interesting information about some of the local politicians.

"Dapper," he says, "I thought I'd drop by and tell you what happened to the Mad Russian. He got drunked up last Wednesday night and I spotted him trying to get out of the trailer park where he lives and I thought I would try to teach him a lesson.

"My partner wanted, and rightfully so, to write him up with a DUI but I talked him out of it. I explained that if we could get his wife, Reba, in on the action she would make life a lot worse for him than the courts ever could. So here is what we did.

"We booked him on public drunkenness and put him in the drunk tank for the night. Then we called the city towing service to come and take his pickup truck to the parking lot of the Pink Pussy Cat Strip Club. The bartender there owes me big time so I had him call Big Reba to see where to put the Russian's truck because it had to be moved out of their parking lot so the lot it could be sealed and have new lines put down."

Reba 'Big Red' Yenderushak is a force to be reckoned with. She was a lady wrestler when Oskar first met her while he was doing a tour of duty in Germany. She had also worked as a sword swallower in a circus. Reba stands a full even six feet tall and still has a knockout figure although she is carrying more weight than she used to. So who ain't?

She has three main interests in life, one is keeping Oskar happy, the second is her job at the UT Vet school, and the third is playing her upright piano. She loves the classic waltzes of old Vienna. Oskar, she claims, saved her from a fate that she doesn't want to contemplate, and she will stay with him even if he occasionally falls off the wagon.

Dealing with what she calls the underside of life, however, will be dealt with in a swift and sure manner. None of us has dared to ask her exactly what that means, but we are all sure that Oskar knows.

I asked Swifty, "Do you know what happened to the Russian after she got him out of the tank the next day?" Swifty said, "No but I know it will be several more days before we see him outside of his quarters. He is under house arrest."

Big Bill looked at me after Swifty left and said, "I guess we can cross Swifty and the Russian off the list for The Great Pool Caper."

I said, "Bill I've got another one you can cross off your list. Small Sam and Wide Wilma were out here over the weekend wearing their new T-shirts that they bought at the Grand Old Opry. They were signed and dated by Waylon Jennings and the date is for the night in question."

Bill took a sip from his coffee mug and then said, "I sure thought Sam was a good bet after that deal the Warthog pulled on Wilma at the last picnic. When that cell phone started buzzing that the Warthog had clipped to her fanny pack and said 'Look out boys, this rig is a fixing to back up,' she would have choked him until his shorts turned brown if she could have caught him."

"Speaking of the Opry," Bill said, "the Crazy Doctor was at the Opera, New York City variety, at the right time so he ain't on the list either.

They didn't get back until two or three days later. I think that Marti had some sort of medical problem."

When Bill left I got to remembering the time that Cleveland had held forth on the topic of gays. His point was that they were all doing what they wanted to do and they could be straight just like every one else. Doc had let him carry on for a good while and then asked him if he really believed that anyone, given the choice, would choose a life style which would bring so much grief on them and their families. That was when the Warthog blew up and said, "Doc you spend so much time defending them queers, you must be about half queer yourself."

THE RENTERS

The renters group includes teenagers to retirees and student pilots to airline transport pilots. Some fly strictly for fun and others are interested in getting advanced ratings. I have heard that some of our young men think that flying at our island gives them an advantage with the ladies.

A certain boat salesman comes to mind in this respect. The big Weenie, as he is called, has been known to bring stewardesses all the way from Atlanta to take them for a ride. I myself am partial to a stewardess, but this guy works in the plural. Hell, he doesn't even stay with the same airline.

Oscar "Weenie" Mayer is the vice-president of sales for the southeastern division of a large boat company. He holds all the records at the club for enjoyment of the descendants of Eve. If there is a lady around that enjoys the apple from the forbidden tree, the Weenie seems to find out about her.

We have seen him bring three different candidates to the airstrip for initiation into the mile high club on the same day. The porch pilots say that he has more time logged at precisely 5280 feet MSL than any other member of the club. One day he took up two fine looking ladies on the same flight. A majority of the young ladies seem to work for the airlines. Big Charley said that the Weenie only took his present job so he could spend more time on airplanes scouting for new material.

Captain Tom told me the other day that he heard the Weenie making a call to Sporty's Pilot Shop. They sell a small set of wings with "Mile High Club" on them. The wings are about three quarters of an inch long and come in gold and silver. He ordered two dozen of each. "You know, Dapper, he must have a black book the size of the New York City Phone Directory."

Big Charley chimed in, "He buys Mile High Pins and the rest of us out here are buying Viagra. By the way, I asked him where he was on P-Day, and he was doing a boat show in Mobile."

All of our members are special people but some are more special than others and I don't mean special as in special education. However, I guess special education could apply now that the gifted qualify under the law. Gene George is an interesting guy who comes out to rent the Club 1941 model Piper Cub now and again.

Gene flew for Uncle Sugar in the Air Force and also did some airline work. He must have shot some really hairy approaches because he quit that line of work and went to seminary to become an Episcopal Priest. If this was a case of promises made and promises kept, the chief pilot upstairs sure got a bargain. Gene is retiring in the spring.

He told me recently of an all day meeting at the diocese where he was informed by the Church administrators and their lawyers that if he was accused of any impropriety that they would pray for him, but that was about all. I wonder if there is any connection between their lack of faith and his retirement? Sounds like my former organization.

Before I could take my first sip of coffee the phone rang reminding me that I wasn't just here to observe the geese walking on the runway. I picked it up and said, "Sky Ranch, this is Dapper." A voice said, "Hey Dapper put me down for the aerobat for about three to four o'clock on the 23rd if it's open."

I looked at the schedule sheet and started penciling in the name of Sam Long on the sheet for the 23rd in the 03M column. Small Sam said, "Every time I have tried to fly for the last month it rains on the day I have the plane. So today when Wilma told me she wanted the yard mowed tomorrow so it would look nice for her bridge group the day after, I just decided I would guarantee a good rain after work tomorrow."

I said, "OK Sam, whatever works for you is all right with me, I just hope Wide Wilma don't find out about your plan. Bye now." I jiggled the switch hook with the intent of calling home, but when the dial tone started it gave me the tone which signaled that the answering service had a message for me.

I called the service, punched in the access code, grabbed a note pad, and waited to see who wanted what.

MESSAGE 1

"Dan, Dr. Hilliard Clanton here, please reserve 57 Foxtrot at 10:00 a.m. for an hour on the 28th followed by an additional hour for Dr. Hilliary Clanton."

The Clantons, Hilliard and Hilliary, both have doctorates in sociology and are quite sensitive that they be addressed with the proper title. They are careful to let the rest of us less educated folks know that they are way ahead in the race for prestige even if they have trouble keeping their club bills paid up. They have the degrees but not a full time job between them.

MESSAGE 2

"Hey Dapper this is Willy Coyote, if the Wanger comes by there today have him give me a call. Thanks buddy."

THE MYSTERY DEEPENS

"Bill, how is the big pool pollution mystery coming along? I heard that you were offering a free night at the Pink Pussy Cat Club for information leading to the identification of the perpetrator of 'The Great Pool Pollution Caper'".

"Well I am, but I'm still not getting anywhere. Every time I get another reason for someone to do the deed, I also find out that they weren't available to do it," answered Bill. "How many suspects do you have?" I asked.

"Hell it's easier to tell you how many I don't have. The only ones that are out of the game are you, Doc Kronk, Small Sam, Swifty, the Weenie and the Russian," Bill groused. I said, "And I know that you were losing all your money on the horses that night."

"So big deal. That's seven out of the whatever the membership is now," fumed Bill. Sometimes Big Bill just wants to be a grouch, so I let him be and went back to the office to play with my various piles of paper. When I came out of the office Bill had left his list on the big round table

Kronk—New York
Weenie---Mobile
Dapper---Charleston
Small Sam---Nashville
The Russian—Jail
Swifty--- Putting Russian In Jail
Me---Horse Races

WHIZZER WHITMORE

A crew of men were pouring a concrete floor in the new hangar that Upndown Ulrick was building beside Smokey Pat Fansler's hangar. The driver was just moving the big mixer away from the hangar when I got there and the bull float man was settling the aggregate down and the liquid up. I watched for a minute. You can always learn something if you watch people who know what they are doing.

Suddenly two big black muscular arms grabbed me from behind and I was a foot off the ground. I was put down slowly and a voice said, "Coach you are putting on some weight but I can still handle you." "Boy, you sure can!" I said as I hugged the big man.

William "Whizzer" Whitmore had played football at East High School back during the early days of integration. Whizzer was one of the four kids on the team who ran a flat ten second one hundred. East owned the state record for the four by one hundred relay, and all four of them were on the football team.

During his high school days if we had a problem with a student that could not be resolved through the usual channels, Whizzer was our man.

Whizzer's first question was, "How is Mrs. Shay doing Coach?" I said, "She is doing real well and I'll call her in just a little bit so I can tell her that I saw you and you were asking about her. How long have you been driving one of these big dudes? The last I heard, you were working up north somewhere."

Whizzer told me that he had lost his job up north several years back and had been with the concrete company for about six years. I said, "Whizzer, did you let Lujacinda get away from you? She was one of the best looking cheerleaders at East." He then told me that they had run off and got married while he was working up north and had been together ever since.

I said, "Whizzer, I know you don't have time to talk right now, so can you and Lujacinda meet me and Shay at the Rib Shack tonight at about 7:30? Here is my number, call me at the house after 6:00 if you can't make it."

Lujacinda hugged me as if I were her long lost uncle when we met them at the rib joint that night. After a lot of catching up about other members of their class and a couple of pitchers of beer later we learned that Lujacinda was working as cook and maid to none other than Mr. and Mrs. C. Grover Cleveland. I started to ask her if she was working the day... and when I said day she said "Lord yes honey, I wouldn't have missed it for a hundred dollar bill!"

Lujacinda continued, "I got there as usual at about eight o'clock and when I got out of the car there was this strange odor about the place. I noticed it, but I couldn't figure out what it was. So I went through the garage and into the kitchen like I usually do.

"Mr. C. called me on the intercom and said for me to open up all of the cans of tomato juice and lemon juice that we had in the house and to put them outside the first floor bathroom door. Then he said for me to go out to the garage and find the yellow five gallon can of kerosene that was in the garage and put it outside the door. He later called again and asked for all of the liquid dish washing detergent. I added two gallons of bleach just for the hell of it."

"Mrs. Willow came in the kitchen wearing her string bikini and asked, 'Cindy what in the world is in the pool?' We went out on the deck to look and then I knew what was causing the odor. You could look up the hill through the trees and see a great big old honey wagon sitting on the road up there.

"When Mr. C. came downstairs later his skin looked as if he had scrubbed it raw. It was all red and blotchy looking. He was so mad that his eyes were coming out of his head. I asked him if he wanted anything to eat and he just snorted and went out and started the Bentley and roared off."

Lujacinda said she asked Willow, "What are we going to do? Mrs. Willow told me to take the week off, that she was going to visit her sister who lives in Kingston and then she wrote me a check for two weeks work just in case she was late getting back.

"As I was leaving I heard her tell someone on the phone that she wanted the downstairs master bathroom replaced with all new walls, flooring, fixtures and decorations, and she wanted it complete before she came back. She also told them to hire the same decorator to oversee the job that had redone the Senator's new house on High Dollar Road."

Billy Bob Wanger dropped in at the clubhouse and told me that he had another damn job on his list and he really didn't want to do it. "Peggy Sue told me I had no choice so I sent a crew over there today to get started. She took the job as a favor to Willow who wants the whole bathroom in the downstairs master suite replaced. She seems to think that the current one is polluted.

"My problem is that she wants me to use the same decorator that I used on the senator's job and if I do it I will break a promise I made to the decorator."

I said, "Maybe you should just ask the decorator whether or not she wants the job and let her make the choice. Are you only doing renovation work now? I haven't heard you talk about starting a new house in a good while."

"Dapper," Billy Bob says, "I done found my niche in the building game and it's in the renovation of the high dollar houses of the rich and shameless. I let them use my name with all of the appliance, light fixture, and bath fixture places so they can pick them out and order at contractor prices. They get it billed direct to them so they know exactly what the cost is and I don't tie up any of my money on the stuff. I do get a referral fee from the wholesalers.

"I also keep an interior decorator, who has a Master of Fine Arts Degree, busy advising these folks about what is current and colorful. She bills direct also and we split any money we make on the things that she adds to the job."

"Billy, how many of the houses across the river on High Dollar row have you done?" I asked. Billy said, "I've worked in 24 of the 150 houses on Hugh Diller Road. I have to be real careful to call it Hugh Diller or I am going to say High Dollar at the wrong time.

"Either I'm going to have to quit taking jobs or hire more people. I've got two carpentry crews, two electrical crews, two plumbing crews, and one general clean up crew.

"All of those people over there just know that they are taking advantage of this old country boy, and as long as they feel that way I'll keep making more money than I ever did building new houses. Now we put our capital in the stock market instead of tying it up in materials."

"Who is your interior designer Billy?" I asked. He said, "Dapper, that's the problem I got right now. When I first talked to her about going into this line of work, she made me promise that I would not ask her to do any work for anyone from the Sky Ranch or tell anyone here that she worked with me."

"I can see that you do have a problem," I said.

"By the way, do you know which sister Willow went to visit, Billy Bob?" I asked. "I get them confused because all of the women in the family are named with a W, there's Willow, Wallene, Winona, Wilma, and Wendy."

"She's staying with Wallene," Billy answered.

DINNER AT HAWKS

Big Bill Henry was working on a magneto in his hangar as I rolled up next door to my hangar. I needed to massage my girl's belly. All old airplanes' engines leak a little oil and it ends up on the bottom of the bird where it gets mixed with dust and dirt to create a dirty mess. The way I clean mine is with a spray bottle of varsol, some rags, and lots of elbow grease.

I was about halfway down the fuselage when I saw Bill's feet and heard him say that he had done about all he could with the mag and was going to the clubhouse and was I ready for a break and a cup of coffee. I told him I was down here and dirty and I would finish while I was here. He told me to come on up when I was finished. I finished the chore, spread the rags out to dry, and started getting the grease off of my hands and my glasses.

I filled my coffee mug and sat down on the porch with Zipper Thomas and Bill. Bill said that he had gotten orders before Beulah left for work this morning to make dinner plans for all of us tonight at Hawkeye's Corner because she hadn't seen Shay and Genie Rae for some time.

The Zipper said that he had heard a similar comment at his house, would six-thirty be a good time for everyone? I stood up and told them that I would make the reservations for a patio table now so I wouldn't forget it. Shay must have been out shopping, so I left her a message on the machine after I called the restaurant.

We were the last to arrive on the patio at Hawks because Shay had to change hats twice after we stood up to leave the house. She gets more like her mother every day. We should have held her mama's funeral at least ten minutes after the scheduled time.

Hawkeye's Corner is a favorite place for us to eat. It opened just before the Knoxville World's Fair in 1982. We have celebrated our good and bad days with a meal at Hawks ever since. The waitress saw us come in and had a couple of frosted mugs and a pitcher of light beer on the table in quick time. Zipper said, "I believe maybe you have been here before."

Big Bill looked up at the sky and said, "I wonder what that wind is going to bring us, some of those darker clouds look like they could start leaking big time." Shay made a quick grab and pushed her hat, one of her wide brim models, back down on her head and told Zipper who was sitting downwind, "You nearly got my hat!"

The wind really wasn't blowing very hard but every now and then there was a little gust strong enough to lift Shay's hat off. She was spending a lot of time with one hand holding her hat on.

Bill was sitting across from Shay and he said, "Shay, you were all right until you lit that cigarette. You had one hand for your hat and one hand for your mug of beer, now what are you going to do?" Shay looked over at him and replied, "Oh I am a talented girl, I can hold my cigarette and a mug of beer in one hand simultaneously."

The Zipper smiled and said, "That may be true but what I want to see is how you cut up and eat that steak with one hand and hold your hat with the other." Shay had a couple of close calls with the wind but managed to keep it all together.

In due time the dinner arrived and we all wondered if the balancing act could continue. I asked Shay if she wanted to put the hat in the extra chair at the table with her pocketbook on it for security while she ate her dinner, but she said no that's not an option. It was a matter of pride with her now, she was not going to take off the hat.

The Zipper offered, "Shay, if the wind gusts while you are cutting your steak, please try to remember not to use the hand with the knife in it to rescue the hat. You could hurt yourself." Bill added, "You could also damage that hat."

The serious eating was over and folks were just picking at a few items that they couldn't leave on the plate when Bill brought up one of his favorite subjects, the unknown perpetrator of the great pool pollution caper. "You know," he said "it looks more and more like either the Wanger or the Coyote might be responsible for this thing. Neither one of them have an alibi that I know of and they both are fully capable of dreaming up and pulling off a deal like that."

"That's true," added Zipper "and both of them wouldn't mind getting even with him for remarks he made about their wives at the club."

"I heard that he called Mai Ling a gook, but what did he say about Peggy Sue?" asked Beulah. "Oh he said that only hookers wore their clothes as tight as she does and it got back to Billy Bob," put in Genie Rae. Bill said, "At least I've got a bunch of them off the list of possibles."

Shay waited for an opening in the conversation and said to Bill, "I think you are missing a whole lot of possibilities in your investigation because you don't have a complete list of suspects."

Bill blustered, "I'm using a club roster and checking on everyone that comes out often enough to know who the players are." "So what?" said Shay. "That's still just half of the list."

"What do you mean?" asked Bill. "All of the members that you have mentioned have wives, and a lot of them are quite capable of driving any vehicle they want to," said Shay.

All of Bill's bluster disappeared and he looked at Shay and said, "Goddamn, you're right, and some of them also have kids that are old enough to drive. I'm gonna have to start a new list. You're too smart to be a blonde." Beulah chimed in, "I don't care who drove that truck, I want to see the dessert menu.

TIM "ZIPPER" THOMAS

Tim "Zipper" Thomas is a quiet guy who just recently became a full fledged porch pilot when he hung up his pediatrician's white smock to embrace the state of retirement. He is finding out what all of the porch people already knew, there are almost as many people asking for your time now as there were when you were working. They all start out with the same old thing, now that you are retired I know you will have time to help us with ...

Zip joined the Air Force after high school and attended several USAF aircraft maintenance schools. One of his assignments while stationed at Lowery AFB was as a member of the crew on the Columbine. The Columbine, for folks not up on their airplane history, was the name of President Eisenhower's private plane. The plane's crew chief, a crusty old master sergeant, had been with Ike since he made his first star and was more than a little protective.

The new help, Zip included, was only allowed to polish and clean the airplane. All mechanical work was handled solely by the crew chief. Zip said he was glad to see the Western White House closed up so he could go back to real mechanical work on the B-29.

Zip was about ten years old when his father was killed working in the mines in Lynch KY. After his father died, the family moved to a farm outside of Morristown TN where they lived with his grandmother. He told me that when he became a doctor and went to work for the coal company in Lynch he was only accepted in the community because the people up there remembered his father.

The Zipper has not completely given up medicine. The porch pilots still come to him for advice and counsel concerning their many ailments, both real and imagined. After a long weekend he sometimes has three or more folks waiting on the porch. Small Sam is a big believer that Zipper is the best doctor in the area, his specialty not withstanding. Big Charley observed one day that considering the size of Sam's mind, a children's doctor was probably the most appropriate choice for him anyway. Zipper's stock answer for most of the complaints is that you are just getting old and the parts are starting to wear out. It is not an answer that we like to hear, but one we are all beginning to have to accept.

KNIFE AND FORK

One of the very important divisions of the Sky Ranch Flying Society is the Knife and Fork section which meets on Tuesdays at 5:30. This group has an elastic roster and goes to the same place for dinner every week. We discussed trying a new place but we couldn't make the switch. Nothing was broke so we decided not to fix it. Besides, if someone is late they can just report directly to the Rib Shack rather than going to the Sky Ranch first.

The charter members of the group consist of G. Gordon Ladde, a lawyer; Tim "Zipper" Thomas, a retired pediatrician; Fritz Fieberg, a drug company rep; yours truly, a retired educator; Caleb Kronk, a shrink; Gale Gamble, an administrator with the local utility company; and Tom "Thumb" Ferris, a retired professional pilot. Big Bill Henry, who has a vocabulary which would make a retired Navy Chief stand in silent amazement and is a retired craft foreman from one of the atomic energy plants in Oak Ridge, makes frequent visits as does Father Gene George.

This very diverse group discusses a large variety of issues and comes up with some very interesting solutions to many complex problems. I think I will suggest at the next meeting that we probably should invite Knoxville Mayor Victor Ashe, Knox County Executive Tom Shumpert, Tennessee Governor Don Sunquist, and Slick Willy to one of our sessions so that they could reap the benefits of such a rare collection of intellects.

Gordon Ladde served in the Air Force for a time and when he got out he came home and went to law school. Gordon was a partner in a C-150 for a while with Ralph Goodman but he does not currently own an airplane.

He still thinks more like an owner than a renter, and also being a former employee of J. Edgar Hoover he probably should have a category of his own anyway. I'm sure you have heard the expression 'there's no drunk like a reformed drunk.' Now Gordon never was a big drinker that I know of but he did smoke a good deal at one time. Since he kicked the habit he has absolutely no tolerance for those poor lost souls that still crave that government supported weed. Sometimes he can be quite lawyer-like about it.

Big Bill Henry survived a mild heart attack a while back and was forced to undergo a treadmill test and other medical indignities in order to get Uncle FAA to return his flight physical to active status.

After waiting for three months and hearing nothing Bill questioned his heart specialist's nurse about the address that she had used when she sent his paperwork to Kansas City. She looked around and found the aforementioned paperwork still on her desk.

Bill did not have another coronary on the spot although he was in the right office, but he nearly caused one. The poor girl may have lived a sheltered life up to now, but rest assured that she has been exposed to a whole new section of the Kings English.

Bill was still very upset with the medical community when he sat down across from Father Gene for coffee at the last K&F meeting and announced that the #/**>/<\` medical community was no *\|>**# good but that he would make a one-time only exception for the doctors present. He then lit a cigar, that he was not allowed to have, and blew a large smoke ring in the general direction of that noted attorney G. Gordon Ladde.

The favorite subjects of the group usually have to do with flying or general aviation and since we have read a lot of the same aviation books and journals it is very interesting to see the different views of the same data from the different personal and professional perspectives. Law, education, and medicine all have their shortcomings and they are pointed out, generally at the expense of the local representative present. If you can't take it, you better not dish it out at this table.

My van full of folks were already on the porch when Gordon Ladde returned from supper in his favorite old Caddie. I said, "Hey Gordon have a seat, we are going to have a brand new member of the 'I have flown an airplane all by myself' club here in a little while."

Gordon said, "I don't remember my solo as well as I remember my first check ride with Ms. Evelyn." "Well, you're maybe right," I said, "but what I remember best about my check ride day was when I got back from Morristown."

Bob Campbell, who had rented the airplane to me, told me to go get Shay and take her for a ride. I told him that I was out of money, that it had taken all my spare money to pay for the check ride and he said "This one is on me, you go get Shay." You know, I need to look around and see if I have any of the old monthly statements from Campbell Aero from that period.

In a little while, we saw Tom get out of 741Lima Foxtrot and stroll up to the porch. The student made two trips around the patch and taxied up to the club tie-down and shut down the engine. He had a grin on his face that was worth my dues for the month.

The new pilot, Sandy Flynn, was a youngster that Swifty was looking after and I wondered why Swifty wasn't on hand for the big day. I asked Sandy and he said Swifty had a court appearance that he couldn't change.

Gordon said, "Let's celebrate! I'll buy you some ice cream or a hot dog at the Greek's place." The kid had had a rough time up to now, but along with a new almost daddy he got a lot of honorary uncles. Sandy asked where the Greek's place was and Gordon told him it was a deli on the corner of Louisville Road and Alcoa Highway that has the best hot dog in the country. They also sell a tee shirt that proclaims 'Be good to your Belly/Eat at Vic's Deli'.

Before we got loaded up to leave Big Bill Henry appeared and announced that he was going to go too. He quickly shifted into interrogation mode, and asked our learned attorney where he was on the night of the big stink. Gordon said he was at the church for the wedding of one of his wife's nephews, he wasn't sure which one, but if Bill needed the name he should feel free to call his better half and ask. Bill just grumbled about one more off the list and sat back contemplating some ice cream.

A TRIP TO NORFOLK

Shay and I decided to make a quick trip over to Norfolk, VA to visit our son who is a career Navy type and working on the crew that is building the Nuclear carrier George Washington. Since the annual was about due on our Skyhawk 02U, I asked Big Bill if he could look it over a little and he said he would squeeze it into his schedule.

On Tuesday I pulled off all the inspection plates, cleaned the engine and firewall with mineral spirits, changed the oil and checked the engine oil screen. The next day, after I had done a little work on the books, I went down to the hangar and pulled off the wheel pants and the wheels so I could look at the brake disks and pads and pack the wheel bearings with fresh grease. Big Bill's hangar adjoins mine so he can supervise my work and meet the FAA requirements as to who can do what to an airplane legally.

Big Bill came over with his flashlight, mirror and a can of lubricant to look the whole plane over and announced that he would have to move the airplane over in front of his hangar to test the compression because the air hose was too short to reach 2U where she sat, but that he was just about done for the day and that he would do that in the morning while I was at the meeting with the EPA people about an alleged oil pollution problem. The inspection was really going well, we had not found anything that would cause worry or expense.

On Wednesday I met with the EPA boys and we all agreed that it was a waste of all our time and that they would send me a letter shortly stating that we were in compliance on this date and that nothing more needed to be done. I met Shay for lunch and we decided to do some shopping and go on home.

At about six that evening Big Bill called and told me, "I would rather tell you almost anything other than what I have to tell you." My first thought was the compression test on the engine must really be bad. Bill followed up with, "I ran the right wing of 2U into the power pole in front of Doc Kronk's hangar. The rear spar is buckled and the tip is mangled. I will pay for anything that your insurance does not cover. I was finished with the compression check and I was taxiing the plane around to come into the back side of the hangar when I hit the damn pole."

You don't have to hit the wing tip very hard to wipe it out. When the force hits the tip, the main spar is in tension and the rear spar is in compression. Usually the rear spar buckles in the bay where the fuel tank is located and it is such a common repair that Cessna has a factory approved rear spar repair part already made up and a procedure to go along with it. Bill ordered the parts and hired a couple of guys from the Tennessee Air Guard to come and make the repairs. Izzy Green and Chub Checker work on the big tankers at the Air Guard and have a good business in general aviation aircraft work on the side. They both have an A&P rating and Izzy is working on his IA.

Friday rolled around and I didn't much want to go to the club and see 2U in her present state so I headed over to Maryville to see what was going on at Jimmy's Radiator Shop. The sign said '*If you have to take a leak take it to Jimmys.*' And a lot of people did. Jimmy Crowe and I had been friends for a good while and we enjoyed each others company.

Jimmy bought a Cessna C-180, a big tail-dragger, which was a real handful for someone who did not have a lot of pilot time so I fly around with him mostly as a confidence builder kind of thing. He is also working on his instrument ticket so he flies some with Captain Tom Dawson, one of the club's flight instructors. The 180 is up the line from my hangar so I check on the tie-down ropes every time I walk by.

The phone rang just as I walked in his office and Jimmy started explaining, "No, Mrs. Banning, your car is not ready yet, the part for it is still on order and I will call you as soon as it comes in. Yes, the part is a factory provided part because of the Ford recall order and there will be no charge. Yes, just like last time. If you need to go to the store before I call just let me know and we will get you to the store. Yes ma'am, goodbye."

I asked, "What was that about? Are you getting into Ford warranty work?" Jim said, "Get yourself a coke out of the box or one of those apples out of that basket over there and come on out to my work bay and I will tell you about it while I put some gas in an air conditioner." I found a good looking apple and wandered out to the middle bay in the shop where Jim was working while at the same time keeping two other mechanics and his son Digger busy at the jobs he had them doing.

After giving Digger some help on just how to repair the radiator for the Maryville police car he was working on Jim said, "The warranty work you mentioned is on that maroon Ford over yonder beside the dump truck." I looked at the only car over there which must have been about a 1972 model but clean as a pin and did not appear to have a mark on it anywhere. "It belongs to Wilma Banning and her son Bill Banning asked me to keep the car over here for a while because he is worried that she may be past driving it safely. He goes by her house to check on the car for her and finds something that needs to be done, so I go out and bring it over here for a while so I can fix it. Bill is out on a trip right now so I will keep the car until he gets back."

Bill is one of the guys over to the Ridge, as the Oak Ridge nuclear plants are known hereabouts, who either rides shotgun or drives the chase vehicle for the special rigs that transport nuclear materials. He must have passed his last physical fitness test and firing range requirements if he was still on the road. He had been worried about being able to carry the weight he had gained around the track in the prescribed time. His weapons range scores were legendary among the people that kept up with that sort of thing.

I told Jimmy about the mishap Big Bill Henry had had with 2U and he said, "Boy, I sure feel sorry for Bill. I bet he feels terrible about bending your bird." I said, "Yes, me too, since I was looking forward to seeing number one son over on the coast."

Jim adjusted the gas regulator on the charging machine and said, "Well I'm going to that bass fishing contest over on Douglas Lake for the next several days so why don't you take the 180 over and see Bunker. You fly that big bird better than I do anyhow and the insurance is set up so that you are covered."

I told Jim that I would take him up on the offer and that I would put in a power jack for my GPS and he would not have to worry about adding it when he got around to buying his own GPS. Jim said, "OK with me, and pick up one of those new Radiator Shop baseball caps to take over to Bunker."

The weather looked good for the next several days so Shay and I packed up and got ready for the trip to Norfolk. The Charley-180 engine run-up checked out fine and she was off the 1800 foot sod strip before we were close to halfway down. I trimmed the bird out and we headed for Tri-City Airport near Kingsport TN. Before too long I called Tri-City approach and told them I was VFR at 7500 en route to Martinsville VA, identifier MTV.

They gave me a squawk code and left me to do my own thing. The clouds were getting thicker and higher over the mountains just east of Kingsport and I climbed another couple of thousand feet to stay clear. We were making good at about 160 knots according to the GPS so it wasn't long till I started looking for a hole in the overcast to sneak down into

Blue Grass Field. The AWOS said we had plenty of room under the cloud base so we let her down and came around to land on runway 12. This is one of Shay's favorite stops. The food is good, the rest rooms are very clean, and she used to be able to smoke inside. Line service is also quick and careful.

I ordered a ham and cheese sandwich while Shay ordered her usual grilled cheese and while we were waiting I got into a conversation with the folks at the next table. A flight instructor and a student who were on the student's first cross country flight had stopped in to eat.

The CFI asked where we were based and, after learning we were from Tennessee, wanted to know if we knew of the Flight Examiner from Tennessee who was still working at the age of 85. I told him that I had her in my log book as the FAA Examiner of record for my Private License check ride back in '67. Come to think about it she was on Unicom 122.8 as we came through Morristown on the was up this morning.

"She is an honorary member of our flying club. We made her a member in the hope that maybe she would be more understanding on some members next check ride. We haven't noticed any change in the number of rejects, but it's nice to have her on the roster anyway."

We paid our bills for gas and food, climbed up into the C-180 and taxied out to the active runway. The engine run-up went well so I announced we were departing runway 12 and we were on our way again. This trip we had decided to land at the Portsmouth/Hampton Roads airport, so I dialed in the PVG identifier and the GPS showed a course of 090 degrees, distance 172.3 miles. As long as the GPS works this navigation thing is a real breeze.

My early days of flying an 85 horse Aeronca Champ with only a whiskey compass, a wrist watch, and a plotter for a sectional map as navigation aids are still with me. I still like to keep a finger or a sticky note on the last reference point as we go along. I haven't had a complete electrical failure, but I have lost a navigation radio while in flight, so why tempt fate? I have always thought I could figure out where I was if I lost all the black boxes, even if my last known position was somewhat old. However, if you use your superior judgment you may not have to show off your superior skills.

Portsmouth airport has two nice runways, 10-28 which is 7,000 feet long and 2-20 at 4,000 feet. Mercury Air Center is tucked into the corner formed by 2 and 28 with lots of tie-down space available. The end of the sock was pointing at the end of 10 so I announced we would do left traffic for runway 10, slowed down and set the bird up for landing. The big tail-dragger settled in nicely and I rolled through the intersection of the runways and turned right to taxi-way and another right turn into the parking area to tie down.

Now I needed to do a 90 degree left turn into the tie-down of choice and the left toe pedal met with no resistance whatsoever. There was plenty of room available so I pulled the throttle back to let the bird slow down and at the next tie-down I stabbed the right brake, started a 270 degree turn to the right and killed the engine as we were passing through the first 180 degrees of the turn and we stopped nearly lined up with the ropes for the spot I had picked out.

Shay made some comment about, "That was a fancy turn but you missed the ropes and we will have to push." We only had to move the plane about a plane length, straight ahead.

We started our usual drill after landing. I take care of getting the airplane tied down and arranging for fuel while Shay arranges for ground transportation. Her job is in the FBO office and mine is out in the sun or the rain, sounds fair to me. I unplugged the GPS, folded up the maps, unloaded the luggage, tied the bird down and headed for the FBO office.

The Mercury folks said they would look at the brake problem later in the day. I told them there was no big hurry since we were planning on being around for several days.

We did some serious visiting with Bunker for a few days and when we were ready to go the brakes were fixed and the weather was forecast to be severe clear. I checked out the bird and we headed for MTV for a coffee stop and came on back into Knoxville with plenty of time to spare before dinner.

THE PICNIC

The club holds picnics whenever it suits us. They are partly pot luck and partly catered by the club. Everyone is supposed to bring a covered dish and the club supplies hamburgers, hot dogs, fixings, and soft drinks. The club in days past supplied a keg of cold beer but we quit doing that when someone decided to emphasize family participation.

None of the pilots then had any trouble with the rule that said if you have a beer you are done flying for the day. We still have the same rule now and there is just as much beer on hand as before, but it is all in private coolers.

Club picnics look like a lot of other social gatherings in the south. There are a lot of women over here and men over there and a few groups which are more eclectic. These groupings are how the party starts out, but as the day wears on there is more and more mixing of the groups. Sky Ranchers don't always agree with each other, but in general they do enjoy each others company.

Peggy Sue Wanger, Mai Ling Coyote, and my better half, Shay, had a ring of chairs in the #1 hangar behind the food tables. The conversation seemed to be mostly about problems associated with the business offices that Peggy Sue and Mai Ling dealt with. They finished up technical details shortly after I arrived.

Peggy Sue, who is four foot eleven and a half and wears a size four shoe, told the group that she had forgotten to close her closet door all the way and Homer, the bull mastiff, had chewed up her last pair of good dress shoes.

"What are you going to do?" asked Mai Ling. "I know you have to special order all of your good shoes and we have to go to that wedding next week." "I'm not sure yet if I will order some and have them shipped next day air or try to get something in the children's department at Shoe World," answered Peggy Sue.

Shay asked, "Mai Ling did you find anyone to help take the emergency calls for the over-the-road boys? The last I heard you were having to do a lot of that yourself."

"Yes, thank goodness I finally got a couple of girls trained. They take the calls and send the guys out on the runs. It was so much easier after I figured out that they could do the work from their house rather than providing them an office. I install them an extra phone line and this way it saves them child care and phone bills. The crews still call me with the billing information, but it can go on the machine if I'm not available."

The Warthog came plowing through the group and asked Peggy Sue, "Do you still do that phony looking estimate on the back of a brown White Store Grocery Bag?"

"Why Mr. Cleveland, whatever do you mean?" Peggy had shifted into her dumb blonde mode which sounded like a role from *Gone With the Wind,* and the Warthog could see that he wasn't going to get any answer to his question and moved on. I guess he frankly didn't give a damn either.

"Peggy Sue, are you going to tell us or not?" Shay asked.

"Well, you remember when I went to that Women In Construction meeting in San Francisco with Mai Ling I picked up that new estimating program that I use on all of our jobs. I had just finished up the estimate on the house for Wendy Higgins, the lady who is in that big public relations firm, when I remembered that Billy Bob had said she had a real nice sense of humor and had enjoyed his poor dumb country boy act.

"So I printed the whole estimate up on the back of a brown White Store grocery bag. I used one of those wiggly fonts that look like it was printed by a third grader with a carpenters pencil. Billy Bob signed it with a crayon and took it to her. She loved it! After the job was over, we went over for the final inspection and she had it framed and displayed on the wall in the new room we built for them. She told me that we might consider doing it all the time, that it was a great signature for the company."

Mai Ling Coyote is a native of Sri Lanka. She is easily the most beautiful woman I have ever seen. Her Eurasian background, with her dark hair and eyes teamed with a perfect figure, make her a knock-out in any company. Ten years ago one of Willy Clyde's secretaries turned up pregnant by one of the Bubbas on a road crew and he had to fire them both to keep any kind of order in the office.

Mai Ling, who was a student at UT, answered the ad for a temp worker and, as they say, the rest is history.

She reorganized the office, shuffled the work crews, lost her heart, and stole Willys' in less than six months. On her first day at the office one of the Bubbas sneaked up behind her so he could feel her shapely butt and somehow ended up sitting in the corner of the office with the water jug off the water cooler emptying in his lap. He hit the water cooler after he fell over a desk and tripped on a chair.

The Bubbas tried to figure out exactly what happened, but their only conclusion was that they didn't want to try for a replay. Mai Ling finished her studies at UT and now she has an MBA degree to go with her third degree black belt. The only cloud in the Coyote's sky has been their inability to have children.

Lee "Loose Lip" Linder came wandering up and sat down with the group. Lee is Willy Clyde Coyote's uncle on his daddy's' side, and works for Billy Bob Wanger as a finish carpenter. Willy Clyde and Lee have been very close since Willy's dad died when Willy was just a child.

Lee had a stroke a bunch of years ago and one side of his face sags and his upper lip on one side hangs down a little bit. Mai Ling and Lee adopted each other the moment they met and Mai Ling cannot stand to hear him called anything but Lee.

Father Gene sat down with a full plate of food and said, "How are you doing Lip?" Mai Ling said, "Gene, priest or not if I hear that one more time I will tell Tyrone he can have you for dinner." "I'm sorry honey, but old habits die hard and Lee and I have known each other for over thirty years," replied Father Gene. Lee spoke up, "You know, I really don't mind that name anyway, it sure beats being called the Warthog."

CAPTAIN TOM DAWSON

Back in the saddle again I picked up the phone at the clubhouse the next day and Captain Tom Dawson wanted to know, "How did the trip in Jimmy's C-180 go?" So I had to tell him about the brake failure and then he got around to asking me to put him down for 57Foxtrot from 2:00 to 4:00.

Tom Dawson is a very successful flight instructor at the Sky Ranch, having helped a lot of us get one rating or another. He is a very laid back kind of a guy who never yells at his students regardless of what kind of bonehead mistake they may make. It is very difficult for those of us who know him to figure out how he could be a graduate of West Point.

His career has been an interesting one including serving with a tank company in Germany. After splitting company with Uncle Sam's Army, Tom became a rocket scientist at the Cape and helped to make the big rockets fly. According to our inside man, it only took about 28 signatures to change the color of a paper tag that hung on a lawn mower that was used to mow grass at the visitor's center.

T.D.'s last regular paying day job was with the Tennessee Valley Authority in the days prior to the arrival of "Carvin" Marvin Runion. If Runion is as successful with the U.S. Post Office as he was with TVA, we are in a world of deep, deep, do-do. There were a lot of good people who lost their jobs at TVA and Tom was among them. We had several members who worked for TVA at the time including Jay Bob Robertson, the Chief Pilot and Administrator of the Aviation Section which operated several planes.

Capt. Tom also gets his share of the lady pilot aspirants who want to learn to fly. Like the men, some of them turn out to be good pilots and some never quite get the hang of it, some finish and some don't.

Tom claims that it is tough duty but, what the hell, somebody has to do it and it might as well be him. It is fun to watch the porch pilots try to make barrel chests out of their bay windows when some of Tom's students go by.

PORCH PILOTS

The porch pilots are a group of folks who may or may not fly on a given day but are always available for consulting work when there is a perceived need for constructive criticism concerning the skill level of a pilot making a landing on the runway directly in front of them. Just as I walked out on the porch Arthur Sandusky came walking up after tying down the Cub. He had been shooting touch and go landings on the south runway and the wind had been playing some pretty mean tricks on him. Art knew what he was in store for but he had no option but to come to the clubhouse because he had to enter his tachometer time on the Cub clipboard so I could charge it to his account.

Small Sam opened the inquisition asking how long it had been since he had flown the Cub, trying to give Art a way to save some face, but Art missed the chance by allowing that he was quite current and had flown no more than a week ago. Smokey Pat Fansler broke in asking, "How many landings can you log for one approach Art? I counted about three landings for most of your trips around the patch."

Art looked over at Smokey and said, "I guess that is about the right number. I just couldn't seem to keep her from bouncing today. I was probably worrying too much about the cross wind and let my airspeed get a little high."

Normally in this situation as soon as the victim acknowledges that he had a problem, the porch pilots would back off. Today the Warthog, wanted to get in another shot and he stated, "I just can't understand how a pilot can let his airspeed get away from him on short final, there's just no excuse for it. You may need to fly some more with an instructor before you bend one of our airplanes."

I don't normally get into these discussions but the opportunity was just too good to resist so I said, "Well at least he can solo in the Cub because he is current. You, on the other hand, are more than 90 days past current so according to club rules you will have to ride with an instructor before we turn you loose again."

"For someone who works so hard at establishing the nickname 'the prez', which no one pays any attention to, he sure got quiet for a politician," said Small Sam after Cleveland remembered urgent business elsewhere and departed.

Father Gene then commented, "Yes, I think the name Warthog that Big Bill hung on him works a lot better for me. He had no call for that last remark bout Art."

Smokey added, "He is not the worst looking man I ever saw, but he is in the running. I was at the fire hall the night all that happened or I guess I would be a suspect on the Warthog's list."

Father Gene added that he too had a perfect alibi, he had been officiating at the funeral of an old friend in Kingsport the day before P-Day and had spent the night there. I noticed Big Charley make a note in his pocket notebook, and I thought I knew what it was about.

As I was leaving to go make a bank deposit Small Sam was asking Smokey when he had to work next and Smokey said his next shift was at Fire Hall 19 the day after tomorrow and they should get together either today or tomorrow if they wanted to fly some.

MISSING GAS

The Wanger came wandering into the clubhouse, picked up a coke, and sat down to chat. He barely got in the chair when in came Willy Coyote, who also dropped into a chair at the table. I said, "I don't know who called this meeting, but I did want to see the two of you about something. Have either of you been missing any gas out of your planes? You both have hangars down in the south forty."

Wanger said, "Yes, I have been missing some gas but I thought it was probably something the Coyote was doing, so I was waiting to see what the game was before I said anything." Willy said he had the same deal and thought the Wanger was responsible. I told them that I thought that might be the case but I was losing gas also.

The Wanger sat a minute and then he said, "I believe we need to stake out the lower forty for a few nights and see what we got. These folks may be coming in by boat to get the aviation fuel to run in their racing boats." Willy put in, "It might just be some of the kids from across the river, and if it is they will know if we are here or not." I said, "We may have to hire some specialist. What would you all think about letting Homer and Tyrone handle the job?" Willy said he would put them on the job in a night or two.

Shay and I were having our coffee on the screened in porch when the phone rang. The Wanger was on the line and more than a little agitated. He told me that Homer and Tyrone had caught the gas thief and that they were holding him down in my hangar, or more precisely holding him in the empty 55 gallon drum in my hangar.

I told him that was fine, just call Swifty to come and get him. The Wanger said he thought he recognized the kid and if it was who he thought it was, that I might not want to do that and I better get my ass out there and deal with it. I told Shay what was going on and told her I would give her a call as soon as I had any details.

In about fifteen minutes I rolled up at the clubhouse where there were a couple of pickups and a police cruiser parked. "O.K. guys, where is the prisoner?" I asked. "Oh, he is still down there in that barrel in your hangar. Homer and Tyrone are looking after him," said Swifty.

"Who do you think it is? I've got to get to the office." Swifty said, "Dapper I think it's Senator Robert Lee Davis' oldest boy. Now do you want me to take him to juvenile or do you want to call the Senator?" I said, "I'll call the Senator. You all go down and give the kid a coke and thank Tyrone and Homer for me."

I went in the clubhouse and called Shay and asked her to track down the Senator and have him call me here at the club, that I had some information about his boy. The phone rang in about five minutes and after a short conversation the Senator said he would be over as soon as he could get a boat cranked up, he lived just a little way up the river.

When Senator Davis arrived he asked Xander Davis what he had to say for himself, then told him to go wait in the boat. Bobby Lee asked me how much gas we had lost and I told him we weren't too sure, but that a keg of beer for the next picnic would probably cover it nicely. He said that could be arranged if he could come and help us drink it and that he very much appreciated that the call came from us rather than from the juvenile authorities.

While he was talking with us, two immense bull mastiffs came nosing up and checked his pockets for anything edible. He had no choice but to give them a good rubbing because they were standing on his feet. The Senator then said, "Someone said that Homer Tyrone caught my boy. I'd like to thank him too." I said, "Well, it was Homer *and* Tyrone and you got one standing on each foot."

The Senator cranked up his boat and headed for high dollar row across the river, Billy Bob Wanger left after letting the two big dogs get in the back of his truck, and only Swifty and I were left on the porch. "You seem to know the Senator some," said Swifty.

"We were fraternity brothers in college and Shay went to high school with him and his wife Sugar," I told him. Swifty looked up and said, "I'm sure we did the right thing, but here comes the man who will tell us that we were wrong. I'm going to work because I don't want to hear it." Sure enough, C. Grover Cleveland, the Warthog, was making big clouds of dust as he roared down the dirt road by the runway in his Bentley.

The Warthog went in the clubhouse and talked with the group inside and returned shortly with a cup of coffee and Father Gene George. The Warthog began his disjointed discourse by saying that everyone should be equal under the law, even the son of a Senator, and that he didn't believe in coddling children, and that the job I was doing for the club wasn't much either.

I was getting a little hot under the collar so I told him, "Mr. Cleveland, I think that getting caught stealing and then sitting in a steel drum for most of the night is about as good a penalty for a 16-year-old as a juvenile judge would have come up with. We have enough kids wandering around with records now. I would also rather have the folks over on high dollar row owe us a favor rather than have them mad at us." The Warthog said,

"Yes, but how long will the Senator remember that he owes us a good turn?" "Not nearly as long as he would remember a bad turn," said Father Gene.

I called Shay and told her the story and that I was going to work a little while in the office and would she please come up with a nice easy plan for the rest of the day after the way this one had started out. She said that the lawn needed mowing and the commode in the back bathroom was running. Oh well…

HANGAR BY COYOTE

Willy Clyde Coyote is a rather special guy, as are most of our members. He is one of the self-made types who started out with a pickup truck, a toolbox full of Craftsman™ tools from Sears, and the ability to look at any piece of equipment and immediately understand its innermost secrets. He could also sell refrigerators to Eskimos, given the opportunity to meet an Eskimo.

Willy Clyde's business provides emergency services to two different groups of customers. If an over-the-road trucker has trouble with a big rig, from tires to transmissions, Willy is your man. There are about a dozen trucks outfitted for over-the-road repairs.

The other part of his business provides construction equipment repair service for all sorts of construction outfits. The trucks are manned by a group of hard-drinking good old boys who require a lot of care and bail money. At least three of these driver mechanics are named Bubba.

Willy once told me that he was really having a problem providing road service on Saturdays when he paid everyone on Friday afternoon. He said he didn't mind getting them out of jail on Saturday morning, but sometimes he had more runs than he had people.

So he still pays everyone once a week but they all end the pay week on different days. It's the end of the pay week for one or two of them every day. His wife Mai Ling still writes all the checks on Friday like she always has, and Willy keeps them in the glove compartment of his truck and doles them out as each pay day comes up during the week.

Willy says the over-the-road operation is steady and makes him a nice living, while the other side is really a gravy train. He says that a small contractor working against a deadline with a machine that he can't fix has to pay whatever it takes to get moving again. He has three crews set up for this kind of work and only goes out on the really interesting cases himself when he wants to.

Willy C's hangar is in the lower south forty section of the island and has been there for as long as anyone around can remember. The hangar itself, supported by old telephone poles, is about forty feet wide by thirty feet deep.

By far the most interesting feature of this old structure is the forty foot beam across the open front of the hangar. The beam is made up of 2"x6"s nailed to a section of three quarter inch plywood which is a foot and a half high. There is a double row of 2"x6"s on each side of the web, top and bottom. The real support of the long span comes from the two lengths of three quarter inch steel cable. Each cable runs from the top of the beam on each end, down to the bottom in the middle, one on each side of the span. Other hangars around it have been blown down or into the river, but this one just stays there.

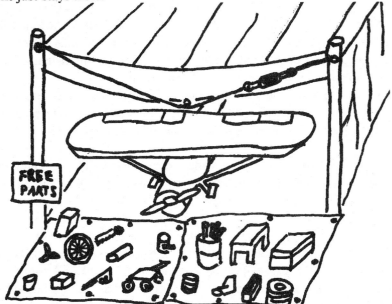

There is a small room in the back of the hangar which had so much junk in it that it could not be used for anything else. Willy decided this was to be his new home away from home. He said that he was going to clean the place out and install a work bench and a couch so he would have a place to work in peace. They had so much work at the shop that he didn't have any place for his own projects.

Before Willy Clyde could start sprucing up his new office, he had an awful lot of junk to get rid of. There were parts from cars, motorcycles, airplanes, boats, and just about anything mechanical you could think of. He picked over it some and put the rest out on a couple of big tarps under the wings of his old straight-tail 182.

He put a note on the chalkboard of the clubhouse that proclaimed free parts in the Coyote hangar and in a couple of days they were all gone. I don't think most of them went very far. They just moved from one hangar to another on the island.

I went to see how the Coyote project was coming and Willy Clyde was just finishing up hanging a door on the back wall of the shop. I asked, "Why are you putting a door in the back wall of this when you already have a door leading into the hangar part?"

"Dapper," Willy said, "sometimes you just have to go with what you got. Wanger had two of these half glass doors left over when that lady changed her mind for the third time on that custom house he is redoing over on high dollar row. I'm going to put both of them on this back wall. They will give me some light and cross ventilation."

"You may need a gutter on this wall to carry the water away from the door," I said. He cogitated a minute and replied, "You may be right, all of the water from the whole hangar roof comes off along this wall."

A few days later, Billy Bob Wanger came in the clubhouse and announced, "You guys got to come out here and see this!" Several of us followed him out to the porch and I asked him what we were looking for and he said, "Just watch the Coyote when he gets down to his hangar."

The Coyote parked his truck behind his hangar, unlocked the back door to his new den and disappeared inside. Big Bill Henry said, "Damn, that sure was exciting," and went back in the clubhouse. We all went back to what we had been doing and about an hour later the Coyote stopped for a minute as he was driving out to tell us he had a run to make but that he would be back in time for the Tuesday night run to Rabbit Hickman's Rib Shack.

I was just about to finish up charging the aviation gas to member accounts when Small Sam Long yelled, "Come here Dapper, you have to see this!" I walked out on the porch and all of the porch pilots were laughing so hard that some of them were close to having health problems. Billy Bob Wanger was standing at the door to the Coyote's hangar drenched to the skin. The gutter was hanging down in a vee shape with the apex just above his head.

The gutter had been full of water and had come down in the middle just at the door. The boy did not own a dry stitch at the moment. "That must be what we were supposed to see awhile ago when the Coyote came in," surmised Small Sam.

Billy Bob changed into a spare set of coveralls he had behind the seat of his truck and settled down with a cup of coffee at the big round table in the clubhouse. He said, "I tested that mechanism three times, so I know it was working when I left here last night. Willy Clyde must have found it and redid the damn thing after I left. When I went down there a minute ago to see why it didn't trip on the Wanger, it just dumped all over me."

"How did it work anyway?" asked Big Bill. "Well it had a trip wire that ran from a loose board on that little porch floor up to a gizmo that held the center part of the gutter in place," said Billy Bob. In a little while Billy Bob's beeper went off and so did he.

Willy Clyde Coyote showed up about four o'clock and we got his side of the story. The first thing everyone wanted to know was how did you find the booby trap in the first place? Willy Clyde told us that he came by early this morning to pick up something from the hangar when he saw a bird taking a bath in a gutter that should have been empty so he started to wonder why the gutter had water in it.

When he found out why the water was there, he modified the mechanism so that you had to press on the loose plank three times before the gutter released.

"By the way, Dapper," said Willy Clyde, "the checks I write from now on will be on the corporate account since the office in the hangar is now listed in the books as the Alcoa Highway branch of the company." I said, "You mean the checks Mai Ling writes will be on the company account. You haven't written a check in years. Does she even allow you anywhere near the checkbook?"

TIGHTWAD WILSON

The day was warm and sunny with a slight breeze coming in from the west setting up a cross wind for our north-south strip. The retired group, we have been tired more than once, was out in force on the porch at the clubhouse when I arrived and I asked them if you had to be overweight to join them or could just anyone sit with them.

T.W. Wilson replied, "I resemble that remark, and if you want to sit with thin people, go over and have coffee at the Krystal Restaurant on the campus of the University."

"We used to talk about all the pretty women we were chasing and occasionally catching" said Captain Tom. "Now we are much more interested in the price of Viagra, and changes in the Social Security Law."

T.W. 'Tightwad' Wilson is a guy that can buy and sell most of the folks in the club. He went to a technical high school for a while and then at fifteen he quit and headed for Detroit City where he worked for a while in an automobile factory.

He quit the plant and opened a shop that did metal plating on parts for the plant that he had worked in. The shop started out reworking parts that were thrown out by the inspectors for defects of various kinds. T.W. paid all his people on a piece work basis, but he only took a small profit so that the men in the shop could make good money. The business prospered and so did T.W.

T.W. was in hog heaven. He had built a house with his own airstrip, hangars and swimming pool. He was enjoying a group of cronies, chugged around Lake Erie on his big cruiser, and was the master of all he surveyed when he sat on his patio overlooking the pool and the airstrip. Wrong.

All of a sudden Gina, his wife of 50 years, announced that it was time to move back to Tennessee so that she could be close to her great-grandchildren. T.W. said, "All those years I thought that I was in charge and then I found out who was really running things."

T.W. is an enigma, a puzzling kind of a guy who is generous with his friends, but would rather die than spend money on maintenance on his airplane.

He painted his current plane, an older C-172, a while back and decided to put the small two inch N numbers on it rather than the twelve inch ones because they were cheaper. The FAA requirement at the time was that if you repainted a plane the larger numbers were necessary.

Tightwad said that they would never know, so what was the difference? Besides, the little ones fit on the vertical stabilizer and he would need less tape to paint a single stripe on the fuselage. It was a nice paint job and the airplane really stood out among its drabber cousins.

T.W. went to a fly-in down at Rockwood and was bragging to a group of folks about the new paint job and what a good deal he got on the enamel. He was violating the first rule of a good public speaker: know your audience. One of the listeners was an FAA man out of Nashville who told him about the twelve-inch requirement. A few days later Wad got the official letter grounding the airplane until the twelve-inch numbers were in place.

Tightwad was in a bind. The N number for his airplane contained five digits and that was too large to fit on the vertical stabilizer. If he put them on the fuselage, he had to paint the whole rear end of the plane because of the stripe.

He worried about the problem for about a week when Big Bill Henry came to his rescue. Big Bill told him that if he had a shorter N number it would fit on the vertical stabilizer and the rudder together, but the down side of it was it would take the FAA in Oke City a while to issue the paperwork required for a shorter number. T.W. said, "Can they do that?" Bill said, "Yes, all it takes is time."

Tightwad said, "Well I can't fly the damn thing anyway, I let my medical run out and I can't get an appointment for three weeks. I was just trying to get all of the good out of the old medical before I got another one." He then said he was making a run to the deli, what could he bring back for us.

There were three of us in the clubhouse and when T.W. got back he had plenty of food for five. When we tried to pay him for our part of lunch, he just said he didn't remember what he paid for the food and whatever it was it didn't matter.

Big Charley told me as soon as I stepped on the porch that the FAA had made a surprise visit to the Sky Ranch and the man had walked around and looked at all the planes. He said that he left envelopes on two airplanes, Tightwad Wilson's and mine.

Before I had time to even find my coffee mug, Tightwad Wilson came rolling in and Charley gave him the news. T.W. tore off down the field in his old truck like Richard Petty in a stock car race. I was going to ask him to pick up the envelope on my bird while he was down on that end of the field, but all that was left of him when I got to the porch was a cloud of dust. He was back in a flash. The form he had stated that he had a non-standard lens on his rotating beacon, and it must be replaced with an approved part. Big Charley asked, "What kind of a lens do you have on the beacon, T.W.?"

"You remember when I was having trouble with the nose strut going down? Well, one of those days when it was low I pushed the airplane into the hangar and hit the rotating beacon, which is mounted up on the tail, on the middle bar beam of the hangar. I replaced it with a shot glass. It has worked good for about six months. Dapper, give me a Trade-a-Plane out of the office and I will order a replacement just to make him happy."

T.W. called six different places and wound up saving a quarter on shipping by paying a dime more for the part and the whole process only took him an hour.

After T.W. left Charley looked up and said, "That is not a shot glass on his bird, it's an old fashioned glass. A shot glass would be way too small." Big Bill Henry chimed in, "Have you ever seen T.W. drink? He can put away more booze than anyone I ever saw and he doesn't seem to be affected at all. Tightwad thinks that is a shot glass.

"One other thing about that situation," Bill continued, "the reason that the tail of the airplane got up in the rafters in the first place was because of another of his bargain replacement parts. The problem in the strut was that little core in the valve where you put the air charge had deteriorated due to old age.

"The little rubber part that does the sealing just gives up after a while. T.W. went to the flea market and picked out a nice one, probably an Edsel part, and it went bad overnight. The air leaked out, the strut collapsed, the nose went down, the tail went up, bang went the beacon, end of story."

"Dapper, what's in your envelope?" asked Charley. I opened the envelope and there was a 3"x5" index card and a business card in it. On the index card there was a short note. It just said, "A long time ago I made a trip in this old girl when she belonged to a former owner. Looks like you take good care of her. Willy Dan Gelmer."

Seeing the name on the card brought back memories of a time long past. The name reminded me of Sgt. Willy Don Gilmer, whom I had served with in the Army. I decided now would be a good time to take a solitary walk around the shore of the island and let the old images come to life again.

WARTHOG SETS UP BUFORD

Big Charley already had the coffee pot going when I rolled into the clubhouse on Monday morning and seemed to be in a very foul mood. So I asked him what put the burr under his saddle and he said that he was sick and tired of the Warthog giving everyone so much grief.

I gave him a quizzical look and he launched into a tale about the latest escapade of one Grover Cleveland. According to Big Charley, the Warthog had been doing his best to make one of the new kid members feel inferior due to the fact that the youngster had not acquired any of the things which were important indicators of a man's arrival at a place of importance in the world.

It seems that considerable time had been spent talking about 'my house in Shang High Hills, my forty-five foot boat at the Marina, my vintage Bentley, my Rolex, my twin Cessna, and my new heated outdoor pool.' Big Charley said, "It was enough to puke a buzzard."

I asked Charley if he had heard about the deal that the Warthog had pulled on his own brother-in-law concerning the honey wagon. He said no, poured us both another cup of coffee and sat down at the big round table, where I was going through some mail, to hear the story.

Cleveland, at the insistence of his wife Willow, set up a septic tank pumping business for Buford Bailey, one of his wife's many brothers. Willow came from a large family. However, it was set up so that Buford did all the work and the Hog made most of the money.

Every time that Buford would come close to paying off the loan something would happen either to one of the big pumper trucks or he would lose one of the long-standing contracts. Then he would have to borrow more money from the Warthog at interest rates that would make some of the Italian organizations green with envy.

Charley then proceeded to tell me that before the pool got polluted the Warthog had been holding forth about how good it felt to go for an early morning swim. He said he did a big dive off his deck and swam twenty-five laps at six every morning. I said, "Yes I know he used to do that because the Wanger who lives up above the Hog has commented that he had seen this diving deal every morning for about two months now. He also says that after the Hog leaves for work it is a lot more fun to watch Willow come out and practice her diving wearing the skimpiest of bathing suits."

Big Charley sat for a while and then asked, "Where does Buford keep that big new honey wagon for the new contract with Port-A-John?" I told him I wasn't sure, but probably on the lot with the rest of the pumping trucks out on 321 there just about where you turn off to go in to the lake and about a mile before you get to the turn-off to Shang High Hills.

Charley said, "I think so too, so it wasn't too far from the Warthog's house. Give me the Wanger's cell number there, I need to talk to him about some fill dirt for the road out to my barn." I gave him the number and headed down to the hangar to change the oil in 02U so it would be ready for the upcoming trip to Charleston SC.

I untied the bird, did a quick walk-around inspection, checked for water in the fuel, cranked up, and started to taxi down to the south end of the field. Before I could get going Big Charley drove up in his van and announced that he wanted to go too. After a routine run-up I announced, "Sky Ranch traffic 2U is departing to the north at Sky Ranch."

I know that I said I was going to change the oil but fifty weight drains so much easier when it is hot and besides I wanted to see how well Wanger could see the back of the Warthog's house and pool area.

When we got over the area there was a paved street between the two estates but no houses, and there was a considerable rise in elevation from Cleveland's place up to the Wanger's. The oil temp gauge was up off its peg so I headed back for the strip. "Sky Ranch 02U is five miles west. Anybody in the pattern?" I called and was rewarded by an answering call. "Hey Dapper I'm on short final for North and I didn't see anybody else, we will be out of your way by the time you get here," said the voice of Captain Tom.

I taxied the bird into her hangar and removed the cowling so I could get at the oil screen on the accessory case, put the hose on the quick drain, and started the oil flowing into the big white bucket that had once contained five gallons of outside house paint. The screens had no metal, just the usual amount of carbon, so I put them back, did the safety wire thing and was ready for new oil. I finished up and headed back to the clubhouse to see who had shown up while we were gone.

BIG CHARLEY FALLS IN HANGAR

Father Gene came hurrying into the clubhouse, picked up the phone, and I heard him say please send an ambulance to this address, we have a medical emergency, not life threatening. After he hung up he told me that Big Charley McGillicuddy, our resident Irishman, was flat on his back in

Tightwad Wilson's hangar with what looked like a broken leg or hip. He had fallen over some 2"x6"s he and T.W. were using to repair the hangar.

After the ambulance was gone Father Gene made a fresh pot of coffee and we relaxed on the porch. Gene said, "I sure hope that old boy comes through this thing. He is getting on up in years. How old do you think he is Dapper?"

"Well I know that he flew B-24's in the big war in '44, so if he was at least twenty then, that puts him at over 75 now. He worked for Pratt and Whitney for lots of years and then came to University Hospital as a facilities administrator when Minnie Bee got tired of him traipsing all over the world trouble-shooting for PW."

"Didn't they live in Vermont, or somewhere up there?" Gene asked. "Yes, they got tired of the winters. By the way, did you hear what he did with the crack house that was next door to him?" Gene had not heard about that little tale so I told it to him.

The house next door to Charley went through a succession of renters with the house and the renters going downhill as they went. When it got down to some crack heads, Charley went to the owner and offered him some cash money to take the place off of his hands.

The offer was pretty low, but it was cash in hand and the property was infested with this drug problem, so the owner took it. By this time the house was really run down and there was the problem of getting the current residents out.

Charley got together with Swifty Swanson to find out just how much dope and money had to be found on the place to put this crowd away for a long time. Then, Lo and Behold! one of the renters came upon some cash in his car which he immediately turned into a supply of dope. When the occupants of the house had time to start getting as high as kites, out of the blue the narc unit of Knoxville's finest appeared and Charley no longer had renters.

Charley then hired Billy Bob Wanger's outfit to come in and do the heavy work of repairing the property and he did the finish work himself. He later sold it to a young couple with a kid and a dog. He says that he came out about even on the deal in money, but way ahead in peace of mind.

EARTHY WOMAN

No one knows for sure how Ms. Cathy Winbigler found the airport, but one day she just appeared driving a VW bus with big flowers painted all over it. She is still a flower child who did not escape the sixties. She has a studio/loft somewhere over on the east side, but also lives out of her bus a lot. I wasn't keeping the books then due to my regular job with the school system so my knowledge of her is limited. However there is a large body of anecdotal data available about her.

When Cathy first appeared at the airstrip she was somewhere in her thirties, but had been rode hard and put away wet on a regular basis. She was about five feet six inches tall and a hundred and ten pounds with long dark hair which she wore in a pony tail down her back. She tied it with a shoe string, a rubber band, a scarf, or apparently whatever was handy when she wanted to get ready for her day.

Cathy was very concerned about her complexion and was always searching for just the right mud for mud-packs. Her first find was in Lake Elder over behind the hangars on the east side of the field. Now Cathy was not a person who did anything half-way. She practiced holistic medicine. Her mud packs were not just for her face, she went the whole nine yards by immersing herself in the shallow water and piling on the mud.

She usually wore an aged T-shirt that came halfway to her knees for this operation. The problem was that the water on that side of the island was not deep enough for her to get all the mud off, so when she was done it was necessary for her to cross the strip, go in front of the clubhouse, between the hangars, and dive off the boat dock into the deep water for her bath.

One of the regular porch dwellers observed that we could sell tickets if we just knew when the show was going to start. Willy Clyde said that he just couldn't decide which he liked better - watching that Earthy Woman walk across the strip with the mud all over everything or watching her walk back by the clubhouse in the wet T-shirt to her van in search of dry clothes. In any case the name Cathy was lost and she was known henceforth as Earthy Woman.

Jimmy Crowe was sunning himself on the porch one day when I came in and he said, "Have you noticed that Earthy Woman may not be here even when she's here?" I told him that we had all noticed there were times when she did not seem to have her act all together, but if we banished everyone from the ranch who was in that shape we would have very few members.

Jimmy agreed, but went on to say that Earthy Woman had come to him this morning to ask him to please move his truck away from her bus because all of those old electric motors that he had in the back of his truck were draining all of the juice out of the battery in her bus. I asked Jimmy what he did and he said that in the light of such obvious electronic intellect that he just moved the truck.

Big Bill said he was sorry that he had missed the parade this morning but he wondered did anyone think that Earthy Woman could have been the driver of the honey wagon?

I said, "Now Bill, just think about that question for a minute. What does she do every time she shifts the gears in that old VW bus she drives? It's a wonder as mechanically delayed as that gal is that there are any teeth at all left on any gear in that transmission. She couldn't drive that big rig, much less figure out the plumbing to dump the load."

Big Bill just hung his head and said, "Earthy Woman's off the list."

THE CONCRETE CADILLAC

The clubhouse was open and the coffee made when I rolled in the next day. Big Charley had it all under control. I picked up the phone to check the service for calls.

MESSAGE 1
Coach, this is Whizzer Whitmore. Ms Shay said you had just left the house when I called. Please give me a call at 555-8898.

MESSAGE 2
This is Laura Lincoln, I would like some information about learning to fly. Please call me at 555-9274.

MESSAGE 3
Hey Dapper, this Pat Fansler, I'm off tomorrow, can I fly 57F tomorrow in the a.m.? Give me a call.

Whizzer's call sounded the most interesting, so I called him first. He answered in the middle of the first ring. "Coach I need to go to Monroe NC as quick as I can get there. How long would it take to fly over there?" Whizzer asked. I told him it would take about two hours more or less and asked "What's the problem?" He told me his sister, Lena, had run off again and her car broke down in Monroe. "Mama says I have to go fix the car and bring her home. Can you take me over there?"

"Sure, it will take me about an hour to pull things together, come on over. How heavy is your traveling toolbox?"

"The box probably goes about twenty five pounds, including some other stuff."

"O.K., I'll expect you in an hour or so."

I called Shay to tell her about the trip and to see if she wanted to go to Monroe or somewhere else after we dropped Whizzer off. She said wait a minute, and I knew that she was considering going on down to Charleston or Savannah for some relaxation. After a moment she decided that the timing was all wrong because she had to get an advertising layout approved for a fund-raiser she was working on.

"Charley, I have to make a trip over to Monroe, can you handle these two calls while I preflight the bird? You can go along for some right seat time if you are interested. It will take about four hours, over and back."

"Jeez Dapper, I would like to, but I got an appointment with the damn hip doctor at 1:00 and I want him to check all of my newly installed hardware." It looked like I would have two hours of my own company on the way back. Flight service predicted the weather to be good to go VFR (Visual Flight Rules) so it should be an easy trip. Even the wind was light.

Whizzer parked his truck and said he was ready to go. We loaded the toolbox and we were off. I worked our way up through a broken layer of clouds and we crossed the big mountains over around Asheville at 8,500 feet MSL. Whizzer hadn't said much, but was starting to look more relaxed as we went along.

"Coach, I appreciate you taking me over here to pick up Lena. Mama says this is the last time I have to go and do this kind of thing for Lena, but we both know it ain't so. Lena just can't help herself from jumping into bed with any man that comes around. She always feels terrible afterward but it doesn't stop her from doing it again. I'm sure all the coaches knew about the time she rewarded the starting basketball team on consecutive nights after the state tournament that year."

She was in my homeroom so I know that she made good grades all the way through high school, but most of the school knew that she couldn't keep her legs crossed. "What happened to her this time?

"Well, she had been doing real well for a long time. She got that job with the Post Office and she understood that if she messed around with the men at the office that she would get fired. Then along came William Q. Mason, who now calls hisself a preacher. He is the assistant pastor at that little church over on Vine Avenue."

"Are we talking about Willy Quick Mason?"

"One and the same."

"Didn't he have the same disease in high school as Lena?"

"Yes, but then he was partial to white girls."

"Well, Mama lives up the hill from Lena and she has a real good view of Lena's place from her front porch rocker. She noticed that there was a big old red Caddy convertible spending time in the driveway there and found out that it belonged to Willy Quick.

"Mama Dorothy called the Reverend John Steele, he is a real Reverend, went to church school and everything, to come up and have a piece of pie and coffee on her porch. I've heard that they were stepping out together in high school, but Mama won't say. The Rev caught on right away when he looked down the hill and saw his assistant's car in the driveway of a parishioner of another preachers flock.

"I got a call from Reverend John that he needed a yard or two of left over concrete when I was in East Knoxville and for me to give him a call when the opportunity arose. You know we often have some concrete left over after we pour a job and it is nice to be able to give it to someone who can use it. I called him three times and he kept saying he was not quite ready yet. On the last call he said for me to meet him at the foot of the hill on Mama's street.

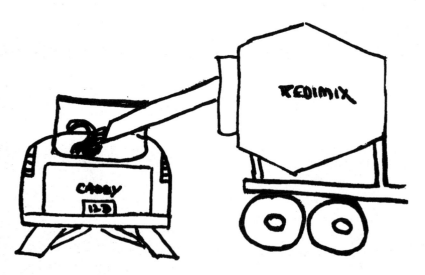

"He was waiting for me when I got there and told me what had been going on and for me to give him about five minutes to get up the hill and then put as much concrete in that old Caddy as it would hold. When I got up close to the house I could hear the music just a blaring at Lena's place.

"I backed the truck up to the driveway and filled that car level full. The tires blew out and the springs bent back so the frame was flat on the ground. About the time I got back in the truck the Reverend John Steele started banging on the back door and singing his favorite hymn. Willy Quick came bounding out the front door with his pants and shirt over his arm and headed for his car. He saw what had happened to it and the last we saw of him he was going into the woods at the end of the street.

"Lena, as usual, was feeling terrible when she called Mama Dorothy the next day to tell her that she was leaving and never coming back. She got as far as Monroe when her old car quit and now I got to fix it and bring her home, again."

We were getting ready to land at Monroe by now and I asked Whizzer if he wanted me to hang around in case the car was past fixing and he told me no.

He said it sounded like either a generator or a battery would solve the problem. "I don't think Lena would want to face you right now anyway. It's one thing for her to know that you know about her problems, but it's quite another to look you in the eye at the same time."

Whizzer called a cab and I put gas in the airplane and headed back up over the mountains for home.

CLOSED CIRCUIT TV

Willy Clyde Coyote left a call on the answering machine that he would be over to see me shortly after noon, he had something he needed to see me about. I was glad to get the message because I needed to see him about something too. He came in sometime after lunch and parked it at the round table. I didn't know how much after noon because when I retired I quit wearing a watch.

"Dapper, I got a problem. Somebody, I say somebody, is using the couch in my hangar for a lot of horizontal recreation. The springs in that poor old couch are getting beat all to hell and the place doesn't smell too good either."

"Yes, I know about the problem. Willy the Wanger said that he was working in his hangar the other day and that there was so much noise in your office that Homer couldn't get a decent nap. He said the poor old dog finally gave up and went swimming in the river.

"Who was in the office?"

"I have it on good authority that it was Hilliard Clanton and some young coed from UT. Excuse me, I forgot to say DR. Hilliard Clanton. By the way, he and Hilliary are both teaching one class at UT, maybe they will pay off their club bill."

"Well do you reckon I should change the lock?"

"Hell there is no use having locks on this airport anyway, the key for every lock on the place is either over the door or under something sitting next to the door. That only leaves the combination locks and those all open with the last four digits of the N number of owners airplanes. The bottom line is if you leave the key out a new lock won't help."

"Dapper, let's get the Wanger, Big Bill, you, and me together for a council of war over at Rabbit Hickman's place. I always work better on a full stomach and some beer.

"It will be at least a week before we can do that because I know that Big Bill just went out of town on vacation. He and Beulah went down to Gulfport MS for a visit with some of Beulah's cousins. Bill made some crack about doing a tour of 'The Great Mobile Homes of Mississippi.' Best I could tell, he wasn't too thrilled about the whole thing. The delay will give us time to gather some more information anyway. I'll set it up as soon as we can all get together."

The next day Big Charley came in the clubhouse and said, "Jeez Dapper, Clanton is at it again down in the Coyote Hangar."

"How do you know Charley?"

"The Smut-mobile was parked in the front part of the hangar when I drove by a minute ago."

"Well, let's get a coke and sit on the porch and see what the rascals latest conquest looks like."

We didn't have to wait long before the Smut-mobile, a tired looking VW bug with hand-lettering on the front proclaiming 'The Doctors Clanton' came motoring up past the clubhouse. However we had a surprise coming, it was not Dr. Hilliard Clanton driving. The car was being driven by Dr. Hilliary Clanton. The other front seat was occupied by a very large black muscle-bound type wearing a UT athletics sweatshirt with the arms cut out to show off his very large biceps.

"Wonder if they fumigated the place?" mused Big Charley. "Why would a nice looking young woman like her want to get mixed up with the likes of him anyway?"

"I don't know Charley, but it looks like both of the Clantons have roving eyes."

"Well maybe one of them is just trying to get even," said Charley.

During the next several days the Clantons visited three times each. Each day with a different conquest. All of the partners were of college age and most of them left with a smile on their face. Captain Tom surmised, "There must be more than one way to earn an A in their courses."

I was working on a little Fats Waller tune on my big piano at home when Shay said I had a call from Willy Coyote. Willy wanted to know if it would be all right to change the meeting from Thursday to Wednesday because he had a conflict and also to invite Shay to come along. It seems that Beulah got wind of the meeting and had explained to Bill that if he was going to the Rib Shack, she was going also. There was also some comment made about the women's presence raising the average intelligence of the group by at least fifty percent. I was the last one called, so the meeting was on.

Rabbit Hickman's place is presently in a converted four bay Esso station on Magnolia Avenue. The business has been operated by an ex-navy type for over thirty-five years in several locations. Rabbit has been successful in everything but choosing a place to do business. Six different locations over the years have been lost either to fire, urban renewal, or street projects.

The rest of the crowd had already staked out one of the long benches with four pitchers of beer and eight mugs. We had places for four on each side. The menu is very complicated. You can have barbecue - beef, pork or chicken. The side dishes are fries, slaw, soup beans, and hush puppies, and they are served family style on the table. The only other choice you have to deal with is which of the barbecue sauces you want, regular, extra hot, or atomic bomb. Rabbit says the atomic bomb sauce sells lots of beer.

The dirty plates and serving dishes had been cleared away and our waitress had just brought us all clean fully frosted beer mugs when Big Bill looked over at me and said, "Who called this meeting?" Peggy Sue said, "We all know what the problem is, what we need to do is find a way to stop it and very quickly. If we can get the Clanton's fighting each other they won't have time to take advantage of those kids."

"What about we just throw their asses out of the club? Then they can't use the hangar for their own purposes" mentioned Big Bill.

"That might solve the club's problem," Mai Ling offered, "but I want a solution that stops them cold. Some of these students may even be minors."

"Let's have them in at the invitation of the board of directors of the club and present them with the fact that we are aware of what both of them are doing on club property and that should start a real fight between them," Beulah suggested.

"In case they don't believe us, let's get Small Sam to install a closed circuit TV from the hangar to the clubhouse so we can record the activity and present it when we talk to them," said Billy Bob.

Shay added, "You'll have time to do that because the Club by-laws state that you must give a member a one week notice before you can require them to come before the board." The group discussed several other important matters concerning the next picnic and adjourned.

The clubhouse has a large TV which is fed by a wireless cable system so we can have access to a weather channel for up-to-date weather. The TV is also hooked up to a VCR for viewing the various training tapes that the club has on file. There are usually some of the tapes laying around on the lower shelves of the roll-around cart that the TV sits on. I've heard rumors that some other tapes have been shown at night by some of the younger members that dealt with pilot proficiencies not covered in the Federal Air Regulations.

Small Sam was tinkering with a new switch box on the cart when I came into the clubhouse and the picture on the screen was a shot of the couch in Billy Bob's hangar. Sam said, "Dapper all you have to do is turn this switch to A for the cable system and to B for the hangar. If you want to record anything on the screen just turn on the VCR and hit the record button." While we were talking, Willy Clyde Coyote's truck passed the clubhouse heading for the south forty, and Willy's big dog Tyrone soon appeared on the screen all stretched out on the Wanger's couch. Sam said, "I must have left the door to the Wanger's hangar open. It sure didn't take Tyrone long to notice, did it? I better go down and find another place for the old boy to get his nap and lock the door again."

Big Charley came wandering in and inspected the set-up and complained, "Jeez, the picture is all right, but ain't we got no sound?"

I don't know how the word got out, but by noon we had a full compliment of porch pilots wandering around. We actually got some of them to mow a little grass. However, most of them did not want to get too far from the clubhouse in case one of the Clantons showed up. Every new arrival had to see for themselves how the system worked so there was a lot more of the empty couch showing on the TV screen than there was of the weather channel.

As usual, Sarge Yenderushak was making book on which Clanton would show up first and what color the partner would be. Sarge was going to make money because in order to win you had to get both calls right.

The Smut-mobile was spotted as it came through the gate and Big Bill Henry hustled into the clubhouse saying, "Turn the damn thing to the weather channel so they don't see what the hell's going on." Dr. Hilliard Clanton drove by the clubhouse and went directly to the back door of Wanger's hangar, retrieved the key from over the door and let a tall redheaded girl precede him into the office.

The couple tried five different positions on the couch before finishing the session somewhere off camera. One of the porch pilots said that he thought he wanted to see this until he did, and now all he could think of was what he would do if this happened to his granddaughter who was away at Penn State. Big Bill commented, "Watching this kind of thing was a lot more fun when I was in the Navy and a lot younger." Small Sam checked the tape, and after it proved to be in good shape I locked it away in my office.

Dr. Clanton stopped just long enough at the clubhouse to pick up two cokes out of the machine before leaving. No one had anything to say to him although he did give his customary greeting of "How do?" as he entered the building. Two days later we got a similar tape of Mrs. Dr. in the arms of an anemic looking white kid that didn't really appear to have much "on the job training" for the task at hand. She helped him through the process and he was a much better educated young man when he left than when he came in.

Big Charley opined that there was very little review of old material involved here, mostly it was just new material for the boy.

The letter requesting the Clantons to appear before the Board of Directors stated that they should appear at the Sky Ranch at 7:30 on the following Friday. They were on time and chatting amiably with some of the members on the porch when I arrived. I'm not on the BOD now, but the President, Dr. Kronk, had asked me to be on hand so here I was.

Doc had been briefed about what we hoped would happen and he opened the meeting by telling Dr. Hilliard Clanton that he had some disturbing information about his behavior with young women on the club's property. Before Hilliard could reply, Doc said that he also had the same kind of information about Hilliary's behavior. The two looked at each other and Hilliard started explaining that what he and Hilliary were doing was part of a research project designed to explore the degree of sexual experience of today's college students through a process of pre-interview, liaison, and post-interview.

Big Bill had had all he could stand without exploding when he asked Doc Kronk if he could ask a few questions. Doc took one look at Bill's face and decided that Bill's blood pressure didn't need any more increase and gave him the floor.

Bill asked, "Are these young people students of yours at UT?"

"Some of them are," answered Hilliary.

"Do you feel any moral discomfort for what you are doing?"

"No, we are doing pure research for the good of society as a whole and there is no moral dilemma involved," answered Dr. Hilliard. He continued, "I just don't see what the problem is."

"There may be no problem for you but there damn sure is one for me," shouted Billy Bob Wanger. "If I catch you near my hangar again I'll fix you so you won't ever be able to bother another young woman again EVER! Just so you know, you asshole, we have tapes of you and your slut of a wife banging away in my hangar."

Dr. Hilliard then rose and announced, "Now if you are through, I just want to tell you that we have anticipated some resistance to our project and we have three complete sets of records of all of our project data, so if you are thinking about killing our project you will have to do more than destroy one set of records. We are leaving now."

Dr. Hilliary asked as she was leaving, "Could we have a copy of the tapes you made? They would be so helpful to the project."

The clubhouse had cleared out and the parking lot was nearly empty when Big Bill sat down beside me on the porch and said, "Now didn't that go well? We tell them we have tapes of their activities, which we think are going to start a fight between them, and they want copies so they can compare techniques. I'm glad Beulah wasn't here, she might of thrown that woman in the river."

When I got home Shay had already been talking to Peggy Sue. The Wanger didn't have as far to go to get home as I did, so he filled Peggy Sue in and she had called Shay. Shay said we were having another meeting Monday night at our house and this time we would have the meeting first and then go out to eat and drink beer.

SMUT PROJECT MEETING

Shay and I had finished eating our supper and I was relaxing at the piano by playing some old standards tunes out of a fake book. Peggy Sue came into the room and I shifted into "Somebody Loves Me," one of her favorite oldies, and followed it with "Blue Moon of Kentucky," for Billy Bob.

Mai Ling came in next and I played "Five Foot Two." She isn't that tall but I always play it for her anyway. Willy is totally tone deaf so I can play anything I want to for him and he never knows the difference.

Big Bill and Beulah arrived and, after I had played Beulah's favorite tune, Bill asked how I knew which couple had just come into the room because he knew that I couldn't see past the piano when I was wearing my special score glasses and I never looked up anyway. I told him it was easy, Shay never wears any perfume and I can tell which of the other three ladies are close to me by the perfumes that they wear. "Goddamn, I can't tell one of them high dollar smells from another," muttered Bill. "If you would quit smoking those petrified dog turds that you call cigars, you could smell better," said the Wanger. "You would smell better to the rest of us too," added Peggy Sue as she hugged him to show him that the remark was all in fun.

I moved off the piano bench into a comfortable chair after I picked up a note pad from the desk and said, "OK guys, the Clantons are way over the line, what do you think should happen next?"

Big Bill, never one to hang back, opened with "I want that pair of smuts out of the club and off the Sky Ranch."

Mai Ling said "That doesn't begin to cover the situation. They are abusing the whole UT system with that bogus research crap they are pulling. I want them out of my University."

Shay said, "I am more concerned about the youngsters they are hurting and the damage that might occur if some of their trashy records should get out somehow."

No one else had anything to add at the moment so I read from the pad the three items that we had listed: Club Ouster, University Sanction, and Record Eradication.

Bill said, "Throwing them out of the club doesn't seem very important compared to those other things, maybe we should drop that." Willy cut in, "I disagree, that's a very public and visible thing for us to do and everyone knows how mad some of us are about this. Also, the ouster may divert some interest away from our more important projects." Beulah added, "I agree and one other thing, we underestimated this pair of smuts last time. We need to plan for three hundred percent overkill this time."

The room got quiet for a moment and I said, "Looks like we are into project management. Bill since you are on the BOD, you are the logical one to handle Project Ouster and have them thrown out of the club. Will you need any resources to get that underway?" Bill thought a minute and said, "No it's just a matter of bringing the motion for expulsion before the BOD and the membership, I'll get it moving."

"Mai Ling, since you mentioned it first, do you want to lead Project Sanction?" She nodded her head and then asked, "Do we have any leverage anywhere that I might use on the Chairman of the Sociology Department in case he needs help in making the proper decision?" Shay said, "Yes, I think we can call on a very Senior Senator, Senator Davis, Chairman of the Higher Education Committee for help in that regard. He pulls a lot of weight in Nashville and that's where UT's money comes from. You and I will go visit his wife Sugar." I asked Mai Ling if she needed anything else and she said she didn't know of anything at the moment.

"Looks like Project Record is next, who wants it?" I asked. Shay said she would handle that one, but she would need some help to locate all the material they had about the students. Willy said, "We could visit their house while they were out and see if they have anything there and maybe follow them around a little to see what else they are doing."

Beulah interrupted, "We would probably just get caught and make the job that much harder. Let's hire some professional help for this part. Who would be a good man for the job?" I said that I didn't know but I knew who did and beeped Swifty Swanson. Swifty called in a few minutes, and I explained that we needed a man who was long on results but that we didn't care much about methods or legalities. Swifty said the man we wanted was Bryson Dwayne "Bird Dog" Brown and gave me a phone number. He also said to mention his name if we called Bird Dog because B.D. owed him a favor or two.

Peggy Sue asked about paying the detective and Shay said she thought she could raise some money for the cause, just give her a few days. I told the group, "I think we should keep the projects separate from each other and that we should only tell outsiders just enough to get them to help us. Any information flowing out should be on a need to know basis. If there is no other business, the first meeting of the Anti-Smut Committee is closed. Let's go eat, I'm starving." On the way out of our house Willy asked the Coyote if he had signed him up for the Gay Pilots Association, because he sure had been getting a lot of mail from that bunch. Billy Bob said that he hadn't signed him up, but that it was on his list of things to do. The way he was grinning, I'm not sure I believed him.

BIRD DOG BROWN

Bryson Dwayne Brown, aka B.D. and Bird Dog, returned Shay's phone call in about an hour after she left a message on his machine mentioning Swifty Swanson's name. He told her that he was working a case, but that if she could come to Cancun's Restaurant on Chapman Highway

he would be seated on the patio and he could talk with her there. He said he would be wearing a gray baseball cap with a blue "P" on it. Bird Dog turned out to be one of those middle-aged, nondescript individuals who had no outstanding features whatsoever. He was so plain as to be invisible, which was a real plus in his chosen profession. Bird Dog worked in basically two areas. The first was in providing divorce dirt for a string of divorce lawyers and his second source of income was from insurance companies who wanted to get rid of fraudulent damage and disability claims. Bird Dog had worked in several law enforcement agencies but had left them, according to him, because they were all more interested in process than results. He had solved some big time cases for a while with the Tennessee Bureau of Investigation, his last employer, before going into business for himself.

When Shay arrived at the appointed patio she had no trouble spotting Bird Dog. No one was seated within earshot so she quickly explained what the Clantons were doing and that we needed to know what kind of records they had and where they were stored. Bird Dog said he would watch them a bit and see what he had to do to get the required information. He said he owed Swifty a day or so and he would get back to her about a fee for any other time he had to spend.

The phone shattered what little concentration I had been able to muster as I worked on reconciling the club checkbook with the bank statement. Shay said that she had gotten a preliminary report from Mr. Brown and that it would curl my hair if I had any.

I asked if she had called the ladies of the Anti-Smut Committee about a meeting, and she said it was on for tonight so I better plan on getting home in time for a nap in my recliner before supper because it could be a long night. Before I could ask, Shay said that we had to be at the Wanger's at seven-thirty and we needed to eat first because Peggy Sue just didn't have time to cook on such short notice.

I went back to work and got the difference between the checkbook and the bank statement down to three cents and decided that was good enough and quit just as Big Bill walked into the clubhouse. I said, "Bill, in case Beulah hasn't caught up with you yet, we are meeting at the Wanger's at seven thirty."

Bill said, "Yes, somebody told me my cell phone was ringing and I talked to her a while ago. I've got to get another cell phone, I can't hear this one for shit and I had the damn thing in my shirt pocket." I said, "Bill, maybe you need to get one that has the optional feature that makes it vibrate rather than ring." Bill said he would think about it.

The Wanger house had two very outstanding features, a wonderful great room which included the kitchen, and a spacious covered deck that is as long as the house. There are two sets of French doors leading to the deck from the great room and another set leading from the master suite. The deck is about twenty feet deep and the middle section is also screened.

When we arrived Mai Ling and Willy were sitting in one of the three large couches that are grouped around a very large fieldstone fireplace talking with Billy Bob. Peggy Sue was busy in the kitchen making a large pot of coffee and a pitcher of lemonade for the group. She was having some trouble moving around because Homer and Tyrone were following her every move in hopes of a handout.

Beulah and Big Bill came in just after we got settled and Bill asked Billy Bob if he had roasted any oxen in his fireplace lately. Billy Bob said that he hadn't tried that yet, but that Fufu, Peggy's white poodle, had spent some more time in the ash pit yesterday when she stepped on the dump door in the bottom of the fireplace and slid all the way to the bottom of the chute and ended up against the steel door down under the deck.

"That's that dumb dog's third trip down that chute," Billy Bob added. "Where is the poor thing?" asked Mai Ling. "She is still over at the poodle parlor hopefully getting all the ashes shampooed out," supplied Peggy Sue as she joined us from the kitchen.

There were a couple of loud noises out on the deck and we looked up to see Homer and Tyrone both chewing on some kind of a bone. Peggy Sue walked over to one of the French doors leading to the deck and tapped on the glass to get the dogs attentions. When they looked up she just shook her head and pointed at the stairs leading down from the deck and both dogs picked up their bones and, looking very guilty, with their heads hanging down, slowly went down the steps. Beulah smiled over at Peggy as she sat back down and said, "It's a shame the way you mistreat those dogs."

There was a moment of silence and Shay said, "Guys I called us together because I'm afraid we have a lot more going on with the Clantons than we realized. I talked to Bird Dog Brown today and he told me that they have a videotaping set-up at their house and they have been recording all sorts of activity there. The attached garage is set up as a large master bedroom with at least four video cameras hidden in it. The cables all lead back to a small closet off the kitchen with a bank of VCR's.

"There is also an office that has been built into the attic of the house that you can only get to by pulling down a door in the ceiling of the hallway. The hidden office has two computers, two phone lines, and there is enough videotape up there to open your own video rental store. There is also a large system for editing videotape."

"How did he find all of that stuff?" asked Willy. Shay said that Bird Dog told her that the first thing he always checked was the electrical box and there he found several new circuits had been added to the old box. Then he just followed the new wire to see where it went. He says there are cabinets and shelves all over the place, overflowing with folders full of interviews, most of them complete with names and addresses on them. There are also lots of computer disks scattered all around.

"What else did he tell you?" asked Mai Ling. "Well, he said the house, which is on the corner of Cherokee Drive and Ellington Road in Vestal, belongs to Bagwell Realty," replied Shay. "Hey I think one of Willow's brothers runs that for the Warthog," said Peggy Sue.

"Goddamn, that don't narrow it down much," fumed Big Bill. "There's Buford, Brody, Baxter, and Bumper in that clan." Peggy Sue smiled and retorted, "If you're going to name the whole clan, you left out Willow, Wallene, Winona, Wilma, and Wendy." "Oh, go to hell," sputtered Bill.

"That's about all I have from Bird Dog," concluded Shay. "Mai Ling, how did your meeting with the Dean of Liberal Arts and the Chairman of the Sociology Department go?"

MAI LING VISITS THE DEAN

Mai Ling shifted around in her corner of the big couch and started out, "Well, after Shay and I went over to visit with Sugar Davis and explained why we needed an audience with the Dean of Liberal Arts, she whipped us out a letter on the Senator's letterhead. It said that a matter of grave importance had come to the Senator's attention concerning the morals and ethics of two members of the Sociology Department and that he would look on it as a personal favor if the Dean would set up a meeting at his earliest convenience between himself, Ms. Mai Ling Coyote, and the Chairman of the Sociology Department so that Ms. Coyote could present her information and to be sure to keep his office apprised of this shocking situation."

Mai Ling continued, "When I first went in the office a young receptionist was more interested in talking to her boyfriend on the phone than she was in taking care of business. She finally glanced at the letter I handed her and said the Dean's Secretary would see me when she was free. I waited about ten minutes and told the girl to take that letter to the secretary now and have her read it. The girl looked a little startled and disappeared. In a minute or two an older secretary appeared, apologized, and led me directly to the Dean's office. Dean Leonard J. Clump looked back and forth from the letter to me for a minute and told me that if I could show him any validity for these allegations he would do anything he could to put a stop to the activity. He put in a call and the meeting was set for the next day at two o'clock."

"I was seated in Dean Clump's office when the Chairman of the Sociology Department, Dr. P. Percy Paddington, came prissing in. The Dean introduced us and Percy handed me one of those cold wet fish handshakes while he looked at the dean rather than at me. The dean told Dr. Paddington that I had some serious allegations concerning members of his department and asked me to put my cards on the table.

"I told them that I had videotape of both the Dr.'s Clanton engaging in sexual intercourse with university students who were possibly members of their own classes. Dr. Paddington immediately jumped in saying that the Clantons had a national grant to study the sexual habits of college students and his department would stand behind educational research and the people who did the work.

"The dean waited until the chairman ran down and then he told him that he did not care how much grant money the Clantons brought in or who had sanctioned the original research. He said there was no way he could condone such a thing and he objected to it morally, ethically, and professionally. He got red in the face and continued that he had already covered for Percy once. Then he told him to sit down and figure a way to stop this mess, not protect it.

"He called his secretary Mary in and told her he needed information about the Clantons in Sociology as quickly as she could provide it and she said she would need a few minutes and did we want any coffee? The dean said he would get the coffee and she should get the information.

"Mary came back in a few minutes and told us that the girl who was providing the secretarial service to the Clantons said that the records for the project were filed in cabinets in the office but that she had to make four copies of each item. One was stored in the office, another was being filed in the dead storage area in the basement. The other two copies were always given to the Clantons and those records were carried out of the office.

"I told the dean that I needed to get back to work and would he please keep me informed. He told me to feel free to call at any time and that if he was not in the office Mary would share any new information with me as it became available. As an afterthought he added that he could guarantee that Dr. Paddington would "cooperate to the fullest degree."

Beulah cut in with, "We are short one copy of this mess."

Shay said, "I forgot this a minute ago, but Bird Dog told me that there is a big old Winnebago sitting on the front of the lot at their house and he saw them carrying some files into it. I bet that is their escape hatch. In case something happens, they will be able to leave town and take all their dirt with them!"

While this was going on the doorbell rang and Peggy Sue came back with Swifty's adopted boy Sandy and he said, "Dapper, a man came by the Sky Ranch a while ago and asked me to give you this letter. He said it was important and that I should only give it to you. So you got the letter and I got a date! See you on Friday when I have my next lesson with Captain Tom."

Handwritten on the outside of the envelope was 'Dapper, I found this in the house after I talked to Shay. BDB.' I opened the envelope and inside was a printout of an e-mail message which stated that the ProPorn Web Site was prepared to start receiving the first group of ten tapes for $2000 per tape one week from today. After re-reading both the note and the e-mail, I picked up a moose call that was on the mantle and blew it for attention. When the noise died down I read the note and the e-mail to the group.

Everyone started at once, but they were all saying basically the same thing. Big Bill summed it up by speaking louder than the others, "I was mad before, now I am so goddamned furious at the no good, shit eating, over-educated, sons of a bitching, low-life bastards that anything we can dream up for them, its not enough."

After the hubbub died down I said, "Looks like we are on a short string here. According to the dates on this letter we have to do whatever we do before Sunday just to be on the safe side. We already know we have to get all the records taken care of and get them out of UT. What else do you think we want to do?"

Peggy Sue said that she would see where the Clanton's stood financially and do her best to destroy any future credit ratings.

Willy said that he thought that Mr. Dr. was one of the worst diseases of the social order that he had ever seen and he was going to try to arrange for the doctor to get some firsthand knowledge of another type of social disease. Billy Bob added, "I think I know just the thing that will put a real hitch in Mrs. Dr.'s get-along."

I put my two cents worth in by saying that I wanted these people out of town for good.

Big Bill said he would arrange for the records in the house and the Winnebago to go away on Saturday morning and so the rest of us should have everything done that we're supposed to do before then.

The group started breaking up. Shay and I headed for home. It was a little out of the way but I cut across Cherokee Drive so I could turn down Ellington Road. The little white frame house sat in the back corner of a very large lot that sloped down and away from Cherokee Drive. The yard around the house had several large flower beds which needed attention. I mentioned to Shay that it looked like whoever had planted the flowers must not be around to look after them anymore. The house was built very low to the ground and the large verandah on the front was level with the yard and only one step up into the house. There was no one around as we drove by.

THE CLANTON FIRE

The Anti-Smut Committee started gathering at the Wange'rs on Saturday morning at nine o'clock to eat brunch and hopefully get progress reports on the various activities scheduled for the morning. We picked Beulah up on the way because Big Bill was out taking care of the records. Everyone except Big Bill and Billy Bob were there. I had just loaded up a plate with biscuits and gravy, county ham, fried potatoes and fresh cooked Granny Smith apples when the first phone call came in from Dean Clump to Mai Ling saying that we could cross off the two sets of records at UT.

Then, before I had time to go back to see if I had missed anything the first time around, Big Bill checked in on his cell phone saying that all the records and tapes on Ellington Road were history, and that he would be over to give us the details in about ten minutes. Billy Bob called in to say that he would see us as soon as one of Willy Clyde's Bubbas could get the junker he was driving running.

Willy Clyde and Big Bill arrived together in Bill's car in about fifteen minutes.

Beulah told Bill to get a cup of coffee and sit down and tell us what happened as she was not going to sit around and wait for him to eat first. Bill talked Homer into letting him sit on a couch with him and started his tale.

"I went out to where I parked the car, raised the hood, and was tinkering under there. The Doctors came out the Ellington Road side and didn't see me at all. My plan was to release the brakes on the Winnebago and let it roll down into the house. Then I was going to throw a match into the place and let it all go up together.

"About the time I was going to cross the street a car came speeding up Ellington with two teenagers in it and came to a sliding stop. A skinny kid got out and ran over to the Winnebago, busted the door with a baseball bat, and got in. He had just got it running when I walked up and slammed the side of the camper with the bat he dropped and the kid must have floored it, because the engine stalled.

"He tried once to restart the thing but gave up and started to abandon ship without setting the anchor. It started rolling backwards down the hill toward the house and the kid finally went out the door just in time to land in a big rose bush. I could see thorns sticking out all over the place as he made a run for his buddy's car.

"The big camper was accelerating down the hill through the yard toward the house and the kids in their old car were peeling rubber up the hill on Ellington. The old car started turning left on Cherokee Drive at the same time as the camper reached the verandah on the front of the house. Then two things happened at the same time. The rear tires of the car lost traction and it wrapped itself around a tree on the other side of Cherokee Drive and the propane bottles on the rear of the camper ruptured as they went through the front wall of the house.

"Ignition was instantaneous. I ran back across the road and turned around just in time to see the big gasoline tank on the camper go up. It was a hell of a fire. If the fire department had showed up right then, they might have been able to save the garage, but the house was past saving.

The last I saw of the two would-be Winnebago thieves, they were running down through the woods toward the river."

"Billy, when did the fire department arrive?" asked Peggy Sue. Billy Bob said "That's another whole story and here it is.

"Like we planned, I had an old junker of a car which I was going to stall in the middle of that one-lane underpass under the railroad down the hill from the Clantons on Ellington Road. The Vestal fire station is just two short blocks on the other side of the underpass so we figured just a few minutes delay would help a lot.

"Well, I was in place about fifty yards from the underpass when I heard the blast go off up the hill. I heard the siren go off in the fire hall and when I started to put the damned car in the underpass, it quit. The car wouldn't start and some man driving a pickup didn't notice that I was stopped on the side of the road.

"He pulled up behind me and started blowing his horn for me to get out of his way. He finally figured out that I wasn't going to move and backed up and came around the old car. The driver had scooted over as far as he could to the passenger side of the truck, steering with his left hand so he could throw empty beer cans at me as he went by.

"He was still looking back waving a finger at me when he met that big fire engine, with all the red lights and the siren going, head-on in the middle of that one-lane underpass. I walked down to be sure none of the firemen were hurt. The pickup was no match for the big, old, heavy, long nosed fire engine. The pickup was badly compressed so that the front bumper was now back behind where the front wheels had been. The drunk had come through the windshield and was stretched out on the hood of the fire truck with a beer can still clutched in his hand, snoring away.

"None of the crew was hurt and they told me that they had called in for a truck from the hall on Highland Avenue to cover the call and the Captain was starting in on the ton of paperwork required by KFD for the traffic accident. The other firemen stretched the drunk out in the back of the pickup so he could sleep better. Other than a few cuts he didn't appear to be hurt. I decided I would walk up to see the fire and I called Wanger's road service bunch to come and pick up the car.

"By the time I walked up to the house, all that was left was the bare frame and the running gear of the Winnebago with the rear end of it in the middle of the foundation and the front end sticking out the front. There were no wooden parts of the house left. Only the metal parts remained, the sinks, bathtub and kitchen stove were laying on the ground. There must have been a lot of gasoline in that old camper. Swifty Swanson pulled up in his cruiser just after I got there and said that he would stay until the Clantons arrived. Bill and I were going down the hill toward the hospital when we passed the smut-mobile going up the hill with a fire truck following it."

Swifty Swanson called to say that he was taking a couple of hours of lost time and he would be over for some brunch in a little while. When Swifty arrived he filled a plate and we filled him in on what had happened while he ate. Then he told us what happened after he arrived.

"Well, shortly after Big Bill and Billy Bob left, the Clantons drove up in their little bug. They stood and looked at the smoking ruin for a minute and Mrs. Dr. turned around and nearly knocked herself out by running into the mail box. She got her bearings and opened the box and took out several things."

Big Bill interrupted, "One of the things was the letter from the Dean that I put in there when I first got there."

Swifty continued, "She sat down in the car and opened one of the letters and just seemed to be in a daze. When her husband came over to sit beside her she gave him the letter to read. He read the letter and reached under the seat for a fairly good sized paper bag and rolled two fat cigarettes. I got them out of the car, cuffed them both, and put them in the back of the cruiser.

"After I had let them stew for a while I told them that I had information that one of the coeds that they had been with was a minor, which meant they might be facing statutory rape charges, and that there was enough Mary Jane in their car to qualify them as dealers.

"I let them think about that for a while and then I made them the offer that we agreed to last week. Mr. Dr. accepted the offer to take the clothes on their backs and two nonrefundable bus tickets to Tuscaloosa AL rather than face the publicity and possibility of jail time here. Dapper, I didn't tell them what you said about going down there and helping out the Crimson Tide. Peggy Sue, here is the mail they left in the car. Looks like they may have a problem."

Willy Clyde spoke up, "Mr. Dr. has a problem that he don't know about yet, and with any luck she will get it too." "What do you mean?" asked Beulah.

"Here is what I mean," said Willy. "I remembered that the Warthogs daddy, Pretty Boy, used to work with Hazel Haskins, Knoxville's most famous madam, back in the old days when his cab company delivered everything from preachers to hookers. The Warthog isn't in that line of business that I know of, but I figured that he still knew Hazel well enough to ask for her professional advice and maybe a favor too.

"I called him and he put me in touch with Hazel and she told me that from time to time some of the girls were put out of service due to medical problems. She gave me a phone number and a name of a girl who was of college age who was currently not income producing due to a particularly virulent strain of the common clap.

"She posed as a student needing counseling in the Sociology office and was immediately chosen to take part in the study. In a week or so Mr. Dr.'s dick will be dripping like a rental house faucet. It just hasn't been the boy's week."

Peggy Sue looked up from her reading and said, "The finance committee will now make a report."

"I checked with Bumper Bailey, Willow's brother, over at the realty company that owns the house they were living in and they were way behind on the rent. Dapper told me that they have also owed the club some money for a long time. I contacted the credit company that we use and reported the debt status and they told me that they already had some bad reports on the couple.

"One of the letters that Swifty just gave me is from their credit card company and it states that their card is maxed out and, until they receive a substantial payment, the cards are void. They also threaten legal action if payment is not forthcoming. Most of the other stuff here is from the utility companies. The electric bill, the water bill, and the phone bill are all over-due, but I believe that service has already been terminated. The insurance on the Winnebago camper lapsed two weeks ago.

"I wanted them to be financially wiped out and it looks like they have handled that all by themselves. Mai Ling, I think this last letter is in your department."

Mai Ling scanned the letter and started filling us in.

"Actually there are two letters here, one to each of the Doctors, but they contain the same things. The letters say that their employment with the university is terminated as of yesterday's date and, since they were on a probationary status, no cause need be given. All university property and any property purchased by any grants to the university are to be returned forthwith.

"The Dean goes on to say that all of the records of the project filed in the Sociology office have been sent to the incinerator. Also, copies of those records which were filed outside the office on university property were likewise destroyed. The Dean's parting shot is a great one. He says, 'after removing all of the university property from your offices we have packed your remaining personal property in a shoe box and will be happy to mail it to you. The box contains three tampons, an autographed picture of Wade Houston, and a string-less yo-yo.'

"The Dean wrote the letter for me on Friday afternoon after I ex-plained to him that we needed for it to be on hand Saturday morning and we were afraid the mail might not get it there in time. He said it was for-tunate that Friday had been a holiday because he had already cleaned out the office but ran out of time before he could get the records picked up. The phone call this morning was to let me know that the second set were headed for the fire."

Big Bill Henry looked and said, "I guess that's about all then."

The Wanger said, "No, I got one more thing to add to the festivities.

"You all know, or have at least heard, about Big Bubba Rhoote who works for Willy Clyde there. He is only about five foot eight but he is called Big Bubba because of his extremely large appendage. That boy hangs down a full twelve inches and is reliably reported to expand to nearly four inches in diameter. He calls it Kong.

"I sent him over to their house on Thursday afternoon and he told Mrs. Dr. that he had heard from one of his friends that she was doing a survey and he wanted to get in on it. She assumed that he was from the university and invited him in. Bubba said she sent him out to a bedroom that was in a converted garage and said she would be right out. He said that she didn't really see Kong until she looked down after she was poised over him, and by then it was too late. Bubba said that he understood from other girls that the next couple of days were usually somewhat uncomfortable for first-timers with the Kong."

Billy Bob added, "I almost forgot, Bubba also has a raging case of the crabs, so this wasn't Mrs. Dr.'s week either."

"Do we have any loose ends here that we need to take care of?" Beulah asked.

"Not as loose as Mrs. Dr.'s end will be for a while," said Peggy Sue.

"No, I mean is there anything else we need to take care of," retorted Beulah. Shay said that she would check with Bird Dog Brown to see what we owed him and she also wanted to see what Bumper Bailey had to say about the loss of the house.

Mai Ling mentioned that she wanted to go by and fill Dean Clump in on some of the other things that had happened, but she would leave out some of the details. Big Bill added that since they were leaving town, there was no reason to complete the club expulsion procedure.

The room was quiet. The group all seemed to be considering all that had happened in such a short time. Shay broke the silence, "I know we had to stop this mess and destroy all of the tapes and stuff, but why is it that now I feel mostly sadness?" I put my hand on hers and said, "Think how bad you would have felt if all of those tapes appeared on the Internet. Your sadness has to do with the Clanton's poor behavior, rather than with what we did to stop them.

KNOXVILLE NEWS SENTINEL

A fire on Ellington road completely destroyed a house owned by Bagwell Realty. The house had been rented to Dr. Hilliard Clanton according to Bumper Bailey of Bagwell Realty. Bailey said that the house was slated to be razed as a part of a plan for a new condo project. The fire was apparently caused by a runaway Winnebago camper, owned by Clanton, which rolled into the house. The Clantons were away from home at the time of the fire and are reported to be moving out of state.

DRY CLEAN ONLY

Big Charley put his head in the office door and asked if I wanted to go with him, the Zipper, and Small Sam over to the tractor place to pick up some parts for the John Deere that they were working on. I told them I would if they could spare enough time to stop at the Greeks for a couple of hot dogs on the way. Somehow or the other I had missed lunch. They said fine they hadn't missed lunch but they would have a dog anyway. After a few dogs we hit the I-40 east and headed for the tractor place.

Small Sam motioned toward a blonde in a convertible with the top down and said, "Will you look at that?" The car was a mid-sixties model Pontiac and it was hard to tell what year model the blonde was. She had very long hair which was blowing in the wind and a Dolly Parton size chest barely enclosed in a pink knit top. Zipper wondered aloud for all of us, "I wonder if that's real?"

She was in the right lane and we were in the left. We passed each other several times as the traffic ebbed and flowed. "There must be a wreck up there somewhere" Charley guessed as the traffic slowed to a crawl. It was stop and go as we would creep ahead two car lengths and stop again. Sam looked over at the woman and said, "At least the scenery is good."

We were one car length behind the convertible, running alongside a big eighteen wheeler when the traffic all stopped again and it started to rain. The gal finally figured out how to get the top up on the convertible and it was nearly on the windshield when the trucker behind her got impatient and hit a blast on his air horns because the traffic in the right lane had started to move.

The trucker's air horn seemed to be directly connected to the blonde's right foot because she floored the big V-8 and left two streaks of rubber in the right lane. The car was accelerating rapidly when the woman grabbed at the locking handle for the convertible top because the wind was starting to lift the top off the windshield. A big gust of wind associated with the sudden rain started taking the whole top toward the rear of the car.

The blonde held on to the locking handle long enough to be lifted out of the seat to the point where her very loose seat belt stopped her and slammed her back down in the seat just in time to slam on the brakes to keep from hitting the car in front of her which had stopped again. The convertible top had risen to its full length straight up in the air, but now it was stretched out upside down on the trunk of the car. Entangled in the top bracing was a blonde wig with long hair blowing in the wind.

The woman that got out of the car didn't look at all like the one we had been watching. Her hair was short with a lot of salt and pepper in it, and it looked like she had been sweating under the wig. Her wonder bra was also a casualty of the accident, her once proud boobs were hanging down nearly to her waist. What had been looking eagerly at the horizon in the east now stared due south at her bare feet. The rain hadn't done anything to improve her makeup either. One minute she had been happy and beautiful, now she looked like the wrath of the gods and she had a temper to match.

She marched back to the trucker who was stopped behind her and started using language I hadn't heard since basic training. The trucker wouldn't even roll down the window. The Zipper looked at her as our lane of traffic moved out and said, "She needs a dry clean only tag on her. Rain water doesn't agree with her."

After we got back from our run, I was working on one of my least favorite jobs, filing away the past years' collection of bookkeeping trivia. There were bills for utilities, fertilizer, aircraft repairs, gas charge sheets, aircraft charge sheets, and other miscellaneous bits of paper from last years' operations. I was putting it in a box to store in the hangar until someone else decided to throw it all away to make room for more of the same.

Zipper pulled out a stack of invoices from Izzy for repairs of the club's rental fleet. The first one was for re-skinning the elevators on the C-172. Zipper said, "This one was caused by someone jamming the tail into the ground while the bird was rolling backward. If they had taken the time to use the tow bar, the problem never would had come up."

I picked up another invoice and the notation on it stated that the tires had flat spots ground down to the cords and said to Zip, "You know, the only way this can happen is for some careless type to land with his feet up on the brakes when he landed on a hard surface runway. There is also a set of brake pads on this invoice."

The next offering was for a new alternator, voltage regulator, and battery with the notation that someone had tried to boost the 28 volt aircraft battery on the C-172 with a 14 volt jeep battery. I said, "We have some slow learners out here." Zip commented, "Education has always been expensive, but this bunch thinks that they are all on scholarship and that someone else should pay for their education." "I sure have made some bonehead moves in my time, but I've paid for all of them myself and I am getting tired of financing mine and theirs. That's the last of this!

"On a brighter note, the guys are having a tough time coming up with the driver of the honey wagon aren't they?" "Yes, Bill and Charley both carry the club roster around with them like a second skin; they have notations as to where members and their wives were on the night of the big stink. The list of possible suspects gets smaller every day," said Zipper.

"You know it will be a little sad when they find out who the culprit is because they are having so much fun with the hunt."

REBA'S REVENGE

I was surprised to see Sgt. Yenderushak on the porch and asked him, "When did Reba let you out?" Sarge said, "I guess everyone in the world knows when Big Red goes on the warpath. This is the first time in a while I have had time to get out."

The Sarge continued, "She was really mad at me this time. I had to come up with something to take her mind off what happened so I went out and bought her a new piano, a six foot grand.

"The boys that came over to deliver the thing said they wouldn't be responsible for damage to the trailer floor. They also questioned if the blocks under the trailer would hold up the weight. I decided to send it back until I could work something out. Reba said that the trailer was too small for the piano anyway and it was time for a bigger place."

"She picked out a nice double-wide and I set it up with a lot of extra supports on those three empty lots next to the old place. I moved all our stuff from one place to the other and now she says that she has to do the hard part. Decorating the new place. By the way Dapper, she wants you to come over and play her new piano, but you better give her a few more days to re-hang all of the pictures a few more times.

"Bill have you all been over to Jimmy's since he got back from the bass fishing tournament in Florida? He left the night before I fell off the wagon and brought back the biggest trophy I ever saw" said Sarge. Big Bill said "Dapper, there goes another name off of the goddamn list."

Father Gene said, "I was over there the other day and Jimmy told me an interesting story about that contest. The way it went is that Charley Bill Franklin had been using a frozen bass he caught up in Norris last summer. He would figure how long it would take to thaw in the fresh water tank on his boat and put it in at the proper time. Jimmy told me that he didn't mind losing when Charley Bill first caught the fish, but enough was enough.

"Jimmy was leading the contest until Charley Bill went back to the boat and put old faithful on the scale. Jimmy said that he had plenty of second place trophies on hand anyway so he just walked up to the scales and stuck a little thermometer deep into the fish. It has a long steel probe and is a very accurate instrument which he uses to measure air temperature when he works on air conditioners. The little dial swung around to about 45 degrees and Jimmy asked the weighing judge how a fish could be at 45 degrees when the water temperature was well above that reading. Jimmy has the first place iron and Charley Bill is out of the fishing tourneys for a while."

INSTRUMENT CURRENCY

I was getting a little behind on log book entries to verify that I had done the things necessary to keep my instrument ticket up to date so I grabbed Captain Tom off the porch and we went out in 2U to shoot a few approaches on the gauges so I would be legal. I checked the bird over and taxied to the end of the strip where I put on the hood which restricts vision to only the instrument panel. I did an instrument take-off and called Knoxville approach, "Knoxville approach, this is 02Uniform, over." They were not too busy so they came right back with,

"02 Uniform, this is Knoxville approach."

"2U is a Cessna 172 just off the Sky Ranch, I would like to shoot a couple of ILS approaches."

"Two Uniform squawk 7034."

"Squawking 7034, Two Uniform."

"Two Uniform I show you climbing through 2000 feet five miles northwest of the Sky Ranch. Turn right to a heading of zero five and climb to and maintain 2500 feet."

"Turning to 05 and reaching for 2500 feet, 2U. Two Uniform turn right to a heading of one niner to intercept the ILS, you are cleared for the approach, call the tower on 121.5."

The marker beacon sounded off so I hit the stop watch, reduced the power to 1800 rpm, and called the tower, "Two Uniform inbound at the marker." The tower came back with, "Two Uniform cleared to land 23 right." Both needles stayed inside of the inner circle on the VOR head, so I rode the beam down to two hundred feet above the runway and called, "Knoxville tower, 2U missed approach."

The tower came back, "2U turn to 270 and climb to 2500 feet."

We went around for another turn and when I called the missed approach I asked to go back to the Sky Ranch. We landed and Tom scribbled in my log book and I was legal again for another six months.

Tom then got to telling me about the big trip to Branson MO. Tom and his wife had driven their fifth-wheel camping trailer out to go to a big square dancing get-together. Tom said that she had insisted on taking their bicycles along but the only exercise that he got out of them was to put them in and take them out of the camper each time they wanted in. I said, "So you were out in Missouri doing the watusi when the fertilizer hit the recreational facility."

Tom said, "I guess so, Big Bill said I was off the list of suspects. You know, nearly everyone in the club has plenty of motive for this one."

SHAY VISITS SUGAR DAVIS

I pulled into the driveway at home just as Shay was unloading some groceries out of the back seat of her old Honda. After we put the food away she said, "Let's go sit on the porch. I have several things to tell you about." We settled in our rockers with our tea and Shay began her story.

"Sugar Davis called me this morning and invited me to come over this afternoon because she wanted my opinion on something. When I got there a big party, political type, was just breaking up. You never saw so much glad-handing in your life.

"Sugar grabbed me and we went in her office where it was quiet. She asked me if I knew who Billy Bob Wanger's decorator was, and I told her that I didn't know who he had on staff but that I had the utmost faith in Peggy Sue and Billy Bob.

"She said that she knew that I had a good eye for decorating and just wanted me to meet with the decorator about the new fabrics for the family room. The decorator was due to show up any time. The bell rang and who do you think walked in? Ms. Catherine Winbigler, also know as Earthy Woman. She was dressed very nicely, had her hair done up on her head, and even had on makeup! She is not a bad looking woman when she works at it."

"Did she recognize you?"

"Sure she did, who else always wears a hat these days? We looked at some fabric combinations that Catherine paired up on the desk and I changed some of them around to suit me and Sugar liked my pairings better than what we started with. The carpet pieces that were previously selected looked better with the new combination too.

"Sugar made her choices and Catherine said she would get the orders in and let Sugar know when the material would arrive. Catherine hurried off and Sugar and I sat still and enjoyed the peace and quiet for a minute."

Shay then proceeded to tell me about their visit and what was said.

Sugar sat with her leg over the side of an overstuffed chair and Shay had her feet up in a big couch. Sugar put a finger in a glass of wine that was on the table beside her, then sucked on the finger a moment and asked, "Shay, how often do you and Dapper get to sit around the house and not worry about someone appearing out of the blue with some damn project or the other? It seems like we have somebody underfoot around here all the time. When we were in high school we use to sit around and talk about who we wanted to be and the kind of life we wanted to have. I have most of what I dreamed about and all I want now is for Bobby Lee and me to have just one night a week to ourselves.

"This is his last term in office. He won't run again. We are worn out with the whole thing. The group that was here today were all trying to get Bobby Lee to endorse one of them after he announces his retirement."

"Is it common knowledge that Bobby Lee is quitting?"

"The crowd that was here today all knew, and that's better than printing it on the front page of the paper, although it probably won't show up there for a while yet."

"I don't see how you put up with some of the crowd that was here. That Quenton Tudberry is a real mess, I would have to count the silverware and check his pockets before he left."

"He is a mess, but hopefully he is so dumb that he is harmless. Grover Cleveland, on the other hand, is trying to use Xander's incident with the airplane gas to pressure Bobby Lee into something."

"What does the Warthog want Bobby to do?"

Sugar started laughing so hard she nearly fell out of the chair, repeating "Warthog, Warthog, that's priceless!"

Bobby Lee walked in about that time and said, "Whatever you girls are drinking, I want some too." Sugar told him about the nickname for C. Grover Cleveland and he enjoyed it as much as she did.

Shay asked them how Xander was doing after the night spent in the garbage can and they said it really got his attention and it also got their attention. Bobby Lee said he might join the flying club so that he and Xander could learn to fly. It would give them a common interest and also give Bobby Lee a place to hide from the world of politics.

The next day at the club I told Bill and Charley about Shay seeing Cathy Winbigler and they said I must have got the story mixed up somehow. They just didn't believe that Earthy Woman had another life.

SHAVING CAN BE DANGEROUS

Billy Bob Wanger settled into the open space opposite me at the Rib Shack. It was not often that Billy Bob got a chance to make a meeting of the Knife and Fork group because he was usually busy with Wanger, Inc. He ordered his usual, a double rack of ribs and a quart of sweet milk and looked over at me and said, "I did what you suggested about the decorator situation. I asked Catherine if she would do the new bath for the Clevelands and she said that she would do the job only if she would be dealing with Willow and not Mr. Cleveland. I called the Warthog and he told me to make Willow happy and to do it as soon as possible so that she would come home.

"We ripped everything out of the bath area to the bare walls. That included the bath, shower, dressing area, and walk-in closet. There were some strange looking stains on some of it but I think we could have cleaned it all up. After we removed it all and the cleaning crew did their thing, Catherine and Willow had their first meeting."

The food arrived and slowed down the conversation for a while. Small Sam, who was sitting beside me, finished up his plate and asked Billy Bob what the girls had decided about the bathroom area. Billy Bob said, "To start with, the girls decided that the bath proper and the drying area should have a heated tile floor. So we ripped out the existing floor and dropped in a box so we could pour a concrete base with the circulating pipes embedded in it. Sometime after we left, the Warthog came in and took a nap in the bedroom.

"He must have gone in the bathroom without his glasses because he tracked fresh concrete all over the carpet in his suite. It left some low spots in the concrete, so when we came in the next day we had to start over on that little project. We never would have been able to make the tile look right on an uneven base.

"I called Catherine to let her know about the ruined carpet and she said new carpet actually would make it easier to blend the whole suite together anyway. She also told me that she had a multiple head pulsating shower, lots of new cabinets, polished granite sink tops, a small refrigerator, a boiling water dispenser, and a heated toilet seat coming in soon."

Loose Lip Linder came in the clubhouse to get some coffee and told us that he had put some shelving material in the parts trailer that had come from the Warthog's job and that he would put us up some shelves out of it as soon as he had a chance. After he got settled at the table he asked us if we had heard about the Warthog's run-in with his electric shaver. We hadn't heard so he filled us in.

"The Warthog, for reasons that maybe only he understands, is still sleeping in the downstairs suite while the construction is going on. There are three other bedrooms on the second floor, each with a bath, and the downstairs suite is empty because Willow is out of town for the duration. She told Peggy Sue that she is allergic to dust. The rewiring of the room is a work in progress and we have a big set of work outlets that we use for plugging in our power tools. It has a long pigtail on it with bare wires that we attach to a hot circuit when we need power.

"The Warthog wired the work outlet up to some wires hanging out of the wall and plugged in his electric shaver. He wired the box to the 220 circuit that will supply the boiling water dispenser, and when he plugged in the razor it knocked him across the room and he landed in that fancy new shower. We had all of the frames up but the glass parts were still in the crate. His head and shoulders were on the inside and his feet were still out. The cord to the razor stayed connected to the box and somehow attached itself to the metal framework of the shower.

"Every time the Warthog moved he got a jolt, but if he could stay still he didn't get hit. Willow's cell phone was in the pocket of the robe he was wearing and he hit the re-dial button by mistake. Willow's last call had been to Catherine and she answered on the second ring. The Warthog was somewhat confused at this point and, thinking that he had reached 911, explained his problem to Catherine. She happened to be near the house and told him she would be right there."

Loose Lip continued, "I was going over there to check on the cabinets and I saw Catherine turn into the driveway just as I turned onto the street. I got to the suite just in time to see Catherine put her toe on the outlet box and pull out the razor cord. The electrical activity had given the Warthog a tremendous erection which had escaped from his robe and was standing up like a flag pole. We helped him up and walked him to a chair in the suite's sitting area.

"Catherine was somewhat uncomfortable with his current state and said she had other business to attend to and hurried out. It turned out that he only had a small burn on his right hand and a very tender area where his scrotum had come in contact with the electrically charged shower assembly. He was still pumped up and ready for business when I left about thirty minutes later."

Big Charley put in, "That may be worth looking into, it sure would be cheaper than Viagra."

The Wanger stopped at my hangar as he was driving by, turned off his engine, and said "Boy, some people really have it made." I asked him how the big job up at the Warthog's place was coming and he said, "You could have gone all day without bringing that up. That job has been a train wreck ever since it started. We have it all done now except the carpet, the wallpaper, and the painting.

"The painters finished up once and then Catherine came out to check the colors. The Warthog walked in, she turned, and walked right into a scaffold which was loaded with paint cans. We had paint everywhere! Ever since that girl saw the Warthog standing at attention the other day, when she sees him her eyes go directly to his fly and that's all she can see. I thought that gal might be gay for a while, now I don't know what to think.

"After we got that mess cleaned up and the walls repainted, the carpet crew was out there stretching the new carpet in the suite when Willow brought some of her nieces and nephews over to play in the pool. She put on her new mini-thong bikini and practiced some of her diving routines while the kids were playing. The carpet laying crew got so excited that they let some of those big long pipes that they use to stretch the carpet get away from them and they broke out three of the French doors that lead to the balcony.

"The black paper-hanging crew was spending all their time in the kitchen watching Lujacinda until the Whizzer came by and explained to them that they had far better things to do than watch his wife. If I can just keep the Warthog away from Catherine and Willow fully dressed for two days, I think I can finish this one up."

ORSON WELLS & COMPANY

The end of the month rolled around and it was time for me to close out the books by getting all the charges for aircraft rental, gasoline, oil, club dues, and tie-downs finished up, along with the work credit for the month. The entering of the work credit book entries would just about finish up the data entry part of the monthly closing if the porch pilots would leave me alone long enough to get them entered. Work credit is the program at the club that helps get the grass mowed, the gate repaired, the clubhouse cleaned, and anything else that needs doing around the place.

The members check the bulletin board for jobs and keep a count of the time it takes to do them. They then enter their name and the date of the chore they did with the hours worked and I convert the hours into money at the rate of five dollars per hour and credit their account for the appropriate amount.

The members either mailed me a check or put their payments in a section of 8 inch steel well casing that had been welded shut on the bottom with a door and a slot on the top that locked with a padlock. The whole assembly was firmly fixed to the wall and the system had worked for years without any tampering that we knew of. The safe, as it was called, was constructed by J. B. "Orson" Wells.

Orson is a big man, about six feet two inches tall and 235 pounds, with no smooth edges anywhere. His hands and his vocabulary have been hardened from years of moving houses and other kinds of heavy work.

Orson is a randy old goat who took his pleasure where he could find it and as a result has been divorced at least three times that the folks here at the club are aware of. His current girl friend is Lilly Lusby, a big strong red-headed woman who works for Orson in his house moving business. It is reliably reported that they often spend the lunch hour or two engaging in horizontal recreation, as they both have substantial sexual drives.

Small Sam recently asked Orson if he was going to marry Lilly, and Orson told him in no uncertain terms that he was not going to spoil a perfectly good relationship by getting a preacher involved in it and 'This old Indian has split his blanket for the last time.'

Orson's philosophy on equipment was the same as it was for relationships, if it ain't broke don't fix it. He has an old truck with a boom on it that one of the power companies must have auctioned off when it got too old for them to keep up. You would swear that the thing was going to die before it got off the airport from the noise that the transmission and rear end makes, but it had done that for at least twelve years because that's how it sounded when he set the bar beams for mine and Pat's hangars. The gear box is so loose in it that shifting is somewhat of a random choice for anyone other than Orson.

Big Bill came in at about 12:15 and we jumped in his car and headed out the highway for the Duck Inn and lunch. As soon as we were on the road Bill said, "The Wanger and the Coyote have been at it again while you were gone.

"While the Coyote was doing a quick test hop of his bird Wanger went by his hangar and put six construction screws through the bottom of his dinner bucket into the top of his work bench and went up to sit on the porch with the other porch pilots to watch the fun.

"The Coyote came back shortly and tied the airplane down and walked by the bench and grabbed the bucket and came away with only the top half. The half with the thermos was in his hand but the half with the sandwiches was still on the bench. Nobody and everybody knew who could have done such a thing, but the anticipation of the next move hung heavy in the air."

We found a parking place and a booth and Bill continued the story "The very next day the Wang was out at the strip working on the John's steering wheel when Small Sam came by and asked him to go for a ride in the Cub and they took off and flew down the river looking for a lost john boat that was supposed to be on the loose.

"They were barely out of sight, when in came the Coyote driving his new all purpose maintenance truck complete with air compressor, short boom, diesel tank, and welding gear. The Wang had left his toolbox open on the tailgate of his pickup with the intention of finishing the job on the John when he returned, but it was a serious error in judgment.

"Coyote lifted out the tray and emptied the box on the tailgate and fired off his new arc welder and laid a bead all the way around the bottom of the box into the tailgate of the pickup. Then he put the tools back in the box and left to go out to a job he had going."

The waitress interrupted about then and Bill said he had a low gravy light burning and wanted roast beef with mashed potatoes and lots of gravy on it all. I had promised Shay that I would be good so I ordered a salad to make her happy and a cheeseburger with a double order of fries to make me happy.

Bill continued the yarn, "When the Wang got back he decided he did not have time to finish the job so he tossed the tools that were still out in the top of the box, closed it and grabbed the handle to put it behind the seat. When he lifted the box off the tailgate all he got were the top and sides of the box. The bottom and the tools stayed on the tailgate. The welding process had attached the bottom to the tailgate, but had so weakened the metal that it separated from the sides of the box when the pressure was applied as the box was picked up."

I told Bill that I guessed we would just have to stay tuned for the next foray and hope we didn't get hit by any stray rounds.

ASHES, ASHES, ASHES

The Warthog flew an old Cessna 337, the inline twin engine job, and most of the porch pilots felt that it was just a matter of time before we had to fish him out of the river off the end of the runway. So far he has managed to prove us wrong.

He had set up a business to own the airplane so he could write off most of his aircraft expenses. His latest venture was using the airplane to spread the ashes of loved ones over their favorite mountain or lake. He could take four members of the family with him to observe the process.

He put together a clear plastic box with two three-inch hoses attached. The exhaust hose went out the small pilot's window and stayed in the slipstream just aft of the opening. Then the other hose was hooked to the fresh air intake in the wing root. The incoming air in the box mixed the ashes with the air and out the exhaust hose they went. The system worked well according to Hal Hooser who flew with the Warthog on the trial run.

Usually the ash hauling trips started at the downtown airport because the runway there is longer and smoother. But because there were only three mourners on this particular day the Warthog decided that he would do the whole thing from the Sky Ranch. Three ladies of various ages, dressed in long black dresses, black jackets and black hats appeared at the appointed time with an urn of ashes. The ashes were duly transferred to the plastic box and the group loaded and departed TN98.

In about an hour I noticed the 337 coming around to land to the south. Everything looked routine as the 337 touched down for a nice landing and taxied to the gas pumps. As soon as the props stopped, the doors flew open and three of the maddest women I ever saw came bailing out of the airplane.

Their black dresses had turned to light gray, their jackets were gray, their faces were gray except for the tear stains. They were completely covered with light gray ashes. They walked toward their car with a small cloud around them and left a white trail of ashes. When the group passed near the clubhouse porch one of the women looked up and said, "I know that none of you gentlemen had anything to do with this, but would one of you please tell that man in the airplane that our attorney will make contact with him tomorrow. I don't ever plan to speak to him again!"

By the time the ladies were gone, the Warthog had put chocks under the wheels of the bird and cranked the rear engine back up. He was standing in the prop wash, beating on his clothes with his hands trying to get the collection of ashes to blow away. The interior of the airplane was a mess. There were ashes everywhere.

The Warthog said, "Everything went as usual, I put the hose out the window and had just gotten the inlet hose firmly attached when the outlet hose blew off the box and all of the ashes started blowing around the cabin. The woman sitting behind me screamed and put her arms around me so that I could not reach up to pull the inlet hose off. I was lucky to be able to keep the airplane upright. By the time I was able to get her off of me the box was empty. I think her screaming in my ear may have injured my ear drum."

The Warthog headed home for a shower and fresh clothes. He probably also called his lawyer.

Small Sam came in my office after Grover was gone and said, "This may have been an accident, but I don't know whether to give credit to the fact the outlet hose was cleanly split where it attached to the box or to the

Vaseline that was on the outlet nipple. Either one would have done the job. It may have been a union job with more people working than were required."

EARTHY WOMAN'S RIDE

Small Sam stuck his head in the office to tell me that he was going to take Earthy Woman for a ride in the Cub and he wondered if I had my video cam with me so I could get a shot for the newsletter as historical events needed to be recorded. I told him that, as usual, the camera was not here. I finished up writing a letter to a member about a check that had been returned for non-sufficient funds and closed the office.

I walked out on the porch just in time to see Small Sam swing the prop on the Cub which was pulled out in front of its hangar heading toward the south end of the runway. The engine coughed and caught and started to purr nicely. The airplane started rolling and Small Sam stepped to the side like a bullfighter, yelling at Earthy Woman, who was in the front seat, to step on the brakes, The Brakes, **THE BRAKES!**

Sam and the porch pilots were in hot pursuit of the airplane when Earthy Woman came out of her trance and tried to step on the brakes. She missed the left brake, and the right brake caused the bird to reverse course and the pursuers became the pursued. The Cub, now moving northward in the tie-down area, scattered Sam and the pursuing porch pilots like a bowling ball hitting the sweet spot for a strike. They went everywhere. The throttle must have been creeping forward a little because things started to happen at a faster pace. The bird was now headed directly for the gas pump and gaining speed as it went.

In every organization there are always some people who never get the word about what is going on. In our club it is Tightwad Wilson. Tightwad, totally oblivious to the rest of the world, was carrying a 4"x4" timber about ten feet long from his truck to the club hangar when he finally saw the plane and Earthy Woman bearing down on him. He dropped the timber and moved out quicker than he had in years. The Cub's wheels hit the timber and stopped, the plane's momentum caused the tail to come up off the ground in the back, and the prop started to cut grass on the front. The tail settled back to the ground just as Small Sam caught up and killed the engine.

Earthy Woman remained strapped in the front seat while the assemblage pushed the Cub back into its hangar where Big Bill Henry inspected the prop for damage. When big Bill pronounced the prop ready for duty Earthy Woman asked, "Sam are we going flying now?" Small Sam looked around a second and said, "What the heck, roll it out, but this time someone please give me a prop."

A VISIT TO MRS. DOROTHYS

Shay and I hit the driveway at home at about the same time. She went on in the house with a bundle of some kind under her arm and I walked back to check the mailbox for the daily pile of junk mail offering me credit cards, Internet access, and lots of other stuff that I didn't want. There were some bills and one small envelope that I thought looked promising. The junk mail didn't make it past the garbage can at the garage, the rest I carried inside. I dropped the mail on the kitchen table and headed for the computer to see if there was any e-mail from the family.

There was a short note from the Navy branch of the family and I told Shay we had mail. She came in and put her hand on my shoulder while she read the message. Then she handed me a small handwritten note.

Dear Mr. and Mrs. Kurlee,

I would be very pleased if you could come and share dessert on my porch on Friday the fourteenth at 9:00 PM. This is my way of saying thank you for the great favor you did our family.

William and his family will be with us.

Very Truly Yours,

Dorothy Whitmore

RSVP 555-2421

Shay looked down at me and said "If you have anything on the schedule for Friday it is canceled. We will be on Mrs. Dorothy's porch in our best bib and tucker. You just better watch your language if you know what's good for you."

I gave the only answer a man married thirty-five plus years remembers. "Yes ma'am."

Dorothy Whitmore was one of the cooks at East High School, where I first started teaching. She specialized in cakes, pastries, and filling up the trays of children who needed all the food they could get at school because their home life left a lot to be desired.

A member of the central office staff who was in charge of the school lunch program came out to the school one day and noticed some of the servings were not meeting the federal guidelines. He came back with a batch of federally approved serving spoons with a memo as to which measured spoonful was to be used in each situation.

When he left, Mrs. Dorothy grabbed up the federally approved 'measured' serving spoons and put them in a drawer and got out her big long handled stirring spoon and continued to give the kids that needed it as much food as they could handle. Someone asked her about the other spoons once and she told them that if the supervisor comes back she would tell him exactly where he was to put his federally approved measured spoons.

We parked out front, walked up a steep driveway and up a set of steps to a big deep porch that was crowded with porch furniture. Lujacinda, wearing a soft yellow dress, met us with a hug at the top of the stairs and took us over to Mrs. Dorothy's chair where she had been showing her granddaughters a recipe in what appeared to be a very old cookbook.

She immediately got up to give us both a hug and started talking about the school dances that we had chaperoned together at the old school as she called it. We all talked together about the world when it was a much gentler place than it is now.

A car pulled into the driveway and the Reverend John Steele climbed up to the porch. Reverend John and I had met many years ago when we were both trying to reassure the community that their children were in good hands in the new school after integration closed the only school people of color were allowed to attend.

Whizzer looked up after opening pleasantries were out of the way and said "Reverend John, you sure seem to spend a lot of time on the property of non-parishioners." The Reverend looked over at Whizzer and said, "Yes, but the difference is tonight I was invited." We all had a good laugh and Mrs. Dorothy said "Lujacinda, let us go out to the kitchen and put a little snack together for these folks."

The little snack turned out to be two cakes, two fruit cobblers, some fried pies, fresh berries, and ice cream. Mrs. Dorothy told me as I was loading a plate that she knew that the fried pies really didn't look right, but she remembered how partial I was to them and there were some in the fridge for me to take home. We had a wonderful evening recalling people and events of times past, but Lena or her problems were never mentioned. Shay said on the way home that she did not remember ever having a more relaxing evening

THE FLAPPER CABLE

Billy Bob dropped in at the clubhouse and poured himself a cup of coffee out of the big green thermos bottle that he always carried in the truck. He claimed that the low octane stuff just didn't have any kick to it. He drank a Louisiana brand that had about half coffee and half chicory that would take the enamel off a set of store teeth.

Billy Bob said, "The Coyote got me again. He almost had me take the whole transmission out of my truck, but I found out what he did just in time." Everyone around the table got quiet waiting for the next chapter in the long ongoing saga.

Billy Bob continued, "I was going out to a job this morning when the truck started making a funny noise. At first I thought that a rod was about to let go in the engine, so I kicked her up in neutral and shut down the engine and the noise kept right on a going.

"I pulled over to the side and checked all of the tires to be sure I hadn't picked up something, and they were all in good shape. When I started up again the noise was back but it quit by the time I got to the shop. The noise seemed to be right under the cab so I figured it had to be the transmission.

I had the truck up on jacks and was just about to drop the transmission out when I saw the clamp on the drive shaft with a little piece of cable sticking out from it. The reason the noise quit is because the cable had a nick in it and just wore out from the beating it was taking."

Big Charley asked, "Why didn't it start making noise the moment the drive shaft started turning?" "There was a little bit of fishing line in the universal joint, so I figure that the free end was originally tied down. Then when the fishing line wore in two, the free end came loose and started beating on the bottom of the frame of the truck," answered Billy Bob. We all had a good chuckle and filed the information away for future reference.

The Warthog had come in somewhere there in the middle of the explanation and asked Small Sam, "I know that one end is clamped to the drive shaft, but what do you do with the other end?" There were several quick rejoinders as to where the other end could go. Everything from up your tailpipe to tie it to the frame of the car. Everyone had a good laugh at the Warthog's expense. The Warthog's poor score in the personality area was equaled only by his poor understanding of all things mechanical.

The phone was ringing when I came back from walking the runway and a voice I couldn't place for a moment said, "Dapper, this is Bobby Lee Davis. I hate to bother you and your bunch when I know how busy you are, but I need the unlisted number of that upstanding member C. Grover Cleveland." I said, "Sure Bobby Lee, anything for a fraternity brother," as I looked up the number. "What has that asshole been up to?"

"Well it went like this," Bobby Lee said. "Mr. Cleveland has been mad at me for some time over a political matter and he decided to come over to my place the other morning and put a cable on my car in the driveway. When I went out the next morning to go to the office all hell broke loose.

"About the time I got to the end of the driveway there was a gawdawful noise and the engine raced but the car was dead still. I got out and looked and the wheels were laying just behind the car on the driveway and the rear end of the car body was resting on the frame.

"I called the wrecker and when they picked up the car, there was a cable attached to the drive shaft on one end and to the frame of the car on the other. The dumb bastard had used half inch cable and must have run it up and over the exhaust pipes and then to the frame, because the pipes were cut clean in two. When the cable wrapped up the slack it snapped off the drive shaft at the front universal and it all caught in the track for the automatic gate which knocked the rear end out from under the car."

"Bob," I said, "I think I understand most of this, but how do you know it was the Warthog?" Bob said, "When Billy Bob did the remodel job for me one of the things that I didn't want that he made me buy anyway was a TV surveillance system. I have him on film and is he going to pay!" I asked, "In court?" Bob said, "That's way too easy." "Will there be any copies of this show available for limited screening?" I asked. Billy Bob said he would have to consider that and get back to me.

When I had a chance to tell Big Bill Henry about the senator's car, Bill commented, "The Warthog has always been mechanically delayed."

After Bill left, I was working on the books when Izzy Green and Chub Checker came into the clubhouse and said that they wanted to see me on a matter of some importance and I knew something was afoot. They told me that they had heard about the Big Pool Caper, and what they really wanted to see was the video of the Warthog hitting the polluted waters of his pool. They had been on a trip to Germany with the Guard and had missed all the fun. They said they had a buddy who could take the tape and make a cassette which ran as a continuous loop. I told them I didn't have the tape but I did give them Billy Bob's beeper number. I made a note to tell Big Bill that there were two more names to mark off the suspect list.

A rain squall had moved the porch pilots all in the clubhouse around the big table. Big Bill said, "Dapper, now that you have retired and have all this time on your hands, why don't you get into something that is for the good of the order." I said, "You mean good for old Bill, don't you?" "Well him too," said Bill. "What I really meant was why don't you get the club to build us a kitchen on one side of the maintenance hangar. That way we could cook for parties and maybe have biscuits and gravy for a breakfast sometime."

The idea appealed to the assembled group, so they started to figure out what they wanted in terms of a kitchen. They all agreed that a stove was the first order of business and a couple of guys headed out in search of a decent kitchen stove.

Word of the new kitchen spread quickly and the hangar started to accumulate various pieces of surplus gear. Hal Hooser came driving up with a three compartment restaurant style stainless steel sink. I asked him where it came from and he told me that it was in a metal building that he and Small Sam were tearing down out in the western end of town. Things were looking up, a little wiring, and a little plumbing, and we would have the big part done.

TIGHTWAD WILSON BUILDING

A new day, a new pot of coffee, and the club was ready for whatever. A check of the answering service netted me a call back to Small Sam, so I gave him a call. "Dapper," he says, "You're just not going to believe this, but I'm going to tell you anyway. T.W. and I were just finishing up taking the last of the metal off of that old building we bought when T.W. went back up to get one last piece of roof metal. He fell all the way to the concrete floor and landed on his back.

"After he got his breath back, we decided that he had to go to the hospital so I asked him if he wanted me to call the meat wagon. He told me he did not want to wait and if I could help him get in the truck, for me to take him on over there. "I called his wife and she met us at the emergency room and I went back to the job site.

When I got there all the metal roofing was gone. Some S.O.B. stole all the sheet metal, three forty-foot bar beams, and the trailer we had it on."

"Have you heard from T.W. today?" I asked. "Yes, he is going to be sore, but there is nothing broken," said Sam. "Sam, did they just hook up your trailer and pull it out, roof and all?" I asked. "No, we were using the Tennessee Security System on it. I had the wheels off the trailer and they were in the back of the pickup truck with me," Sam said. "They must of had one of those trucks with a crane built on it or maybe they used one of the fork lifts that hook to the back of a truck. They sure had been watching and were well prepared."

DINNER AT JIMMY'S

Shay's air conditioner on her old Honda wasn't doing the job very well anymore so I told her that I would drive it to the Sky Ranch so I could run over to Jim's Radiator shop to let him check it out. I gave Jimmy a call and he asked me to bring it by at around five and he would have a look.

It was about four thirty when I pulled in the lot and there were still several cars parked here and there. Jimmy was charging two air conditioners, supervising two other jobs being done by other mechanics, and talking on the phone to someone about a bass tournament in Mississippi. Jimmy looked up and asked me to get us both a coke out of the machine.

He finished up the two in his bay and said, "I'll back this car over to that open spot on the fence and you put that one in front of it. When I get the Ford from over there, you get the Chevy that is behind and put it right here." We moved the cars and in short order Jimmy had them diagnosed. He added a charge of gas to the Chevy's system and checked the temperature at the vent. He pronounced it cured and said put it back.

"Jimmy," I asked, "is it possible that that thermometer might have a slight odor of fish, maybe frozen fish, about it?"

"If you want to get Shay's car fixed, you better start treating the help a little better," Jimmy said. "So you heard about that, did you?"

Six o'clock rolled around and Jimmy said that's all of them but Shay's, let's have a look. I put it in the bay and Jimmy took a quick look and said all it needs is a little squirt of gas and we are through.

The phone rang again and Jimmy talked a minute and asked if I could come on up to the house for supper. "Prenny has plenty and you have been promising that you would come up." I said "Sure, Shay has a meeting tonight and I am on my own anyway. She is probably a little miffed that she will have to drive the van." We locked up the shop, let one of the original junkyard dogs loose inside and I followed Jimmy to his house.

I had seen Jimmy's place many times but only from the air. We often left the Sky Ranch and flew through the Walland Gap in Chilhowee Mountain and turned south in the first valley on the other side of the mountain. The house was about halfway up the east side of the mountain and just a few miles from the gap.

The two-story house had a deck running the length of the house with a spectacular view of Mt. LeConte. Prenny was in the second floor kitchen which smelled wonderful. She gave me a big hug and asked where Shay was. She turned me loose to check the cornbread and told me to check out the view on the deck.

Prenny came out in a minute with some iced tea which she put down on the big wide wooden rail going around the deck. She came over to me and started to give me a big hug again and I kidded her about where is your ugly husband. She said he is getting a shower but this hug isn't just for you it is also for Gretel over there.

Gretel turned out to be the biggest German Shepherd I ever saw. Prenny went on to say that "once she sees me give someone a hug and a kiss they are family to her and from then on she will treat you as such."

We settled in around a table loaded with green beans, slaw, mashed potatoes, pork chops, and gravy. When the meal was about over, Gretel came and put her head in my lap for a minute and then picked it up and looked up at me. I knew I was accepted and gave her a pork chop bone to seal the bargain. She walked away with the bone and put it in her bowl and came back to check everyone else for a donation.

We sat on the porch eating a dish of ice cream and looking at the big mountain as the sun settled over the mountain behind us. About the only sounds you could hear were the ruffle of the night birds coming out for the evening and the pork chop bones being systematically crunched over on a corner of the deck. We sat and talked a little but mostly just listened.

A faint breeze mixed the soft fragrance of the woods around the house with the aroma of our dinner. The deck had that same warm feeling of home and contentment that I had felt on Mrs. Dorothy's porch. Everything that was here belonged here. You could get lost without leaving your chair.

"Hey you guys, I'm going to have to get through the gap and find South Knoxville before you have an extra for the night. This has been great, next time you all will have to come over to South Knoxville."

THE INVESTIGATION CONTINUES

Big Charley and Bill Henry were deep in deduction and conversation when I arrived at the club on Monday. They had a club roster out and were making notations on it. I knew that they were engaging in their favorite pastime, searching for the elusive honey wagon driver.

"Well Sherlock and Dr. Watson, what have you deduced?"

Big Charley said "Well, when I went up there with Buford Bailey to pick up the honey wagon, there were motorcycle tracks leading away from the truck but none leading to it. Whoever it was brought the bike with them so they could leave as soon as the load started to drain down into the pool."

Bill grumbled that didn't help a hell of a lot because every SOB in the club rode a damn motor or had at one time. Charley mused "That's true, the only one I can think of who does not ride one is Earthy Woman and she is scared to death of the things. Do you think that Buford could have done it?"

"No, I'm quite sure he is too afraid the Warthog would take his business away from him if he were to get caught. He was on a big 'coon hunt up in Union County that night anyway. I know that because Willow was worried about him being blamed and she asked Buford's wife Mozelle about it. Willow told my wife about it and she told me over breakfast this morning."

REBA'S NEW HOUSE

The big leather recliner in our living room had sneaked up on me again. I woke up from a nap at about 4:30 in the afternoon and walked down the steps into the new room on the back of the house. I added the room to the house more than twenty years ago and have made other additions since, but the family has always called it the new room.

Shay was working on some sort of advertising document at her computer and I went to the piano to play. I worked my way through some Fats Waller, some Harold Arlen, and some George Gershwin tunes, finishing up with several choruses of "Five Foot Two". Shay made the appropriate comments as I moved over to my desk to find out how her work was going.

Shay said that she had just faxed a proposed layout to the major sponsors of her current fund-raiser for what she hoped was the last time. Some of the sponsors get real touchy about the relative placement and size of their logos.

Shay also told me that she had talked to Reba Yenderushak earlier in the day and we were invited over to see the new digs. "She said to tell you to bring a fake book so you could play some of that 'wonderful American Jazz music.'" I said, "She sure knows how to turn a guy's head. When do we go?"

"We'll go over tomorrow night at around eight, no dinner, but you know she will have all sorts of desserts on hand."

"Sounds like a winner to me, what do you want to do about dinner tonight?"

"Let's go over to the strip and find a patio, a pitcher of beer, and take it from there. I've had about all of this computer I can stand today. "We parked next to Oskar's truck and headed for the new house. Before we got to the door Reba was out giving us a hug and nearly carrying us in the house. She is an enthusiastic woman.

The house was a wonderful mixture of things from all the places where both of them had lived. They had been posted to the Far East, Hawaii, and Germany since they had been married. One wall was filled with the career of Sergeant Major Oskar Yenderushak.

There was a picture of a young GI, not the Sarge, next to Oskar's Silver Star medal from the Vietnam war and I asked him who the other trooper was. Oskar told me that he was the other man in an operation and that he didn't make it. Sarge said that he promised himself that he would remember the ones who did not come back and this was one of the ways that he did it.

Reba's memories of times past were quite different. She had framed handbills of a circus appearance in Hamburg, and piano concerts in Bonn and Prague. She said the piano concerts featured her mother and that she had worked in the circus.

There were interesting silks and laces from all over. Reba loved fabrics of all kinds. The great room just seemed to reach out to you with interesting things, including a Young Chang grand piano. Reba said that she had played our Chang and liked the action so much that she had to have one of her own.

I asked Reba what she was going to play and she said that she had a couple of Strauss waltzes, "New Vienna" and "Treasure", that she knew I would like. She played them beautifully and the Sarge looked up and asked her to play his favorite. Reba turned back to her piano and played "Tales From the Vienna Woods." The way she played, the song obviously meant a lot to both of them.

Reba stood up and said "After we have a little strudel and coffee, some jazz from you I want to hear. Maybe some Fats Waller you could play."

The strudel was truly sinful, it was so rich and good. I put my plate on the counter and headed for the piano. I opened up my gig bag and pulled out my dog-eared Hal Leonard "Ultimate Jazz Fake Book". I had yellow sticky notes on "Honeysuckle Rose", "The Joint is Jumping", and "Squeeze Me". Reba slid in beside me and we finished up with "Ain't Misbehavin". She played the melody line very correctly and very straight and it was quite difficult for me not to add a lick here and there. I did one chorus solo my way and then I thought the evenings entertainment was over.

Reba pulled out a four hands waltz and said, "Come on Shay, let's see if this arrangement you and I can play?" It sounded great and I told Shay that I wished I could sight read a full arrangement like that. Oskar said, "They've been practicing all week, don't let them pull that sight reading gag on you." We said our good-byes and headed home.

THE GAS TANKER & ONE LEG LILLY

"Dapper, the gas tanker got stuck up the hill there, you better come and see if maybe you can pull him out with the tractor," said Big Charley. I asked him if the tanker was blocking the railroad crossing and he said no, that it was in the first turn off the main highway.

We jumped in the van and rode up to the main highway and there in the first turn of 180 degrees sat the big tanker with eight thousand gallons of aviation fuel aboard. The right front dual on the tandem axle trailer was down in some soft gravel and that took most of the weight off of the left driving wheels of the tractor, so there he sat.

We tried putting some planks and gravel under the driving wheels, but they were no help. Doc Kronk pulled up and suggested that we jack up the trailer, but we didn't have a jack on the place that would lift that kind of weight. While we were standing around a tandem dump truck pulled up with a load of gravel for Hal Hooser's hangar. The dump truck driver said that he would get on his radio and call the wrecker service that his company used.

When he came back he said they were sending out Big Bertha to give us a hand. Big Bertha turned out to be a great big wrecker mounted on a Mack tandem truck body when it rolled up a short time later. The driver was One Leg Lilly.

Leg took a quick look around and said the thing to do was tie Big Bertha to the trailer and pull the whole rig back about six feet, unhook it, and then let the rig move forward under its own power fast enough to pull on through the loose gravel. It worked like a charm. One Leg followed the tanker on down to the clubhouse to be sure that it didn't get hung up on the rail crossing. He parked Bertha, scrambled down out of the cab, and came in to see me and to get a cup of coffee.

"Leg, what are you doing driving Big Bertha for Bergen Wrecker?" I asked after One Leg got his coffee. One Leg answered, "Acey Deucy McClanahan dropped a big tractor towing assembly on his foot and he can't drive with his foot in a cast. They hired me to run all the heavy duty stuff for them until he gets the cast off." I said, "You're telling me that this outfit has a man off on a medical leave with a bad foot and they replace him with a man who doesn't even have a leg?"

"That's about the size of it Dapper," One Leg said. "What you have to remember is that one leg is my natural state and Acey Deucy just ain't used to the idea." Big Charley asked One Leg, "What kind of transmission does that big devil have in it anyway?" Leg answered, "It has the old two stick twelve speed with a real low rear end for power." The radio in Big Bertha started squawking and One Leg grabbed his yellow wooden crutches and hurried out the door. "Come down and see me the next time you come over to Jimmy's," he said over his shoulder.

We watched and listened as Leg took the big rig through her gears going out of the Sky Ranch and Big Charley said, "I couldn't shift that damn thing that smoothly when both of my legs were working, he must be a busy S.O.B."

I said, "I rode with him one time when he was putting a fourteen-wide house trailer up on the side of Chilhowee mountain. You had to cross a little bridge that was a measured sixteen feet wide and then turn off on a little side road that had been cut out with a dozer leading up to the home site. We came down the hill to the bridge with him stomping the brake, clutch and gas pedals with that one foot as he down-shifted through a bunch of gears to slow down.

"When the wheels on the trailer cleared the bridge he dropped the hitch ball to the low point so the rear of the house trailer would clear the bridge rails as we turned off. Then he had to raise the hitch point back up so the front of the trailer wouldn't hit the ground when the drive wheels on the tractor went through the ditch before we started out on that little track of a road up the side of the mountain."

"How did he lose that leg anyway?" asked Small Sam, who had come in while we were talking. I said that I had heard several stories about that, but the one that I liked the best and the one that was probably true was this one.

Lilly had been out coon hunting all night and had come home somewhat the worse for wear after having drunk a sizable amount of homemade liquid corn. His wife Gertrude had the door locked, which was her practice if her husband didn't show up before midnight. So when Lilly got home he leaned his shotgun against the porch wall and he and the dogs bedded down on the porch.

The next morning Gertrude came out on the porch and told him that he better get off of that glider and down to the barn to do his chores. Lilly looked up at her through his hangover and said, "God I feel awful, you just ought to shoot me." So she picked up the shotgun that was leaning against the wall and blew his leg off.

Leg told me that they both thought that the gun was empty, because he always took the shells out of the gun before putting it down where kids could pick it up. Gertrude was able to get him to Blount Memorial Hospital in time to save his life, but not his leg. It came off at the hip. There is not enough stump left to support even a peg leg so he has been on those yellow crutches ever since.

"Are they still married?" Big Charley asked. I told them, "Oh yes, this happened more than twenty years ago and they had a couple of kids since the accident, so I guess she missed all of the important plumbing."

THE STOLEN TRAILER

Swifty Swanson came in the clubhouse and was immediately button-holed by Tightwad Wilson. T.W. wanted to know if the Knoxville's finest had made any progress on finding his stolen trailer and the load of material that was on it. Swifty sarcastically replied that he was not on the task force that Chief Piker had set up to handle that crime.

Tightwad settled down and mused, "I just invested so damn much work and sweat into taking that building down, it really pisses me off that some Bubba is sitting out there with all that metal and the trailer too." Big Charley chimed in, "You also have to include the pain and suffering of falling off the roof and landing flat on your ass on that concrete floor, that's also part of the investment."

Swifty sat quietly stirring three packages of sugar into his mug of coffee and offered, "T.W., you might try putting an ad in that free newspaper for the trailer wheels that you have left over after they took your trailer. Some Bubba out there has a trailer but no wheels.

"You could use the phone here at the club and I can check out the license plates of anyone who shows up to take a look at the merchandise. After I find out where he lives, you can go see if he is building a new shed at his house. Even if you don't find the right man, you may sell the wheels that you don't have any use for anymore."

Swifty continued, "By the way Wad, I hear that you think that the club needs more members. What kind of new folks do you think we need?"

T.W. offered, "Well, I just thought that if we had more members we would have more money coming in and we could reduce the amount of the monthly dues." "Yes," said Big Charley, "the only thing wrong with that line of lackluster logic is that with more members we would need more airplanes to rent. So to get more planes we would have to assess each member about $150 to buy another bird. Tightwad, you would let a gimp-legged, cross-dressing, gay, IRS tax lawyer join the club if it saved you a dollar a month." T.W. grinned and looked at Big Charley and said, "I guess you're right."

After Swifty left, Tightwad and Big Charley started working on an ad for the paper and finally settled on one which read:

EXTRA UTILITY TRAILER WHEELS COMPLETE WITH TIRES & TUBES FOR SALE. CALL 555-5555.

We received five calls about the trailer wheels and three guys came out to look over the goods. Big Charley noted the license plate numbers on each of the trucks while T.W. talked to the suspects. The first two offered only $5 each for the wheels and T.W. said he would rather keep them at that price, but the third man offered $75 for all four and T.W. settled for $80. Tightwad asked the guy where he was from and he said he lived just outside of Oak Ridge. He loaded the wheels up and departed.

"Where did he say he was from?" asked Big Charley.

"Oak Ridge."

"Oak Ridge is in Anderson County and his plate is out of Blount County. Something's wrong. I'm going to give Swifty a call."

"No need," Small Sam put in, "While you were getting the number of the back I looked in the cab and he had a past due KUB bill laying on the dash and it says he lives in Knox County. I have the name and the address."

DIVORCE

Little Al Nance walked into my hangar while I was trying to find an oil leak that was keeping the belly of old blue dirtier than usual. Alvin Nance, Little Al to all his friends, is a little guy about five foot six and weighs maybe a hundred and forty pounds, works for the big aluminum plant in Alcoa TN and plays the mandolin in a popular bluegrass band. He had been through a very messy divorce from Wallene, his wife of over twenty years and who is one of Willow's sisters. The divorce made him a real pain in the ass to have around. The porch pilots usually retreated from the area if they had the chance.

He only had one tune in his repertoire and most of us were tired of hearing "How could she do this to me?" regardless of what key he played it in. Little Al jumped right into his favorite theme by saying, "Have you heard what that Lesbo Bitch of a Lawyer wants now?" 'Lesbo Bitch' was Little Al's endearing term for his wife's divorce lawyer, Billie Jean Kingston. Billie Jean is a very successful divorce lawyer in the area who only works one side of the street. She hates all men and any women that she considers to be to the right of dead center, and she moves the center to suit herself on a daily basis.

"What's on her mind?" I asked, knowing that the comment was not needed but since I was stuck in the hangar until I could find the oil leak anyway I figured I would act sociable.

Little Al continued, "She wants my goddamn hangar. I forgot to list it as an asset and now she claims that I am in contempt of court. I told her I was saving all my contempt for her, but it didn't seem to bother her. Dapper, I would like for you to sell the hangar for me. I want $2500.00 for it, but I would like to have a check for one thousand dollars and the rest in cash." I told him that I thought the hangar would sell at that price pretty quickly, but that the terms of the sale would be between him and the buyer.

Hangars at the Sky Ranch are the property of the individual members who either built them or bought them from other members. The land that they are built on continues to be the property of the club and is leased to the member on a monthly basis. If your medical or your marriage goes south, you either have to sell it to a member of the club, or you can tear it down and take it home.

I didn't have to wait long to hear the often repeated bit about the country song. "Dapper, you've heard that tune that goes, 'She got the coal mine and I got the shaft.' Well, in my case its the God's truth. She got the new Lincoln Town Car and I got the '82 pickup. She got the farm and I got the garden. I had to sell the bass boat and she got to keep the houseboat. She has had the airplane tied up in court for two years and now she wants the hangar too."

I didn't say anything for fear that it might lengthen the number of verses he was going to do in this set. Someday maybe someone would get it through Little Al's head that, other than his own stupidity, his biggest problem was the total ineptitude of his own lawyer. Al had engaged the services of Wiley Bright, a lazy good old boy type lawyer who walked around town with cow manure on his boots. On the other hand, Ms. Kingston cheated, she only came to court after she and her staff had thoroughly investigated and researched her clients husbands professional, financial and private lives. She very seldom got any surprises in court, but her opposition couldn't say the same thing.

During Little Al's first day in court she handed him a copy of a canceled check made out to the pilot's club and asked him what it was for. He told her that it was a club for boat pilots. Then she handed him a printed club invoice that listed Dues and Tie-down and several aviation gas purchases all of which added up to the same amount as the check she had just shown him and asked, "What do you put on the tie-down space that you rent at the Sky Ranch?" He spluttered a little and she said, "I will save you the trouble of remembering, here is a picture of the airplane, tied down at the Sky Ranch, that, according to FAA records in Oklahoma City, belongs to you." It didn't get any better. Wiley missed filing dates and didn't explain any of the processes and the penalties attached to them to his client until after he had been slammed repeatedly by Ms. Kingston.

I knew he was about to wind down when he got around to talking about how much he had to pay the lawyers. He finished up with his usual line, "I also had to pay that Lesbo Bitch a ton of money." Big Bill Henry had come in the hangar just in time to hear the closing line and said, "Well Al, at least you got to pay one good lawyer. Wiley Bright should be named Wiley 'Not So Damn' Bright." Little Al continued as if nothing had been said, "I did everything in the world for Wallene, I taught that country girl everything I know."

After Little Al left I said to Bill, "It seems like I've heard that story before." Bill answered, "Me too, too damn many times. I saw him coming up the road when I was sitting up in the clubhouse and I hid in the shit house. I didn't want to hear any more about what his wife and her lesbo lawyer did to him."

The leak turned out to be coming from the rocker box cover on the number three jug. I tightened up the screws and we were ready to put the cowl back on. Bill was holding his side of the bottom half of the engine cowl while I put a couple of screws in my side when he asked if I was around when Little Al made his comment about the perfect wife in front of Wallene. I said, "You mean when he said the perfect wife is one who greets her husband naked on her hands and knees on the living room floor with her mouth open and a can of cold Blue Ribbon Beer on her back?"

Bill added, "It would have been so much better if he had just left it at that, everyone could have laughed it off, but when he looked right at Wallene and said that his wife had all of it down pat except the part about the beer, she looked like she had been hit with a baseball bat. I think the little asshole deserved everything he got." I said, "You mean everything he lost, don't you?" Bill shook his head in agreement.

NEW WIVES

The Knife and Fork society had finished eating and were working on another glass of iced tea when Fritz Fieberg said, "Did you see that middle aged dumb-ass at the Ranch yesterday?" Small Sam jumped in with, "You'll have to narrow the field a little more than that, you just described most of the club."

Fritz returned, "I mean the dumb-ass who was walking around with the young redhead with the big tits and the short skirt. She was some woman." I put in, "I sure hope Smoky Pat doesn't end up like some of our other middle aged crazies who have gone out and married much younger women."

The resident attorney, G. Gordon Ladde, added, "Pat will have to get a divorce first and then, if he has enough money left, the redhead may still be interested in him. If there isn't enough money for the first wife, the lawyers, and the girl friend or the new wife as the case may be, very often the client gets mad at his attorney and that's just one of the reasons I never did do divorce cases."

Doc Kronk said, "Do you guys remember Wally Winslow? He was the one who used to have the nice Bonanza in the hangar that Fred Forrester built. He also stored a forty foot cruiser behind the hangar in the winter time. His first wife took lots of cash when she left, so he kept the boat and the plane."

"Yes, but it wasn't long after he married the new young one that she started digging in her heels," said Small Sam. "He sold the airplane because she didn't like to fly, and the boat had to go because she didn't like to cook in the galley. She also made him quit bowling in the Big Blue League on Wednesday nights so he could sing in the choir at the church."

Zipper Thomas said, "You know, I tried to talk to her a few times when they were out at the Sky Ranch and she didn't seem to be the sharpest knife in the drawer. After a man got out of bed for the day, I'm not sure she would be good for anything." Big Bill added, "On my good days, I remember what they were good for in bed."

TIGHTWAD'S NEW TRACTOR

As I drove up the gravel road beside the runway I noticed a tandem trailer with a John Deere tractor on it parked by Tightwad Wilson's hangar. He was sitting in his hangar so I pulled in to look at the new toy.

"Where did you get the tractor and trailer, T.W."

"Well the trailer is the one I lost out in West Knoxville when the metal was stolen and I made a deal for the tractor."

"Is there more to this story than you have told me so far?"

"Yes, I guess there is. I drove out to the address on that KUB bill and there was a newly built shed with a John Deere tractor sitting in it and while I was passing the house the fellow pulled into the driveway with my trailer. I called Swifty and he asked me if I could positively identify the trailer and I told him that I had reinforced the trailer frame with some heavy angle iron and that I had put my welders mark, TWW, to it. He said that was plenty.

"We went over there and the old boy tried to deny the whole thing, but when we tilted the trailer bed up the angle irons were there along with my TWW. Swifty told him that if he could make it right with me, he wouldn't bother him except to keep his eye on him in the future. So I told him that since he already had the shed built I would let him trade the tractor for the metal. He didn't like the deal, but when Swifty said he had plenty of room in the back of the squad car, he agreed. We hooked the trailer to my truck, loaded the tractor, and now you know the rest of the story."

"T.W., you didn't mention the forty foot bar beams. Did he have them too?"

"Yes, come to think of it! He used them in the shed that he built. I plumb forgot about them. I guess he got them for nothing, I must be slipping more than I thought I was."

OLD MAN HICKMAN VISITS

I had the books all caught up, the Trade-a-Plane read, the airplane washed, and for once even all the grass was mowed. Boy, I was on top of the world! A vehicle that looked familiar, but didn't, was coming down the road. It was an old step van and before it got close enough for me to see inside, I knew it would have an altimeter and a compass mounted on top of the dash.

Herb Hickman stepped out of the old truck and took a seat on the porch. Herb is a former member who lost his medical several years ago. I said, "I had a little trouble identifying the van, it's been a while since I've seen it or you. How are you doing?" He allowed as though, "Things are going pretty well for us. Me and Maudie figure that every day that we both wake up and know who each other are we got a hell of a start.

"Are you still the president of this organization, and I use the word organization loosely," Herb asked. "Not since we bought the property in 1992, although I have spent some time on the BOD," I told him.

We sat for a while without saying much. "Those were some pretty boisterous meetings we had in those days," Herb said. He went on to say that he was glad it was me and not him that had to deal with all of the problems associated with raising the money to buy the place. I said, "I'm going to get the bird out and go over to DKX for a few minutes, do you want to go along?" "Dapper, I would love to," he said.

We did a quick walk around and took off to the south and headed over to what Herb still calls Island Home Airport. As soon as we were headed toward downtown I asked Herb if he wanted to fly the airplane, and he declined, saying it had been too long and it would make him nervous.

After we landed, I told Herb that I needed to see someone in the maintenance shop and I would meet him in the office in a few minutes. I killed some time in the maintenance shop and then went into the front office. Herb said he was ready, so we headed out to the airplane, wound it up and departed for the Sky Ranch.

IS IZZY JEWISH

Captain Tom and Big Bill Henry were in deep conversation around the big table when I went in the clubhouse. I unlocked the office, turned on the computer, and picked up my favorite coffee mug. When I sat down Bill said, "Is Izzy Green Jewish?" I said, "It probably depends on the tense of the verb." "What the hell does that mean?" asked Captain Tom. I said, "Well, the way I understand it he was, but now most people would say that he is not." "Oh, that really clears it all up." said Bill. "Will you please get down to an answer."

We settled in and I told the tale that Izzy had related to me.

Israel Timothy Greenbaum was born into a strict Orthodox Jewish family in the lower east side in New York City. He was brought up in the faith and was a dutiful son until sometime shortly after puberty.

Izzy discovered that blondes did have more fun, or at least he had more fun with blondes than he did with the girls with dark hair that he met at Temple. Sex at once set this young man free and at the same time made him somewhat a prisoner. His father absolutely forbade him to be seen in the company of any of the young ladies outside the faith, read blondes.

Izzy was able to sneak around to visit some of his newly found more liberal blonde friends but was in a constant battle with his father. The day after Izzy graduated from high school he joined the Air Force and left New York, the 'baum' from Greenbaum, and the strict confines of the Orthodox Church. I.T., as Izzy was known in the Air Force, worked on the big birds during the day and bedded the blonde birds at night.

Life was good for Izzy who was now about twenty-six-years old when nineteen-year-old Miss Ramonda Mae Maloney appeared in his life. Ramonda Mae was not blonde nor would she be bedded by Izzy and the more she refused his advances the more smitten he became.

They were both working on Tinker AFB when Ramonda received word that she was needed in Knoxville to help care for her sick mother. A short time later Izzy was working for the Air National Guard at TYS Knoxville. The way Izzy tells it, there are some things you can do without, but for him Ramonda wasn't one of them.

Captain Tom looked up and said, "Dapper, as usual, you haven't answered the question about is Izzy Jewish. Are you going to get around to that?"

I said, "Well I think that we have established that he was Jewish. Now comes the other part, is he now Jewish?

"Izzy decided that his only course to true happiness was to marry Ramonda. So when the chance came he proposed to her and she accepted with the provision that he join her church. Izzy told her he would join the church but that he would probably not attend on a regular basis.

Ramonda set up a meeting with her preacher, Bishop C. William Love, aka Charley Bill Love and Loving Charley Bill, the leader of the Pilgrim Holiness Church of Absolute Faith and Hope. The Bishop asked if Izzy had been saved and Izzy said no, not that he remembered.

The Bishop said he would be happy to officiate at a dipping ceremony at the boat dock at the Sky Ranch because he preferred that these rites be performed under God's own sky. Izzy said he had always thought God owned the whole place and wherever anything happened it was under the eye of God, but somehow that point was lost on the Bishop.

"Captain Tom," I asked, "Is a man who was born, raised and circumcised in the Orthodox Church, who was later saved and baptized into the arms of Jesus and the Pilgrim Holiness Church of Faith and Hope still Jewish? I personally have no idea. Come on Tom — you answer the question."

"Tom," Big Bill asked, "do you know why the Bishop won't hold outdoor tent meetings?" "No, but I think I'm about to," replied Tom. "They lose too many snakes in the grass," chuckled Bill.

RADIO THIEF HITS AIRPORT

The airport was hit on Wednesday night by a radio bandit. I went out to make a trip to Norfolk to see that the Navy was doing a proper job of commissioning the new carrier George Washington when I discovered my loss. My sister-in-law and I loaded 2U and then found the radio missing during preflight. The weather was so poor I had already filed IFR, but didn't want to go with just one navcom.

Di and I drove to Norfolk. When the three of us returned I had a call from Charley at the avionics shop who relayed to me that Gulf Coast Avionics in Tampa had bought my radio from a man, stopped payment on the check, and called the FBI.

I have the radio back, and if the courts don't get this guy maybe the club can contact the Tennessee Game and Fish people to have a special open hunting season declared. A bounty would be nice too.

Father Gene looked up and said that he thought that the story was good as far as it went but he had a question for me. I said, "So go ahead, what's the question?" "Who was the woman you took to Norfolk, because I was here when you flew your wife to South Boston and I was here when you didn't fly the other lady to Norfolk?" I said, "You have a good eye, the second lady was my wife's younger sister. We were all planning to go together but Lady Di and I couldn't get our work schedules to work out so I took Shay over early and Di and I went later."

Father Gene looked up and said, "That's a good story, you stick with it. No, now that you tell me, they do look a lot alike." I told Gene, "The three of us have fun together wherever we go. When the Big Orange played basketball in the old Stokely Center we only had two basketball tickets. So we took turns going to the games. One night during half-time a man came up to me and said that he could understand how I could bring two different women to the games on different nights, but what he did not understand was how I got the two of them to come together when I was out of town."

CHARLESTON TRIP

Shay looked up at me over our morning coffee and said, "I need several gifts for people. My drawer of goodies for any occasion is about empty." "Well, why don't you call someone and do a safari up to the Pigeon Forge Outlet Heaven and stock up," I replied, although I knew from the tone that there was more to come on the subject.

"I think I would like to do the City Market, they have such a nice selection, and besides you could have lunch at Hyman's Seafood, and then we could eat at Jestine's Kitchen too. How long does it take to get down there?" she asked.

When you have been married for over thirty-five years, it's easy to tell when a decision has been made. The thing to do is to go right along, but to try to make some points for some future plan you have in the works. I said, "Let me fire up the flight planner and I'll see."

I have a flight planner on my PC which lets you enter your destination and it will give you distance, time in route, fuel used, and show it to you on a map. It will also let you use more than one airplane's performance numbers to create the trip data. I punched in the request and now I had some numbers for Shay.

"Honey, the trip is about 273 miles to Charleston Exec and should take about 2 hours and 45 minutes, plus or minus the wind. Just for fun I also checked on how long it would take if we went in a Bonanza. It would only take about 1 hour and 53 minutes and use about the same amount of gas," I reported. Shay ignored the superfluous data and asked, "When does the weather look good for a two day down and back?"

The weather was severe clear as we lifted off from the Sky Ranch and started our climb up over the Smoky Mountains. The area around the Asheville Airport, some twenty-five miles off to our left, was clearly visible as we crossed the big mountain at 7,500 MSL. Greer and Columbus came and went and about two hours and fifteen minutes later I gave Charleston approach a call.

"Charleston approach this is Cessna 02U."

"02U this is Charleston approach."

"2U is a Cessna 172 VFR, 21 miles out of exec JZI heading 136 at 3,500 descending."

"2U squawk 3535, descend and maintain 2000 feet, report Exec in sight."

"Maintain 2 point 0, call the airport, 2U."

We found the airport, or the GPS did, and we were soon loading the rental car. I mentioned that the car was a bigger model than we usually rented and Shay said that it had a nice large trunk.

There was no change of command ceremony, but the control of the expedition moved smoothly from the left seat of the airplane to the right seat of the rental car. I drove us across the big bridge into Charleston and we checked into the motel of choice for the trip.

The quarters were minimal and inexpensive, which meant that the shopping probably would be a maximum effort operation. The bird would be at or near max gross weight or volume for the trip home.

What the heck, when Shay's happy, I'm happy, and I had a big plan sitting out there.

We hit the City Market, which sits between North and South Market Streets just off of Meeting Street, by one o'clock. The City Market is a series of mostly open buildings with vendors selling all kinds of interesting items, from junk to junque. I made one pass through with Shay as she did her scouting run. Then I found me a nice bench in the shade near a coffee shop, so I could watch the happy shoppers and the men with them.

My only real function from now until dinner was to keep the meter supplied with quarters and carry assorted parcels to the nice large trunk when the occasion arose. The only decision making that was going to be required of me the rest of the day was which entree at Hyman's Seafood did I want.

I was wearing a baseball cap with Skyhawk 02U on it so I had several pilots stop by to shoot the breeze while their copilots were shopping. The highlight of Shay's shopping was the purchase of a primitive carving of a man done in a dark soft wood, which Shay dubbed 'My African Man.' He sits in our living room as a memento of the trip. Our house has a lot of those.

After a little more shopping the next day and lunch at Jestine's Kitchen, we loaded up and flew home. We went over in about two hours and a half and returned in about three, so the wind was about the same both ways.

HEAVY BOAT

Billy Bob pulled into the Sky Ranch towing his new big bass boat with the big Mercury outboard tipped up on the transom. The big boat and trailer were about all the '55 pickup could handle and if it had been a stock engine there was no way it could negotiate a very steep grade. The suitability of the '55 as a towing vehicle had been brought to his attention before but Billy Bob was not going to hear it. Willy Clyde let him off light with only one or two short remarks.

Billy Bob pulled the boat on down and parked it next to his hangar where he usually kept his boat. The boat had a full cover on it so it didn't matter that it was outside.

A day or two later I was cleaning the accumulation of oil and dirt off the belly of 2U when Willy C. stepped into my hangar and asked, "Can you get the tractor and give me a hand? I can't move my boat. The wheels must have settled down in the damp grass and I just don't have enough power to pull it out."

Before I could get my hands clean to go get the tractor, Billy Bob Wanger pulled up in his truck and asked what was going on. As soon as he heard that the '55 wouldn't pull the boat out of its spot he started touting their new four-wheel drive SUV.

After a lot of conversation it was decided that the Wanger would bring Peggy Sue and her SUV over at 10:00 tomorrow to show the Coyote that it was the application of four-wheel drive, not just the pure horsepower of the '55 Ford, that got the job done.

The word had spread and when 10:00 rolled around there were several of the porch people to see if the SUV could pull the boat out. Homer, the mastiff, and Billy Bob arrived in the '55 truck and there was a short wait until Peggy Sue Wanger arrived. She had stopped by to pick up Mai Ling

Coyote. As soon as Homer spotted Mai Ling he immediately wanted in the new car with her.

After putting the proper size hitch ball on the SUV, Peggy Sue, coached by Billy Bob on how to use low range four-wheel drive, pulled the big boat up beside the clubhouse and stopped. She told the Coyote, "Now maybe your little truck can handle it from here."

The Coyote nearly exploded, but he was raised right and actually thanked Peggy Sue for helping him move his boat. His parting shot was, "If you had not had Homer in the back seat for extra weight, you couldn't have done it." I am not entirely sure about the financial arrangements, but I know it did include an exchange of pictures of dead presidents between Billy Bob and Willy Clyde.

Peggy Sue walked over and said, "I think since I did the towing with my SUV, this little pot is mine." The boat was unhooked and Peggy Sue left on an urgent shopping trip with Mai Ling.

Small Sam Long asked me later in the day if I knew why there was so much water in that low place in the south forty. We looked it over a little and it seemed that the wet area started at Billy Bob's hangar and extended to the low spot in the lower end. Sam said, "I think a light just came on. Let's go look under the cover of that boat."

We walked back to the clubhouse chuckling and pulled the cover off the stern of the boat and it was still wet. You could see that it had been nearly full of dirty water very recently. "Sam what would this rig weigh in at if it was full of water?" I asked. Sam said, "I don't know, but it would be more than a '55 Ford and an SUV together could handle." I said, "Looks like this round goes to the Wanger, but I'm sure he'll be out to get even."

"Well, who have you cleared of suspicion today?" I asked. Big Charley replied, "Izzy Green and Chub Checker were in Germany, and Captain Tom was in Branson MO square dancing, Jimmy Crowe was bass fishing in Florida." Big Bill added, "G. Gordon Ladde was at choir practice and Father Gene was conducting a funeral and here is a list of the women:

Marti Kronk— Opera in New York
Shay Kurlee— Shopping in Charleston
Wide Wilma— Grand Ole Opry
Beulah— Horse races
Mai Ling Coyote— California
Peggy Sue— California
Bett Ladde— Choir practice
Marge George— Funeral
Prenney Crowe— Florida with Jimmy bass fishing
Bea Dawson— square dancing in Branson

"I left off Izzy and Bib's wives because they are too new to know what an asshole the Warthog is anyway."

"Charley," I said, "you are spending a lot of time looking for this perp, but I haven't heard where you were on the appointed night." Charley hung his head and said he wished it were him, but that he had had a flare-up with his heart the night it happened and he and Minnie had spent the night in the emergency room with him wired to all kinds of machines. He said he hadn't told anyone because he didn't want to hear anymore about it than he already had.

Big Bill chimed in, "Hell, I knew you didn't do it anyway, but who do we have left to find out about?" Charley returned, "Well we still have Tightwad Wilson, the Zipper, Coyote, and Wanger left and I favor one of the last two myself.

SAMUEL GREEN COMES TO KNOXVILLE

Izzy Green was working on the starter on 220 in the #1 maintenance hangar while I stood around and watched. We had the place to ourselves so I asked him a question that I had wondered about for a while. "Izzy how did you come to have Samuel to raise? I know he isn't your son."

"Well, about ten years ago I got a call from Samuel at the Greyhound Bus Station, would I please come and pick him up. He said he would explain it when I got there. When I arrived he handed me a letter and said please read this first. The letter was from a lawyer who was representing the estate of my brother Saul Greenbaum. It stated that all the members of the family except Samuel were killed in an explosion in the apartment building where they lived.

"The lawyer, a member of the firm Goldberg, Lopez, MacTavish, Johnson, and O'Toole, reported that fortunately, after liquidating all of the assets, the estate contained enough money to pay the funeral expenses, the court costs, the attorney fees and had enough left over to buy Samuel a bus ticket to Knoxville so he could be with his only living relative. So suddenly we had a ten year old boy. He was a good boy, but I am a little worried about this religious phase he is in now that he is out of school."

UNCLE ANDY'S CLOSES

Izzy Green came in to check the squawk sheets on the airplanes at about five o'clock and asked if I had heard that the best place on the strip was closing down for good? I told him that I did indeed know about the sad event and that Sam Venable was asking for letters about the place to use in his column.

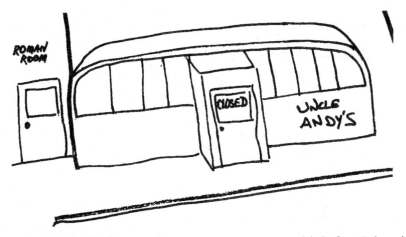

"I've just finished up my letter, so you want to read it before I drop it in the mail?" I asked. He said sure, so I fished out a copy from the carry bag and pushed it across the table to him.

May 2, 1997

Knoxville News-Sentinel
Attention: Sam Venable

Re: Sam-and-Andy's

Dear Sam,
    My first visit to Sam and Andy's, or Uncle Andy's as it was known then, was in 1955 when I ventured off to school from the mountains of southern West Virginia. In those days Uncle Andy, complete with handlebar mustache, presided over the cash register in the converted streetcar which was the diner on the front part of the business. In those grand days if you dated a girl who lived in the dorm, you knew that she was securely locked up for the night at 10:45. If you happened to know an airline stewardess who did not live in the dorm, then you were perfectly safe to take her to Uncle Andy's for a cup of coffee or what-ever.
    Things went quite well until the star of this little soap opera got his days mixed up and was having a little late supper with Shay Stewardess when Debby Dorm walked in with a group of her sorority sisters on a Friday night. The situation rapidly escalated from surprise to anger to ugly. Have you ever tried to find a fraternity pin in a bowl of Uncle Andy's Chili?
    Change is what got the boy in trouble. The witching hour for the girls dorm changed from 10:45 on week nights to 12:30 on Friday and Saturday nights. The boy in the television ad who says thinning hair is the most traumatic experience of his life obviously never tried to deal with two very upset ladies at Uncle Andy's.
    I am still having to learn to deal with change and two women at the same time. My mother-in-law has moved in with us for the duration. My wife of 35 years says I should get along just fine considering my previous experience.

I will miss Uncle Andy's, just as I miss the big Delta Tau Delta house on the corner of 15th and Laurel, the Ellis and Ernest Drug Store and the smell of the book store in the shop behind the E&E. We have been eating at Sam and Andy's about once a week recently, the beer is cold, the food is good, and the memories are legion. However, I don't eat the Chili at Uncle Andy's anymore.

Yours,

Dapper Kurlee

PS: The Young High Finishing School for South Knoxville Ladies surely must have taught a course in long term memory, because Shay Chris Kurlee never seems to forget some of the things that happened a long time ago. You may have made the same observation from your own data.

SMOKE DANCERS

The porch pilots were admiring the landings Sandy Flynn was making in 220. He was consistently getting a full stall at about six inches off the ground hitting on the mains only. He taxied up to a club spot and tied the airplane down. After filling in the clip board and his log book Sandy came out to sit on the porch with the pilots. He was now a certified member of the brotherhood of pilots.

He got plenty of advice, some of it relevant, about flying from the assembled group of experts. The conversation died down after a while and Sandy asked, "The other night I saw some video of the Smoke Dancers in an air show. How do the guys that fly the shows make all that smoke?"

Several experts paused to draw a breath and were left behind when Big Charley started his discourse on the art of making smoke. Come to think of it, no one was better qualified to blow smoke anyway.

He said it is a very simple process, you just put a small tank of oil up on the firewall so it can drain out by gravity through a small tube to a fitting placed fairly near the end of the exhaust stack. You put a valve on the tank with a control in the cockpit to start and stop the oil. When the stack and the exhaust gases are hot you open the valve on the oil tank and the oil runs down and burns to make a lot of smoke. You just have to experiment a little to get the right amount of oil flow to make the best smoke.

"Can you put that on any airplane?" asked Sandy.

"Hell, you could put it on a lawn mower and it would work, but if you put it on an airplane you would first have to get an IA to sign it off for you. Then you have to file an FAA form 337 and get FAA field approval."

Soon we had a regular rash of smoke making vehicles on the Sky Ranch. It was poetic justice that Big Charley was the first victim. He had said his adieus and started up the van in front of the clubhouse. He drove down to Tightwad Wilson's hangar and picked up some tools that T.W. had borrowed and came back up toward the clubhouse when his old van started making more smoke that a 450 horse Stearman Biplane.

One of the porch pilots sang out "Drive around the strip Charley, maybe you can kill some of the mosquitoes!" Charley drove about half-way down the field and the smoke quit. "Small tank," commented one of the onlookers.

Charley drove the old van up in front of the maintenance hangar so he could roll a creeper under it to see how the unwanted smoke system worked. He rolled out in just a minute and asked for a pair of pliers and some wire cutters to remove the device.

When he came out in just another minute he held up a plastic bottle with a plastic tube coming out of the cap and running to a piece of aluminum tubing about a foot long. The bottle still had some duct tape clinging to it. Charley told us that the bottle had been taped to the firewall and that there was a hole bored in the exhaust pipe with the aluminum tubing sticking into the pipe and wired on with safety wire.

Everyone was admiring the simplicity of the design when our resident rocket scientist stopped the crowd with a question. Captain Tom wanted to know why all the oil didn't drain out into the exhaust system when the smoker was first installed. Where was the control valve that delayed the flow until the pipe was hot enough to make smoke?

No one had an answer and there were three more victims, including one on my old pickup truck, before I found out the last secret of the smoke system.

I went out to mow using the John Deere tractor. It started up fine, but the transmission refused to shift into any gear. When this happens you have to remove some bolts and lift the shifter handle and the shifting forks out of the transmission so you can place the gears, the forks, and the handle in the same relative position. If you are lucky it will work again for a while. The catch was, I needed a wrench to get started and all of my tools were in the garage at home instead of in the van where they were supposed to be.

Small Sam's truck was parked nearby and he had his truck toolbox on the back with hopefully a wrench that I wanted in it. I opened the box and there on top of his tools was a complete smoke system ready for installation. There was also a battery powered drill laying there with the proper bit already chucked up. There being no one around I picked it up to see how it worked. It was quickly apparent that the aluminum tube was sealed with paraffin or candle wax. So the oil couldn't drain out until the exhaust system was hot enough to melt the wax. Ergo, if it would melt the wax it would make smoke.

Small Sam was out flying and I figured I had plenty of time so I rolled under his truck and installed the smoker on his truck. I aligned all the gears in the John transmission and was mowing the grass in the south forty by the time Small Sam landed and tied down the plane. I was still mowing when Sam left the Sky Ranch. I saw the smoke come on just as he got to the main road. He must have put some extra wax in this model. I finished up mowing the south forty and headed for the house.

TUDBERRY'S BOMB

Big Bill Henry was reading the paper on the porch of the clubhouse when I came wandering in several days after the smoker hit Small Sam's truck. Bill waited for me to check the answering service, get a cup of coffee, and sit down. He then asked if I had seen the morning paper and I told him that I had mowed the front yard but had not seen the paper yet. He held up the front page of the paper with the leading headline 'VICE MAYOR'S CAR BOMBED'.

The story went on to say that Vice Mayor Quenton Tudberry's car was bombed in the City-County Parking Building. Tudberry was shaken up but unhurt in the incident. Police Chief Paul Piker said that no details would be released at this time and he was seeking the advice of the law director to determine if there were any federal statutes to be considered. "That last part means he has to find out which way the political winds are blowing," Bill filled in for me. He added, "It's a damn shame that somebody didn't use a bigger charge so we would be rid of another lawyer. Come to think of it, Tudberry is the lawyer that the old ladies hired to relieve the Warthog of some change on that ash hauling caper he pulled."

"You might call it change, Bill, but I thought $25,000 was a little steep for a dry cleaning bill."

Swifty Swanson parked his pickup under one of the big trees and joined us on the porch. "Good morning guys, it sure is a pretty day. Boy, what a mess that was last night at the City-County Building. The chief hit the panic button when that thing went off on old Tudberry's car. He called in all the reserve officers and as soon as it hit the radio, all the press that wasn't already there to cover the council meeting showed up.

"Tudberry wanted to be hauled away in an ambulance, but he didn't want to get on the stretcher until the TV people were set up, and by then the medical people said there was nothing wrong with him. Tudberry told the EMT that he was a sick man and needed to be transported. The EMT told him that he was sure that he needed help but he did not deal with head cases and left.

"By this time every politician in the area was doing an interview with some member of the press. Some of them talked about how brave the Vice Mayor was. When Channel Ten shot the interview with Tudberry, they had to be real careful to show him only from the waist up. He had pissed in his pants."

"What kind of a bomb was it?" I asked.

"It wasn't a bomb at all." Swifty told us. "It was an imitation of the smoker that was on Big Charlie's van. There were a couple of differences. This one was plugged into the catalytic converter and the bottle that should of had oil in it smelled of gasoline. It blew the whole exhaust system off the car and made a hell of a noise. Tudberry is really lucky that the gas tank didn't go up at the same time."

"Sounds like someone with a low mechanical IQ was trying to pull a joke," said Big Bill. "I wonder who that could be?"

"Whoever it is, he sure was lucky that the surveillance camera for that section of the garage was not working last night," Swifty added. "Don't tell anyone who is short and ugly that there are no witnesses or that the camera wasn't working. Whoever he is he should sweat some more."

After Swifty left, Big Bill looked over at me and said, "You know, I think I would pay the Warthog's club dues just for the entertainment value of having him around. That asshole can stir up more shit than a manure spreader."

THE BISHOP'S CHURCH

Swifty Swanson, Izzy Green, several others and I were sitting around the break table in the hangar one. Izzy was making a maintenance entry in a log book and the rest of us were drinking coffee from the hangar pot. Several of our members are ex-military so a coffee pot is mandatory in all work spaces.

Swifty said "I sure had an interesting run last night. A little before nine o'clock we got a disturbing the peace nuisance call on the Pilgrim Holiness Church of Absolute Hope and Faith over in Happy Hollow. The neighbors were tired of having to listen to the church service being played on the big speakers in the church steeple.

"We went over there and you could hear it more than two blocks away. They must have spent a lot of money on their speakers and amps. They were singing and a'shouting something fierce. You could hear a big set of drums, guitars, organ, choir, and somebody was playing the slide trombone."

"Did you all shut them down?" asked Big Charley.

"No, about the time we pulled up to the church, a bunch of shots were fired from more than one location and the speakers took direct hits. I don't know what they were using for firepower, but it was some heavy shit. It made a hell of a noise, and the top of the steeple just seemed to explode.

"Let me tell you, the service was over. The faithful didn't wait to take up an offering, or invite any lost souls to join the church. They didn't even pause to say amen. In less than sixty seconds, that place was empty.

"The preacher, Bishop Charley Love, was the last one out. He came out the front door with his slide trombone in one hand and his bible in the other. The slide on that horn had some strange looking bends in it and there was a big angry looking rattlesnake all wound up on the end of it. He had a rather dazed look in his eye and we didn't want to get too near him or the snake.

"My partner looked around a minute and said 'Well, the call we got was about the noise and there ain't no more noise, let's go get something to eat. I don't think the neighbors are going to complain about the alleged shots that were allegedly fired by persons who will remain anonymous. I don't care who all we ask.'"

"By God, I would have liked to see that," said Big Bill.

"Not from the inside you wouldn't," said Izzy, "I was there.

"My wife makes me go to church twice a year and last night was one of the nights. I take all the precautions I can. We sit near that side door on the left side of the church and I wear the best ear plugs that the Air Force has. I also wear steel-toed high-top boots. I needed it all last night.

"The service was coming down to the home stretch. I don't have any trouble listening to the music at all because I play a little game of changing the lyrics. I use one stock phrase and last night my phrase was 'her ass looks bigger with no pants on,' and every time anyone said amen, I substituted 'big ass.' Try it the next time you go to church, it's very entertaining.

"Anyhow, the Bishop had just finished up preaching about a big noise from the sky and had started another hymn on his slide trombone when the steeple blew up. The slide on the preacher's horn got down in the box of snakes he had up on the stage and he turned the whole box over onto the main floor of the church. Those snakes fell about two feet and started doing a rapid deployment all over the area. Some of the parishioners haven't moved that fast in years. We were sitting right by the door and three fat ladies with no shoes on beat me to the door from three rows away. I did have a handicap, I was carrying my wife. I would have dropped her in the doorway when another old heifer stepped on my foot if it had not been for the boots."

"What kind of firepower do you reckon was used on the steeple?" mused Big Charley.

"Let me have a talk with Loose Lip Linder, he lives about two blocks from that church and generally knows what goes on over there," offered Swifty. "I'll let you know when I find out."

Swifty dropped by the Sky Ranch a day or so later to tell me that he had talked with Loose Lip Linder and all that he would say was that some unknown someone had let it be known in the area that if anyone wanted to take a pot shot at an unnamed church steeple it should happen at one time.

Now the Methodist Church in that same general area has a set of Westminster Chimes that announce the hour. They play a set hourly tune and then chime the hour. The idea was that all activity should coincide with the third bong of the hourly group.

"I went by the church on the way over here and, from the looks of the space where the speakers are, everyone in the community must have cranked off a round or two.

"I still don't know what caused the big noise in the steeple, something had to explode up there, but there is no sign of shrapnel from a grenade. Loose Lip said he was coming over here to put some cabinets up in the new kitchen, you may learn more than I did. I probably know as much as I should anyway."

Loose Lip appeared later in the day and hung some cabinets in the hangar. He told us pretty much the same thing that we had already heard so there was no new news. As he was leaving he told me I should ask Jimmy about the new tater cannon that Bill Banning had rigged up. The last comment was an aside to me only and I knew I better check it out.

Jimmy's Radiator was covered up as usual when I arrived. Jimmy looked up when I walked in and asked, "Have you had any lunch yet?" I shook my head and he hit the quick dial for the Deli up on Alcoa Highway. The order was for twenty-five hot dogs, ten orders of French fries and two egg salad sandwiches on plain, not toasted, bread. I asked who was on egg salad and Jimmy said that One Leg Lilly had gotten drunk and lost his upper and lower plates over the weekend.

I drove up to the Deli and brought back the food. There were three mechanics, two customers waiting for their cars, Jimmy, One Leg, and me. We sat around a small coffee table in the waiting room/office to eat and swap stories, mostly about fishing.

When lunch was over, I asked if Jimmy had seen the new tater cannon that Loose Lip Linder had said that Bill Banning built. Jimmy said, "You go look in the locker on my bass boat over in the last bay."

Now a tater cannon, for those of you who may not be up on the latest in good old boy technology, is a gun made of a three foot length of plastic pipe which shoots a potato by igniting a charge of flammable gas such as ether, carburetor cleaner, or hair spray. The pipe or barrel is sharpened on one end to aid in the sizing of the potato, and the other end is threaded to receive a screw-on cap. A potato is placed on a firm surface and the sharpened end of the barrel is forced through the potato with a solid plug of potato remaining in the pipe. The potato plug is pushed down the barrel with a measured ramrod and the gun is ready to be charged. The cap is removed from the other end of the cannon and the open chamber is sprayed with the aerosol. The cap is replaced and it is ready to fire. The firing is triggered by applying a spark from a cigarette lighter wheel to a touch hole drilled through the pipe.

The one I was looking at was several generations past what is described above. It was larger, to start with, and it had a much more sophisticated ignition system. It was fired by a spark plug attached to a small electronic package which was attached to the stock. It was designed to be a shoulder fired weapon.

I went back over where Jimmy was working on a car radiator and told him that it sure looked good, but it would take a big potato to fill up that barrel. He said, "Oh, it wasn't built for taters. Bill was having trouble with the geese messing up his boat dock. It looked like it was whitewashed part of the time. He asked Game and Fish about it and they told him he couldn't shoot them out of season but he could scare them. So he built this special tater cannon. It fires a special round that he builds himself. It acts just like a concussion grenade when it hits something solid. It's all noise and no shrapnel. Whatever he is using to hold the charge of powder together just disappears when it goes off. It makes one hell of a noise and the geese don't have to be re-educated very often."

I was beginning to feel a little like Swifty Swanson, I already knew as much as I wanted to.

JIMMY'S GONE

Sometimes phones ring happy and sometimes not. This was one of the not kind of calls. Captain Tom said, "Dapper have you heard the news yet?" I knew from the tone that I didn't want to know what was coming next but at the same time I had to know. Terry continued, "Jimmy died at about five o'clock this afternoon. He was on a hunting trip and drowned in a farm pond while retrieving some geese that he shot... Dapper are you still there?" I was too stunned to speak, I just couldn't take it all in.

"Yeah, Tom, I'm here. What I'm having trouble with is that Jimmy isn't."

I called and left a message on the machine for Prenny and went out to sit on the screened porch and remember.

The funeral home was overflowing all over the place. It looked like a politician or a lawyer had died, and everyone had come out to celebrate. There was a large difference however. These folks were out because they had all lost a friend. Everyone I talked to had a story to tell about something Jimmy had done for them.

We were all feeling sorry for ourselves, but we all knew beyond a shadow of a doubt that he was in a much better place. The EMT's that picked him up were there and they told me that they felt sure that Jimmy was dead before he went under the water. He either had a stroke or a heart attack.

I also talked to the old gentleman who owned the farm where he was hunting who said that he was watching him through field glasses about a half mile from his house. He said "Jimmy shot a couple of geese and they fell into the pond. Jimmy waded out to pick them up and was returning to the bank. The water was up to his chest and he just seemed to relax and slip under the surface. I called the 911 number, but I knew he was gone. I can't walk very well anymore, so I couldn't get up to the pond, but it didn't matter. I'm sure going to miss that boy, he kept all of my old junk running. All he would ever take for it was for me to let him come up here and hunt this and that."

SKY RANCH AIR MAIL
JIMMY CROWE DIES (Dapper)

Jimmy Crowe, age 51, owner of the big C-180 down in the lower forty died while on a hunting trip on Friday 7 Oct 94. Jimmy served his country as a Marine in Vietnam where he was assigned to an elite rifle sniper group. Jimmy had the physical ability to see things very clearly at long range. I have flown a lot with him and he always saw other aircraft long before I did. Jim had many strengths, the determination to see a job completed, the intelligence to unravel a mechanical mystery, and a good sense of humor. However, his greatest asset was his feeling for people, not just some of them but all of them. I have often watched him tell folks who just had their car fixed at Jim's Radiator that the bill was $10,000, but for them to go ahead and take the car and send him a little something when they were able. The best wishes and prayers of the club go to Jimmy's family. ETPC has lost a good and loyal member. I have lost a good and true friend. Dapper

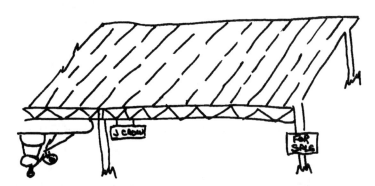

TIGHTWAD WILSON'S ROAD TRIP

Tightwad Wilson came wandering into the clubhouse and started looking through the latest issue of Trade-a-Plane. He religiously perused the publication which comes out three times a month, but had not bought an airplane in over thirty years. Big Charley let him look for a while and then asked, "T.W., where were you on the night the pool got polluted?" T.W. responded, "I knew you would get around to asking me that and I'm glad you waited as long as you did because it is still painful for me to think about that night. I'm sure you have heard about the world's longest yard sale that runs from up in Kentucky all the way down into Alabama. Well, it took me four days to make the trip down that thing and I found some real bargains let me tell you. I had the back of the old truck nearly full of stuff when I heard about this fabulous flea market that they have in Chattanooga, so I came back through there on the way home. I found some stuff there too, but the only way I could get it home was to buy another trailer. So I picked up a real nice looking covered utility trailer and loaded it up with the good stuff I found in the flea market.

"I got about as far as Cleveland when the left rear tire on the trailer let go. I got her pulled over and when I checked it out the damn bearings were dry and the wheel was seized on the axle. I tried to call up here to get One Leg Lilly to come and get me but my phone battery was dead." "Is that the battery you found at the flea market in Maryville?" asked Charley. "One and the same," continued T.W.

"Anyhow, I decided to unhook the trailer and go on into Cleveland and get some breakfast and call Leg from there. Leg said for me to just wait on him at the restaurant and he would come there and follow me to the trailer. He showed up in a while and we went down to get the trailer. When we got there, it was gone, lock stock and barrel. I called the sheriff but he told me not to hold my breath. Next year when I make that trip I will take the big truck, and hook a horse trailer and a utility trailer together so I have plenty of room for stuff."

BIG BILL LOSES THE WAR

Big Bill Henry had some serious surgery six months ago and now his FAA medical exam is coming due. All of us who fly know that at some point we will lose our medical if we live long enough. Bill had some chest pain a couple of years ago and one doctor pronounced the problem a heart attack and another said not. Bill told the truth on his next physical and the FAA chose the bad news and required a treadmill stress test, all sorts of affidavits, and lab work. If the file was any larger, Bill would have needed to use Roadway Express to ship the file to the FAA in Oklahoma City.

Bill waited a while and then called the folks in Oke City only to learn that some of the tees weren't crossed with horizontal lines and the dots on some of the i's didn't look good either. He was grounded for awhile until the paper work all suited the FAA. "They are so goddamn careful with their @#$%%$%* paper, I wonder how they deal with the paper that comes on a roll in the small smelly cubical. It must take them an hour to get the paper ready to wipe their rotten goddamn no good sorry asses," growled Big Bill.

I covered Bill's most recent trip to the Baptist House of Pain, read hospital, in the club newsletter when it happened.

SKY RANCH AIRMAIL
BIG BILL HENRY'S GALLBLADDER (dapper)

Big Bill is going to have to go into the hospital for a spell of surgery here in the next few days. If you remember, the surgeon went in a while back and determined that he could get several more boat payments out of this deal, so he expanded the field to include the gallbladder, a resection of the bowel, a hernia repair, and the removal of the appendix.

The experts on the porch are divided as to whether or not this should count as a major repair requiring an FAA form 337 or not. Some feel that the removal of equipment, even if it is not required for general operation, requires that the paper work be filed. Most of the porch people agree that the resection is just a minor repair in that both ends are still hooked to the same places and no functionality is changed.

The hernia repair is a quandary. It is a structural repair but the question is, is it a major or minor repair? One requires a log book entry, the other a log book entry and an FAA337. One thing is for sure, Bill will need a new weight and balance calculation for a new center of gravity.

Bill's log shows a lot of hours, but with the good wishes and prayers of all of you, I'm sure that the blank pages will be filled with lots of interesting entries of travels yet to be.

Bill told me that in light of his previous experience with Oke City that he was not going to attempt another round with them. He had decided to sell his Champ and buy an ultra light that he could fly without a medical exam blessed by the FAA.

A TRIP TO ABINGDON

Bill and I were sitting in some lawn chairs in his hangar in front of Aeronca 8557. It had been sold but not yet moved to her new hangar. Bill mused, "I sure did hate to sell that bird. After doing all that restoration work, I had it just like I wanted it." I said, "That little bird has a long history on this field. I bought her from Dick Cox in the sixties and we kept her for several years. Well, we kept her until Bunker got too big to sit on his mother's lap when we went on a trip.

"I remember one time we flew up to Abingdon VA (VJI) when my cousin, Jocko and his wife Annabelle had their last baby. We had all the stuff you have to have: a diaper bag, bottles, formula, etc. They picked us up when we got there and drove us to the house. My Aunt Ophelia, the Grandmama of that branch of the family, organized what was supposed to be a quick lunch. Quick didn't work out due to the long discussions comparing the new baby to all the previous family babies.

The next order of business was for the women to organize a safari to the hospital to see the newest addition. I told Aunt Ophelia that we needed to start home by about six o'clock because the airplane did not have any lights.

The short version is we were late getting out of Abingdon and it was dark by the time we made Morristown. I landed and we were lucky that there was a student pilot there who was going to Knoxville. We hitched a ride with him and had to stop somewhere along the way and buy some milk for Bunker, because we had planned to be home a lot earlier

Bill looked off over the ridge line in front of us into the past and remembered trips that he and Beulah had taken in the Champ. "I wonder how may people have learned to fly in that air knocker over the years? I taught Beulah to fly in it.

"One time there were five of us flying to Tullahoma to the Old South Fly-In. There was Billy Bob with his Aeronca Chief, and Old Folks Ferringer, Swifty Swanson, Tightwad Wilson, and me in Champs. The weather wasn't very good and we agreed to follow the interstate and land in Crossville. All of us but Old Folks landed in Crossville. About thirty minutes later we saw a Champ enter the pattern, but it didn't look like the one we were looking for. When it taxied up it was indeed Old Folks and his Champ but it had been redecorated. It had big splotches of fresh cow manure all over it. Old Folks said that he got lost and had to land in a cow pasture and ask where the airport was. He must have hit every fresh cow patty in that field either on landing or take-off.

The word spread rather quickly at the airport and the FAA guys working at the Crossville Flight Service Station all took turns coming out to see the Cow Champ.

We all gassed up and Old Folks hosed the worst of the decorations off his plane and we headed on down to Tullahoma. We put Old Folks in the middle of the group and told him to stay in sight of the one in front and in back of him.

He was afraid he was going to run over the plane in front of him so he reduced the power. When he slowed down everybody else had to also. Then he slowed down again and so did we. Pretty soon we all had just enough power on to stay in the air. We got tired of that and went on to Tullahoma and let Old Folks do the best he could.

We didn't see him again until the next day. He got lost, ran out of gas and had to land in a field. After spending the night with a farmer, he left the plane and hitched a ride back to Knoxville. The next week a couple of the boys took some gas and picked up the airplane for him. Old Folks was good at handling the airplane, but he could get lost in the traffic pattern.

THE SHERIFF BACKS DOWN

Willy Clyde Coyote settled in on the porch and said, "I talked to Bill Banning the other night and he was telling me about his latest trip to the left coast and back for Uncle Sugar. I think that you guys know that I have a contract with DOE to do emergency road service on the big rigs they use to haul nuke products around the country. I mostly just collect the money for being available, but every now and then something comes up that they need a little help on.

"The other night I got a call to go look at a rig out near Kingston. Bill was riding chase and he was my escort while I was anywhere near the truck. He told me that they had been somewhere out in Texas the day before when a local county sheriff wanted to show off while they were at a refueling stop. They had three full teams covering the truck stop. That truck was being watched closer than the collection plate at a Baptist tent meeting.

"The sheriff was up for re-election in a few days and there was a group of his followers looking on when he announced he was going to inspect the tractor. Toby John Ratliff, who was putting fuel in the truck, told the sheriff that this was a DOE truck and was covered under a federal directive which was required to be on file in the sheriff's own office. He then handed the sheriff the standard law enforcement card and asked him to please call the telephone number listed on it and ask for confirmation about the truck.

"The sheriff didn't want to back down in front of his people and started to force his way past Toby John to the cab door. Toby let him get fairly close to him and then he told him, 'Sheriff, if you really are a Sheriff, you better look down on your chest. There are three little red dots there, any one of which can make you very dead if you lay a hand on me.

There are six men stationed around this truck stop with weapons ready to take out you or anybody else that we feel is a threat.'

"The sheriff had worked himself up to a full red-faced bluster, but when he saw the red dots dancing on his chest he suddenly remembered that he had not shown any official identification, and the men who were guarding the DOE rig really didn't know who he was, and were going do their jobs. The red face turned white and the sheriff backed down, election and all. We had enough fuel aboard to make an alternate stop and rolled out of the truck stop with one unit up front and another in chase. The third unit kept a single red dot on the sheriff until the others were gone and then moved out to catch up."

Big Bill commented, "I'll bet that old boy is a little more careful in the future about who he is dealing with. What was wrong with the truck that you went out to check?" "It was just a fault in one of the warning light circuits in the cooling system," replied Willy Clyde. "What night did you make that run?" asked Bill. Willy replied, "Well, Mai Ling was in San

Francisco and it was also the night Reba called me to get the Russian's truck moved when he got put in jail."

Big Bill sputtered, "There goes another name off the list and I really thought you were an outstanding suspect after the Warthog made that comment about you marrying a Gook."

SAMUEL GREEN, PREACHER

The porch people were all drinking their coffee out of the pot in the maintenance hangar when I arrived. Izzy Green was checking the compression on 220 as a part of a hundred hour inspection. I'm not sure if Izzy enjoyed playing to an audience, but around here it went with the territory. Tightwad Wilson asked Izzy if he had been back to church since the big boom.

Izzy said no, but from what he was hearing from his wife Ramonda, the church was growing by leaps and bounds. Just last week they had to go out and buy another batch of folding chairs. Fritz Fieberg spoke up and said, "I had to go to a funeral there once. I thought they had pews to sit in." Izzy said, "Yes there are pews, but they only come about half-way back. The preacher sold the rest of them to a brother preacher who has a church up in Union County."

Izzy continued, "A bunch of the other chairs that were there had to be placed on the out-of-service list after the last evacuation order. That night I saw one big tall strong looking woman with a baby under one arm and a pocket book that was bigger than the baby under the other over on the other side of the church. She was stepping in the seats of the pews going from pew to pew until she came to the rows of chairs.

"Her last step from the pews was to an old green kitchen chair. It gave up the ghost immediately. The four legs went in four different directions and the seat was flat on the floor. The big gal wanted no part of the floor and stepped up into the seat of the next chair. It was an old folding chair with the name of some long extinct funeral home on the back in fading paint. It too promptly folded up.

"She gave up on stepping up and cut a wide swath through the rest of the chairs. She looked like an All-American Tennessee offensive tackle cutting a swath through the Vanderbilt defense."

"Izzy, I heard that Samuel got saved by Bishop Love just like you did," said Big Charley. "Well it isn't the quite the same thing," Izzy said. "He may believe all that stuff. I just did it so I could marry Monda. He is so wound up now that he has finished the Bishop's night school course, 'Teach to Preach in Ten Easy Lessons'."

"Yes, I saw an ad on television about that course," said Big Bill Henry. "The Bishop listed five areas of special interest for up and coming preachers. If I remember right, the first two were 'Tithing' and 'Church Music'." "You mean Plate Passing and Psalm Singing," said Small Sam.

Big Charley said, "Yes, and two other areas were 'A Show of Faith' and 'Immersion Baptism'." "OK, those courses are Rubbing the Rattlers and Deep Dipping." translated Small Sam.

"What was the last one?" Big Bill Henry asked. "Oh I don't remember what it was, but I make a motion that before we continue this discussion, we have a lightning rod system installed on the hangar," Big Charley solemnly intoned.

Father Gene said that he could not resist when he saw the ad and that he called to get more information. It seems that each course requires the student to attend two four-hour sessions on succeeding Thursday nights with a tuition fee of two hundred dollars per night. So for two thousand dollars you can become a preacher.

"Not quite." said Izzy. "Samuel scraped together the money for the ten weeks, but when he finished he found out about the rest of the deal. You also have to preach ten sermons on the Bishop's outreach circuit and then lay out a five thousand dollar anointing fee. Samuel said that he did get a two hundred dollar finding fee for an applicant who joined the program from a Union County Church where he preached."

"How is Samuel planning to raise the anointing money?" asked Big Charley. "Well," answered Izzy, "he told me he was leaving it up to the lord and long shots and, judging from his effort last month, it may be awhile before he wears the robe of the anointed. He laid a fifty dollar three-way parlay on his bookie for Vanderbilt over Alabama, South Carolina over Florida, and Kentucky over Tennessee at home." "Goddamn!" cried Big Bill, "I thought bookmaking was supposed to be a risky business."

"Where does Samuel want to do the lord's work when and if he gets anointed?" asked the Mad Flaming Russian. "Does he plan to give up his regular job at the Post Office?"

"He will keep his Post Office position. It gives him a nice place to sleep during the day" said Izzy. "As to his other plans, the last I heard he was undecided as to whether to save the bikers or become the Chaplain for the exotic dancers of our fair city."

About a week later Izzy was making entries in some aircraft and engine logs in the clubhouse when I came in. He stopped and told me that Samuel had decided to become the Chaplain to the exotic dancers in the city rather than trying to save the bikers.

Sometime last week he had been out trying to save one of the bikers at the Two Wheeler Bar over in Lonsdale when one of them had a flashback of some kind and beat Samuel up pretty bad. Two of the dancers working the bar found him in the parking lot and took him home with them. They really fixed him up. He said that his face was still swelled up the next day but he had another part that probably wouldn't swell up again until the day after that.

RATTLERS AND RATTLERS

Billy Bob Wanger pulled up in front of the clubhouse and came in to give me a piece of paper which had the date of his new flight physical on it for me to put in our computer system. Each month when the bills go out the system looks at the dates of your last flight physical and flight review and if either is coming due it prints a reminder on the bottom of the invoice. The old system has some nice features to go along with its faults. One of the things it won't be able to do is function normally after the year 1999. It just loses its grip after that.

Big Charley asked Billy Bob if he had a flush valve in the truck as the one in the men's room had quit and the water had been turned off. Billy Bob said he would look and see. He thought he had one on the truck. He came right back in the clubhouse and Big Charley said, "Well did you have one?" Billy Bob said he didn't know yet because when he unlocked the tool bin on the truck he must have disturbed a visitor.

We all went out to see what he meant. Billy Bob slapped his hand on the top of the front tool bin and you could hear that a serious sized rattlesnake was very unhappy. Big Charley said "Wait just a minute, I've a little 410 shotgun in the van loaded with bird shot." Billy Bob said "I don't think you want to do that, there are about five sticks of dynamite in that bin and you really don't want to shoot anything in there."

Small Sam Long had been watching the proceedings and came up and asked Billy Bob if there was a hole between the front and back bins. Billy said there was but it was not big enough for the snake to go through. Sam said open that back bin and I'll slow your snake down for you. After the bin was open Small Sam picked up a CO_2 fire extinguisher and removed the large nozzle from the hose. He put the hose of the extinguisher over the hole and sent a long blast of cold CO_2 in with the snake. He waited about thirty seconds and did it again. After about four tries there was no response from within when Billy Bob beat on the side of the tool bin.

The snake was a very slow snake when the bin was opened. Billy Bob picked him out with no trouble at all. Sam said "I think he will be all right if you put him out in the sun to defrost." Billy Bob took the snake over across the runway and put him down in the grass next to the woods. He was starting to get in the truck when Big Bill Henry said, "Now that you are done playing with the snake, when are you going to fix the shit house?"

The story enjoyed wide circulation among the clan. They all wondered what who would find where next. We didn't have long to wait.

Willy Clyde came in a few days later and told us that he too had heard a rattling noise in his big toolbox. He said there was no hole in that big toolbox before but that he had one now. He had drilled a big hole right under the lock and used all of a CO_2 bottle before the noise quit. Big Charley asked how big was the snake? Willy Clyde pulled a battery driven tape recorder out of his pocket and pressed the play button. While it was rattling along, Willy said, "About this big."

EARTHY WOMAN'S FLYING MACHINE

Big Charley was drinking coffee on he porch when I rolled into the clubhouse. I had parked next to Earthy Woman's bus so I asked Charley if I had missed the parade from the mud flat already. Charley told me that there was no parade today, she was down in the Wanger's hangar looking at her new flying machine.

"Is she going to put it together herself?" I asked and Charley said that he heard that Billy Bob was going to come over and help her with the assembly. While we were talking, Billy Bob drove up so we jumped in his truck and rode down to his hangar.

Cathy had a booklet of instructions open and was looking them over carefully. Billy Bob spread out a large tarp on the ground saying that he did not want to lose any more parts in this batch of grass. We opened the first crate and spread the contents out on the tarp. It had most of the fuselage, what there was of it, and lots of hardware items, bolts, nuts and so forth. The second crate contained the wings and tail feathers, all covered and hopefully ready to go. We pulled the lid off the third crate and found the engine, and another box of goodies.

I asked Billy Bob if he needed any more help before I went back to the office because I had some club bills that I needed to pay and he said they could handle it. We both knew that he would have more help and hindrance than he could handle once the porch pilots all started to show up.

Big Bill Henry stuck his head in the office at midmorning and asked if I had been down to see the flying circus that was being constructed in the Wanger hangar. I told him that most of it was still in the crates when I left Big Charley down there earlier. Bill continued by saying, "Billy Bob could get the damn thing built a lot quicker if he could shoot about half of his help. Some of those mechanical geniuses couldn't pour piss out of a boot with the directions written on the bottom of the heel.

"The flying machine came with two complete sets of directions and they don't know each other. Earthy Woman is reading one set to Billy and Big Charley the other. I don't think Billy is paying a lot of attention to either one."

"I'm sure he will figure it out," I said.

"Do you think she can fly that thing after it is put together? She has flown with every instructor on the place and still can't land a Cessna 150 more than once out of four times around the patch and that's with an instructor sitting there for security."

"Maybe it will go slow enough so that she has more time to make up her mind about what she has to do."

"Maybe so."

The Warthog was the next interruption when he said, "Did you see that flying lawn chair down in Wanger's hangar? We need to have a meeting to vote on letting those things fly around here. There could be a real problem for those of us who fly the heavy iron with longer approaches and higher air speeds."

He did have a point, but as usual his approach to the problem was to ban it rather than looking for a solution that would let everyone live and fly in peace.

I walked back down to the Wanger establishment and sat down beside Cathy on a crate. "It looks like it's going pretty well." Cathy said that there had been a few problems but that she was really happy to see the little bird go together. She added that some of the colors were not what she expected but with the addition of a few accent stripes it would come together nicely.

I told her that Shay had told me about meeting her at Sugar Davis's house and asked her if Sugar had settled on the upholstery fabric. Cathy ignored me completely, acted as if I hadn't said a word. Then I asked her what colors she needed to bring this thing together and she said three shades of green. I figured her mind must have been somewhere else when I asked the other question.

Cathy, aka Earthy Woman, decided she needed a mud bath to help her relax, and when she mentioned it to Billy Bob he said in a voice loud enough for all the 'helpers' to hear that he thought that she should have a mud bath and relax. The exodus of helpers was immediate and complete. I felt sorry for Big Charley, as slowly as he walked all the good seats on the porch would be gone by the time he got there.

Billy Bob looked over at me and said, "Boy it's a relief to have that bunch out of here. I got more suggestions on what to do than a young rich widow gets at a funeral."

Billy Bob worked a little and then he said, "I'm sure you have known who my decorator is and why I couldn't tell you about it. I knew it was just a matter of time until someone found out."

"I haven't told anyone about it Billy because I'm really not sure what to tell them anyhow."

"Hell, she has been working for me for nearly two years now and it is the strangest thing I've ever seen. We put an ad in the paper for a decorator and Catherine came out and talked to Peggy Sue and she hired her. She has a wonderful portfolio. Peggy kept it for a few days so I could see it.

"One of the strange things about it is if I call at her place and she answers 'this is Catherine, can I help you?', we can make appointments, do business, whatever. But if she just says hello and I ask about some work related thing, the phone goes dead. If I call right back I get the answering machine and I leave a message for Catherine. She usually calls me back within an hour. If I need her at a job she always shows up in that Black BMW within five minutes of when she says she will."

"Boy, that is strange. When you are working with Catherine on a job, have you ever mentioned the Sky Ranch?"

"Yes, she will talk about the people here and the planes and so forth. She also talks about Earthy Woman and the ultra light, but I have never asked her about the mud baths."

"Billy, it looks like this kid is a prospect for Doc Kronk's couch. Catherine knows about Earthy Woman but do you think Earthy Woman knows about Catherine?"

"Hell, I don't know Dapper. I have problems enough with people when they answer to one name and have one personality. You take the Warthog for instance, he's an asshole now, he was an asshole last year, and I have great faith he will be an asshole next year. I like it that way.

"I can even deal with Earthy Woman and Catherine if I can see them because the hairdo tells me which one I'm dealing with, but when you're talking on the phone you're working blind. Whoever it was that said 'she ain't all here when she's here' was wrong. She is more here than he knew. She just may not know who is here."

I walked over to my hangar and piddled around with the airplane a while and then went back to the clubhouse. I asked how the parade of mud went and Tightwad Wilson said that by the time Earthy Woman got back to the clubhouse, she had forgotten why she came and got in the bus and left.

In due time, about a week in this case, the new bird was all together and ready for a test flight. Big Bill Henry looked the machine over carefully and said it was put together according to the drawings as best he could tell. He also said that everything was as safe as the design would allow. He then stated that he would not sign any log book or any scrap of paper stating that he had even seen the damn thing and, if possible, would like to have ten minutes notice of when it was to be flown so he could get off the island.

One of the porch pilots standing in the back spoke up just loud enough for everyone but Bill to hear, "Bill, why don't you lean back and tell us what you really think about this machine." While the porch pilots were having a long discussion about who should test fly the new machine, Earthy Woman came putting up in her VW bus and drove down to the hangar. The discussion was still in progress when the bright little machine started up and taxied to the middle of the runway and took off to the north.

After a short roll it was in the air, flying at about the same height as the club hangar. She hung a hard left around the flag pole, with the wings nearly parallel with the pole, barely made it over the trees behind the clubhouse, and went cruising down the river. Zipper Thomas commented, "Did you expect her to fly a conventional traffic pattern?"

It didn't take long to get some money up as to what kind of landing was coming in the near future. The group was having trouble getting the bets narrowed down so there could be clear winners declared. They were still at it when Earthy Woman came taxiing up the runway. She had approached and landed on the south end of the runway so quietly that no one heard her coming so no one saw her land. All bets were off.

HIGH FAT LUNCH WITH BIG BILL

Big Bill Henry stuck his head in the clubhouse to tell us that it was time for Big Charley, Small Sam, and me to get our asses in the car if we were going to go to lunch with him. "Bill isn't much for subtle, is he?" Sam chuckled. We loaded up and headed out to try a new place on Kingston Pike that Bill had heard about.

We had just gotten the menu when Big Charley looked up and said, "I thought we were in trouble when we walked in. They sure don't have much on the menu that looks good." Charley measured restaurants by the variety of sandwiches that contained ham that were on the menu. His golden dinner bucket award went to the places that offered three kinds of ham, five kinds of cheese, plus multiple offerings of dressings, pickles, and other options. As usual there were several things on the menu that looked promising to me. If it's classified as food, I will most likely give it a shot.

The waitress was standing at the next table trying to answer all the questions sent her way by a big gal in a yellow and black dress. She wanted to know if the salad dressing in question was low fat or no fat. Then she wanted to know the family history of the olive oil so she could determine for herself if it classified as extra virgin. Next she wanted an exact analysis of the sodium content of various items on the menu that she may or may not consider for consumption. After an inquisition concerning the content and lineage and exact freezer temperature of the frozen yogurt she let the waitress escape.

The waitress turned to our table and said with a smile of relief, "What do you guys want today?" Charley, Sam, and I all gave our orders and the girl turned to Big Bill Henry.

He turned his chair so that he was perfectly aligned with the ear of the big heifer at the next table and said in a voice much louder that he usually used, "I'm a little hard of hearing, so you will have to speak up a little. This meat loaf that you have on the menu, if it is made with a mixture of real pork and beef with all the fat left in it, I'll try it. I want some home fries fried in hog lard with plenty of salt, and I'll also have some of those green beans but only if you can bring a piece of the side meat that was in the pot when they were cooked."

The waitress and about half the tables around us were soon enjoying Big Bill's luncheon order, but the lady who caused the whole thing was not a happy camper. She looked around for some support from the surrounding tables but saw only smiling faces. She started gathering up her various bundles preparing to leave. As soon as she started to push her chair back from the table, Small Sam made a noise like the OSHA reverse beeper on heavy equipment. Our table nearly broke up on the spot.

As we were paying our tab on the way out, Big Charley told the owner at the register that he hoped we had not caused him to lose a customer, and the man said that he hoped that we had because she had been nothing but a pain in the ass ever since he opened. I told him that we had heard about his place from Nick the Greek who runs the Deli out next to the airport. He said, "Yes, he goes to the Greek Church with me." "It seems as if most of the restaurants in town are run by Greeks," said Bill.

DOG TRAINING

In the south forty of the field there are a batch of hangars. The first hangar in one of the rows belongs to the Coyote and there is space beside it for his boat. On the other side is Small Sam, then Wanger, and next to him is the Warthog.

The Warthog's current airplane, the C-337, is too big for the hangar and it sits out on an outside tie-down over next to the river. So he keeps boats, motorcycles, and other rolling stock in the hangar. Whenever he uses his airplane he also uses the hangar to store the Bentley.

The Warthog's dog Prince, an Afghan Hound, has to be the one of the dumbest dogs on record. Zipper says he is the only left-handed dog he ever saw. Small Sam, after tiring of watching the dog come and pee on each of the poles supporting his hangar, developed a system which should have worked with one lesson. Sam installed a copper band around each pole starting just above ground level, extending up about twelve inches, and tied them all to an electric fence charging system.

Sam said the first time the Warthog came over with the dog, he watched for the dog to come up and wet down the first post. Sam said Prince howled for a minute or two and then sat down and stuck a leg up in the air to inspect his equipment. He sat there for a while and started nosing around the area some more.

Pretty soon he came up to another pole and raised his leg and got slammed again. After getting hit five times in one day, he finally let the sixth pole go, but three days later when he came back, he had to start learning all over.

Homer and Tyrone, on the other hand, came to the hangar and found that something had changed since their last visit. They looked over at Small Sam who just shook his head and said no and they walked away without as much as another glance at the poles.

OLD NEWSLETTERS

Big Charley McGillicuddy sat down at the big round table with a folder in front of him and as usual waded right into an ongoing conversation. He said, "Dapper, I borrowed this folder of old club newsletters from Big Bill Henry and by Jesus there's some good stuff in here." He fished around in the folder and said, "This end of the year story is a pip".

THE SKY RANCH AIR MAIL
12/94
THAT WAS THE YEAR THAT WAS (dapper)

The club must be in pretty good health as the year closes. We have been probed, inspected, questioned at length, and had our time taken away from flying by several specialists at wasting time. We have been visited by Dr. FAA, Dr. EPA, and Dr. OSHA. The collective doctors all practice various subspecialties of proctology (Painus-Assus).

Dr. FAA arrived and said he was here to help us with our flying problems. He then looked over every exhaust stack on the place. He then selected our most outstanding example of a flight instructor (Flyus-Teachus) for a complete physical out on the picnic table. Captain Tom's eyes were a little crossed when it was over but Dr. FAA and his assistant went away with smiles on their faces and we have not heard from them since.

Dr. EPA arrived at the Sky Ranch and announced that he was concerned that we were suffering from a rash of problems resultant from various irritants and pollutants which were dumped on the property. The good doctor was unable to locate a rash or a cause for a future rash anywhere on the island. He concluded that if anyone had a case of rash (Redus-Assus) it must be off-site. Several days later Dr. EPA returned to say the rash was caused by the dumping of oil under the house trailer or our property. NOT TRUE. This time the Dr. left in such a hurry that he did not ask who carried our health insurance.

We also had another specialist in to check the health of our fuel tanks and they are in good shape for another year. Dr. OSHA sent us a long medical history to complete, rather than making a house call. We are so lucky. This good doctor was concerned about the hangar door (Bigus-Doorus), our antique tractor collection (Tractus-Johnus), and our runway lights (Minus-Litus), and too many other items to list in this epistle. After much searching of the soul and other extremities, the completed history was returned and Dr. OSHA is looking for other places to practice his specialty.

We heard a rumor that Dr. IRS is looking for a space in his appointment book for us, but that information may not be valid.

"Just across the page there was another story that I remember, because I was here," said Dr. Kronk.

THE SKY RANCH AIR MAIL
12/94
PAUL POBEREZNY VISITS (dapper)

Paul Poberezny was a visitor to the Sky Ranch on Saturday, the day that he spoke at the EAA Chapter 17 banquet. Paul sat and chatted about the things that most pilot groups talk about, machines that fly and the people that fly them. I was a little surprised to learn that he drove rather than flew to Knoxville for this trip.

As we sat and talked, I was reminded of the other national figures that have visited the Sky Ranch. General Chuck Yeager and Dwayne Cole have also walked on our grass. Dwayne Cole parked his airplane in our hangar and there is a picture of it on the wall in the clubhouse to prove it. I don't remember at the moment if we have a picture of Chuck Yeager or not. If we do not have that picture, we need to tend to that. The talk that Paul gave at the dinner meeting was fine, the Chapter 17 folks put on a nice program.

WE LOST THE LEASE 1992

Captain Tom Dawson came up to me just as I parked the van in the lot at the airport and said, "Mr. President," to alert me that there was serious business afoot. "I hate to tell you this, but the city of Knoxville has canceled our lease and plans to put the property up for sale to the highest bidder. It also seems that our grand bookkeeper, Reginald Roach, has not paid the damn rent for the last two months and I wonder if that had anything to do with their sudden need to sell this out from under us." I asked Tom how do we know this and he says that the letter came today from the Knoxville Utilities Board.

It seems that KUB has held the property since the City took it away from those two old ladies back when a former mayor tried to construct a water treatment plant here. I asked, "Who all knows about this and have you called the members of the board yet?" "Just opened the letter," Tom said. "All right, let's get the members of the board together tonight at 6:30, and you better hit the emergency fund for a couple of six-packs, because we will need some free thinkers to come up with a plan that will get us through this one."

The folks on the clubhouse porch who had heard about the letter all started preaching gloom and doom about how some big wheeler dealer would come in and bid a million dollars for the property so he could put condos and boat docks all over the place. Billy Bob Wanger was just sure that some rag head S.O.B. will pop up out of the sand with oil money dribbling out of every pocket and buy the place.

The group gathered in the clubhouse for the BOD meeting and, as soon as everyone had a beer and was settled in at the table, I asked them what was their pleasure. Small Sam said, "You know the last time we had to fight city hall we had the help of all the high dollar property owners in the area because they didn't want a sewage plant on their doorstep. This time they may be happier with some other option than this airport." "Yes," Doc Kronk chimed in, "a man with a llama ranch in here would be a lot quieter than we are."

There was more discussion about who might want the place and what they would want to do with it, but I grew tired of that and shut off the discussion with a bang of the big gavel which had started out life as a meat tenderizer. "Guys let's spend more time figuring how we are going to buy the place instead of what someone else may do with it if he gets it," I said.

"What I want you all to do is consider what mix of the following money raisers you want to use to get the cash necessary to bid on this place.

"First, we can lay an assessment on the membership for some amount of money. The assessment could range from $100 to $1000 dollars. The higher the assessment the more members you will run out of the club.

"Second, we can sell land bonds at above market interest rates to raise cash. If we sell this kind of bond it would have to be backed by the land and should only be sold to members so that control of the club is maintained.

"The third option is to borrow some money from a bank and have a mortgage like everyone else in the world. Get out and talk to the members and see what they want to do. The next big club meeting will be a dilly and I would like to know what some of the brain trusts are thinking ahead of time if possible."

The next day an ad appeared in the paper.

> NOTICE OF PUBLIC SALE
> The Knoxville Utilities Board will offer
> COX SKYRANCH
> 58.1 acres on Fort Loudon Lake
> off Alcoa Highway
> For information call
> (615) 555-2513 M-F 8:00AM through 4:00PM

Just below the KUB ad there appeared another ad for river front property.

> 10 ACRES on Holston River
> Excellent building sites.
> $4,500 per acre. 555-2069

The day after the ad appeared in the *Knoxville News-Sentinel* the interest in the property really picked up. We had folks prowling around all over the place and asking questions about all sorts of things. One of the most asked things was about how often the water gets up and how high does it go. The members gave some interesting replies to some of these folk and some of them actually believed that the whole place was totally underwater at least twice a year.

The truth is that we do have water over about three-fourths of the area about every five years or so. One man lost interest after he learned that TVA actually controlled all of the land below elevation 817. The club has had an agreement with TVA that any hangar that we put below elevation 817 would have all electrical outlets and wiring above that level.

"Hey Dapper," said the Mad Russian poking his head into the cockpit of 2U where I was stretched out with my head under the instrument panel, "There is a newspaper gal from the *Sentinel* up at the clubhouse asking all sorts of questions and you better get up there PDQ or she may get some strange quotes in the paper from the porch pilots that are here today." I had my head under the panel, my back on the floor, and my feet up in the pilot's seat so it took a while to get unwound and out of the airplane. Planes are built to be flown, not worked on.

The reporter was Pam Park and she had lots of questions and I gave her more answers than she had questions. When she left she seemed happy that she had plenty of grist for her mill and at least I knew more than I did before she came because she had already talked with Larry Fleming at KUB. Mr. Fleming had told her that he would be happy if we won the bid.

The following day we got the lead story on the East Tennessee page, just above a story about a local lawyer charged with theft.

KUB TO SELL STRIP; FLYING CLUB WORRIED ABOUT FUTURE

The Knoxville News-Sentinel 3/92
By Pam Park

The Sky Ranch Flying Society which operates the Cox Sky Ranch, a sod strip sport aviation airfield off Alcoa Highway, is in danger of losing the property it has used for 22 years. Tom Dawson, Treasurer, wants to prevent the Knoxville Utilities Board, which controls the airstrip property along Fort Loudon Lake, from declaring the airfield surplus property and selling it by closed bid.

The City of Knoxville, or the Knoxville Utilities Board, is planning on having a closed bid sale of this property. If they go through with a closed bid sale, the pilots could lose it. "We want to keep the place if we can. We hope to keep this kind of aviation in Tennessee," said Dawson.

Dapper Kurlee, president of the club, said "When the lease was originally drawn, City Council promised the club first rights to buy the land if it was ever sold. I don't know that we can do anything but plead our case with KUB, or city council, if that becomes necessary. If the club is unable to buy the property their second choice would be to have KUB keep it and continue to lease it to us," Kurlee said.

The club has about 300 members; 35 planes are based at the field. It is one of the few sod-strip sport aviation fields left in East Tennessee, Kurlee said.

Larry Fleming, superintendent of the bureau of water and wastewater for KUB, said the city originally bought the 58 acre tract as a site for a waste water facility. Plans changed and the property is now considered a non-performing asset.

KUB intends to solicit closed bids because that is the procedure for the sale of surplus property, Fleming said.

The club's 10 year lease expired Dec. 31, so this is an appropriate time to make the change, Fleming said. KUB is not trying to bounce the club from the property, he said.

"We would be thrilled if the club is the highest bidder," Fleming said.

Fleming said KUB is not in the land management business, and it has a responsibility to rate-payers to make sure the land sells for the best price it can bring.

He said he would review the sales procedure this week to make sure KUB is correctly interpreting the regulations and meet with club representatives on Tuesday.

Air Club members say the property is on a flood plain and most of the property is unusable from 100 to 200 days per year. Of the 58.1 acres, about 24 are under water six or seven months of the year. In the 1981 flood only one acre was above water. "There is nothing to do with the property except what we're doing," Dawson said.

The story in the paper brought out a whole new batch of folks who wanted to buy the place and do all sorts of wonderful things with it except use it as an air strip. One of the groups that really concerned Swifty

Swanson was the Blue Blood Polo Club. The very thought of a bunch of people playing polo on our air strip, just drove him up the wall. Swifty, serving as a beat cop for lots of years, had run into the landed gentry more than once. He had come up the hard way in life and felt that the law should be the same for everyone, but he had had the facts of life and money explained to him by various representatives of the gentry, as he called them, enough times that he knew about the golden rule. If you've got enough gold, you make the rules.

Big Bill Henry walked in the clubhouse and caught me staring off into space and said, "What in hell's wrong with you? You look like a one legged man that's been invited to an ass kicking contest."

I told him that I had just gotten back from a meeting with Joe Willy Davis, the First American Loan Officer that the club had done business with before, and he had laid the word on me. In order to process this type of business loan the bank as a matter of policy would have to have an appraisal by a professional real estate appraisal firm and an EPA study by an engineering firm. If the EPA study came up clean, then the bank would consider loaning us 70% of the value that the appraisal firm said the property is worth. The kicker is that the appraisal and the EPA study would cost us about two grand each.

The thing that really worries me about that is if you look in the right places around here there may have been some oil spilled over the years. Bill looked at me and asked, "Don't you ever have any good news?" I thought about it a moment and told Bill, "At least everyone that wants to borrow money is in the same boat."

I had just put the last word in place for the *SKY RANCH AIR MAIL* when Father Gene walked in so I asked him for a quick read of the item.

The big item in the newsletter was the announcement that there would be a general membership meeting on Tuesday to discuss the amount of the assessment. I wanted a big turnout and I knew that the use of the "A" word would bring them out.

After some rough days at the office, Tuesday finally rolled around and there were cars and pickup trucks everywhere. People who had not been to a meeting in years showed up with all kinds of advice. The wildest idea I heard was that we should consider giving all city council members free membership. The idea was not without precedent because a local county court member had been greased pretty good by the local cable company when they gave him free access to the Playboy Channel.

We had people spilling out of the clubhouse, standing on the porch, and looking in the windows. They all had opinions and it took two parliamentarians and Swifty Swanson as master of arms to help keep order. At one point I had two motions that had been tabled, one motion on the floor with six amendments, and most of the membership talking about something that had no relationship to any of the above.

I finally told C. Grover Cleveland that if he called for one more point of order or one more point of clarification, that I would have Swifty throw his skinny ass off the dock so we would not have to listen to him any more tonight.

Big Bill Henry stood up and I banged the hammer and gave him the floor. Bill said, "I was president of the club in '82 when we leased the property from the city. During the city council meeting, as I remember it, we were promised the right of first refusal if the property ever went up for sale in the future." There were several amens around the room and G. Gordon Ladde said, "That's all well and good but is that language in the lease?" Three more lawyers were on their feet in a split second, all with different views as to what the lease contained.

When I finally got the group quiet by nearly beating a hole in the desk with the meat tenderizer, I announced that there would be a fifteen minute break during which time all of the lawyers present would meet privately in the hangar to evaluate the lease. I handed the lease to Gordon and walked outside where the air was a little cooler and certainly calmer. Sergeant Yenderushak handed me can of cold beer and said, "Dapper, that's the last of the Mohicans. I'm going to make a run for beer. Everyone's coolers are empty and some SOB forgot to stock the beer machine." I traded someone the beer for a root beer and went back inside.

The lawyers came back and said they were ready to report to the club. Gordon reported:

"The lease runs from the first of January 1982 and terminates the 31st day of December 1991 at 12:00 p.m. midnight.

"The lease made no mention of right of refusal.

"All prior agreements between the parties were terminated.

"ENTIRE AGREEMENT: This agreement represents the entire agreement between the parties and no representations, inducements, promises, or agreements, oral or otherwise, between the parties not embodied, herein, shall be of any force or effect.

"The Law Director, Jon Roach, did a good job of protecting the city's interests.

"The document is duly signed by Mayor Randy Tyree and Bill Henry.

"We strongly suggest, however, that the club pursue any hard information concerning the promises made by the politicians in the City-County Building."

Swifty Swanson said, "Dapper, I move that you get the tape recordings of the council meeting and see just what there is on tape."

"Point of order Mr. President! Can the Sergeant at Arms, an officer of the meeting, legally make a motion in that meeting?" asked C. Grover Cleveland. "Hell yes," I snapped. The motion passed unanimously.

After much more tedium we passed a motion to require that all members buy a two hundred dollar bond which would be paid back over a twenty year period at $15.25 per year. The payment is to be shown as a credit on the October club bill each year.

After most of the crowd had cleared out I said to Swifty, "If everyone stays in the club, that will raise about sixty thousand dollars. How many members do you think we will lose because of two hundred dollars?"

Swifty said, "Well there is a bunch here who are living in the past and still expect the club to provide the same services that we did twenty years ago and at the same prices. There is another group here who have wives that have been looking for a good excuse to quit writing a check to the flying club for a long time. There may be twenty five or thirty in each group." I said, "Come on Swifty, I'll take you for a ride and we will look at the lights of our fair city."

We rolled out 2U, checked the gas and the oil, did a quick walk-around and cranked the engine. The old bird waited a little longer than usual with the extra weight of Swifty and me before getting off, but she came on out, climbing up toward the big moon. It was a clear still night with just the blinking of the city lights and the drone of the engine and neither of us had anything to say for a while.

Finally Swifty said, "This is better than a cold beer for relaxing." I agreed that it was and thanked him for all the help in keeping the crowd in order. I turned back to the strip and made a low pass so I could check for deer on the runway, and finally put the bird down and taxied to the hangar. We tied down the bird and walked back to the clubhouse where I made a note on the chalkboard that we had a couple of field landing lights out. We drove out and I locked the gate before heading for home. It had been a long day.

The next day I went up to the City Government floor of the City-County Building to find out how to get tapes of city council meetings. The tapes, it turned out, were easy to get, but it would take a few days for them to be reproduced and the only cost would be the cost of the cassettes.

There were three tapes for the city council meeting of 9-1-81, and it took awhile to find the part of the meeting that was of interest to me. There were two of them:

One was a statement made by the Vice Mayor:

"You have our word that if someone in the future offers us more money for the property you will have the first right of refusal."

An act by council stated:

"Council must have a workshop to discuss with the administration any action relative to the Sky Ranch Property."

I wrote Larry Fleming a letter giving the club position and requesting a meeting with him to discuss the matter.

Friday Shay said I had received a call from Larry Fleming at KUB and she had set up an appointment at 4:00. Larry told me at the meeting that the lawyers had decided that he should bid the property as originally planned and gave me a copy of a memo that was being sent to the KUB Board of Commissioners. I asked Mr. Fleming if KUB would consider a lease purchase as a viable bid for the property and he smiled and said, "I would have to consider any offer that would produce income for the rate payers." His statement really started a bunch of wheels turning in my head.

In a few days the official bid documents arrived.

ORLANDO TRIP

Shay and I were enjoying the last of a pitcher of beer after having dinner at Cancun's when she looked over at me and said, "You know if the school system's stress load doesn't get to you the Sky Ranch's will. What we need to do is get you out of town for a few days. Let's run down to Orlando and see our number one son." I agreed with her and after consulting our schedules we decided that Friday would be a good day to go.

Friday rolled around but it was not clear and sunny by any stretch of the imagination. In precise aviation jargon, it sucked. I filed IFR with the first stop in Vidalia GA (VDI). I slipped up through an overcast and we were on top at 9,000 feet. We cranked along at about 105 knots over the ground according to the GPS. I had the flight planned for 2 hours and 25 minutes, and when we were about ten minutes out of Vidalia the overcast became just a scattering of clouds and we were told to expect a visual approach into the airport.

Vidalia is one of Shay's favorite stops because the rest rooms are so clean and the people are nice. We hoped they would have bags of onions for sale but they didn't.

Orlando had some low clouds and light rain in the area when I checked weather, so I filed IFR into Orlando Exec (ORL). The trip on down was uneventful. When I got handed off to the Orlando Exec tower, we were in and out of the clouds and light rain. Exec wanted to know about the ride and I told him that it was smooth. We were cleared for the ILS and broke out into the clear at about 800 feet. I hope I always get that feeling of pride when the approach breaks you out on the center line of the runway. We had been in the air a little over 2 hours and 15 minutes.

Shay went to find a phone to alert Bunker that we were on hand and to do the paperwork for the rental car we had reserved. I stayed to unload the bird and get it topped off with fuel. She took about 20 gallons. I always have to totally unload the plane because the locks on the old Skyhawk doors no longer work, so leaving anything in the bird is not an option. Bunker showed up pretty quickly in his new car and he was correct in telling us that we would need a rental unit. His car was very pretty, but very small. The Italian two-seater was cute as could be, but there was no way that three people would fit into it.

We mostly just sat around and talked a lot. Bunker did take us out to see the base and I visited his quarters. They were not unlike the barracks that I had lived in during my tour with Uncle Sugar in the late fifties. We also visited Church Street Station, where we listened to a very good roaring twenties band. It is never easy to leave your pride and joy, but he seemed to be working hard to get through Nuclear Power School and was determined that he would see it through.

Flight Service recommended a more westerly track for the return trip so I filed for Columbus GA (CSG), home of the Benning School for Boys, as Colonel Willy Strunk used to call Fort Benning.

Flight Service had promised that the thunderstorms and rain between Columbus and Chattanooga would be gone by the time we got up there but as we got closer to Columbus, I could hear lots of chatter on Atlanta center from folks looking for an easy route through there. I told Shay that, unless she really wanted to get bounced around a bunch, we should probably spend a night in Fort Benning Country. Shay said, "Great, we were going to get back home too late for a decent dinner anyway."

By the time the fuel truck had come and gone and 2U was tied down, Shay had worked out a motel at the FBO corporate rate and had a cab on the way. She also had a line on an interesting place for dinner.

The next day was severe clear and we came on back to the Sky Ranch VFR without a hitch. In order to stay away from all the traffic going into Atlanta, I headed direct to Chattanooga (CHA) before tracking to Knoxville (TYS), which kept me out of the ATL control area altogether. Knoxville approach brought us around the big airport and I told them I had the Sky Ranch in sight. They said squawk 1200 and the trip was just about over. We tied the bird down in her hangar, transferred the gear, and headed out to find a pitcher of beer and a pizza.

There had been an addition to the property while we were gone. As soon as we crossed the railroad track, I could see the sign up near the highway.

FOR SALE
COX SKY RANCH
58.6 ACRES
CALL 555-5555

Shay looked over at me and said, "What a homecoming! I've known that KUB was going to sell the property but that sign really makes it for real, doesn't it?" I said, "It does. I'll have to get the board together to get all of our ducks and ducats in proper alignment."

BUYING THE DIRT

The board meeting attracted the usual folks and we started the process of trying to determine first how much money we could raise and second how much we could bid. Those two amounts were considered to be related but not necessarily equal. The board also had the strong feeling that if some of our uglier members knew exactly what the club was bidding, we might lose the bid by a few dollars.

Therefore a bid committee of two people was appointed to make the final bid when the time came. Those two were the noted attorney, G. Gordon Ladde, and me, Dapper Kurlee. The board also decided to take two other motions to the membership to help raise more money. The idea was to offer five and ten year notes at 6% interest, available to club members only, and to be secured by a lien against the property.

G. Gordon and I went out to Hardy's for a cup of coffee and a look at a crystal ball for guidance in what to bid. I told Gordon that I would leak the idea to a few big mouths that we could not afford to go more than one hundred grand or the debt service would eat us alive. He agreed and we decided the most we could raise was about 125 grand so we settled on $127,557.50. Gordon said that 27 was a lucky number for him and 5575 was a number on a big Sikorsky helicopter that I crewed in the army in the late fifties. We also put the finishing touches on the lease purchase and the straight lease plans.

The bid opening was attended by Big Bill Henry, G. Gordon Ladde, Small Sam Long, Billy Bob Wanger, and me. There were some mid-east type folks in the bid room when we got there. The bids were opened in the following order.

Skysports	$71,000.00
Sky Ranch	$127,557.50
Abu-Ragheb	$120,000.00
George Harb	$105,000.00
Ron Watson	$101,500.00

The purchasing agent for KUB then formally announced the club to be the high bidder and the new owner of the property. He said we could get together later to work out the time and method of payment, but that there was no great rush.

Big Bill Henry offered the best comment of the day when he said, "I was real worried when I got here and saw all those camels tied up in the parking lot."

On the way back to the Sky Ranch we knocked down the ulcer producing sign which had advertised, "Cox Sky Ranch for Sale." The plywood sign was later retrieved and used on saw horses as a party table at picnics. I think we need to keep it around so we can always remember the old days when someone else owned our airport.

The group that had been to the bid opening sat on the porch of the clubhouse for a while and just looked out over the runway and had very little to say. Then the Warthog's Bentley came billowing up in a cloud of dust and we knew the peace and quiet were over. After he found out about the bids, he started in on Gordon and me about wasting so much of the clubs money. According to him, anyone else in the world should have known that 121 grand would have done the job and that we had left too much money laying on the table.

Big Bill chimed in with, "The thing that I noticed is that most every bid there was over the 100 grand that I heard you talking about on the phone a while back. Come to think about it, that Watson guy sure looked a lot like the fellow that was out here talking to you about what a great polo field this would make." The Warthog quickly looked at his watch and said he was late for an appointment with the Metro Planning Commission and hurried off. "You know," said Billy Bob, "that idiot is getting harder to take all the time."

I set a BOD meeting for the following day and got the numbers ready for them to see. Basically it was a simple picture. We had about 200 of our 300 members who were willing to buy the required $200 note, which raised $40,000. We also had an additional $20,000 raised from the sale of $250 five year notes. We were short about $70,000.

The BOD meeting was very upbeat and the members all said they would get out and twist a few arms on the $1000 bonds and that it would be a piece of cake. The headline in the *SKY RANCH AIR MAIL* proclaimed: 'SIXTY GRAND ON HAND'

After a full page of projections of debt service, and other high sounding terms there appeared a small story of another kind of finance.

THE SKY RANCH AIR MAIL
9/92
THE GOOD OLD DAYS (dapper)

A bill from Campbell's Aero fell off the back of my old desk at the house the other day and it set me to thinking about how flying used to be for the Kurlee family. The bill was for 9 gallons of gas and a quart of oil. The oil cost 65 cents and the total was $4.70 including 18 cents for tax. I'll save you the trouble of looking for a calculator, the gas was 43 cents per gallon. The date on the ticket is May 1970. I was teaching at the high school level in those days at the princely salary of about $7,500 per annum. Our son was two years old and life was good.

Nine gallons of gas in an air knocker will buy you lots of time in the air, but it may not be able to take you very far. A big trip in those days was going home to West Virginia. Come to think of it, it is still one of my favorite trips. There's nothing like going home, even if it doesn't look like you think it should when you get there.

I worked out the first two pieces for the newsletter and gave them to Shay for editing. It is hard to find the mistakes in your own work and she has pointed out my errors, both written and otherwise, for a long time now. I wouldn't have it any other way. Here is what they looked like after she cleaned them up for me. I'd rather you didn't see the first draft.

THE SKY RANCH AIR MAIL
10/92
THIS LAND IS OUR LAND or WE BOUGHT THE DIRT (dapper)

If all the people who have committed to buying notes and bonds come through with their money by Tuesday, we will complete the sale this week. It has been a most trying time for all of us at the club as we wrestled determining a winning bid and building a consensus for funding to support the bid.

In spite of our differences, it looks like we are about to buy the dirt. I would like to thank all of you for the cooperation and help you have given me during this long and sometimes messy process. We will send KUB their check and they will give us a deed to OUR AIRPORT.

THE SKY RANCH AIR MAIL
10/92
DIRT PARTY AND PICNIC (dapper)

The big "we bought the dirt party and picnic" will be held on Sunday the 18th of October at OUR AIRPORT with the knife and fork work beginning at about 1400 hrs. The weather will be fair and warm and the BIG ORANGE will have sent the Alabama crowd home in defeat the night before. Come out and see your friends, eat more than you should, impress everyone with your entry in the spot landing contest, tell tall tales, and have a good time in general. Most of all though, come out and take a look at the DEED TO OUR AIRPORT.

Crazy Doc Kronk came wandering up at the picnic and asked, "Do you think you ever saw all of this group so happy at the same time before?" "No, not since we quit having two kegs of beer in the engine shop," I said. "Are you going to enter the spot landing or the bomb dropping contest?" "I'm going to try the bomb drop in the Woody Pusher," Doc answered. "That is, unless the rules committee claims that it flies too slow." "You have to admit that you have longer to make up your mind than the average bear since that thing does go slow," I said.

The bomb dropping contest is an exercise of dropping a small plastic bag of lime from an airplane flying at 50 feet above the runway and trying to hit a cross chalked on the grass strip. We haven't had much trouble with getting too much lime in one place. You put a dollar in the pot to buy three bombs and the pilot hitting closest to the target takes home the pot.

The rules for the spot landing contest vary from year to year, but basically it is who can land with the main gear touching down the closest to a line chalked on the runway. Usually, if you touch down before the line or if the bird bounces off, you are disqualified. One year we tried a more complex system where there were three landings. For the first landing, the pilot had full use of all controls. During the second landing the flaps could only be set once on approach. For the final landing both the flaps and the throttle had to be set on short final over the water before landing. The complex system was thrown out after one year because it was too hard to keep the score. It did get folks involved, that is if you count arguments as being involved.

Smoky Pat Fansler won the spot landing contest with a perfect full stall landing touching the mains down exactly on the line. The Warthog claimed the wind wasn't as strong when Pat flew as when everyone else did so Pat should be disqualified. "Not in this life," ruled the chief judge, Sergeant Yenderushak. When Sarge said it was over, you could bet the farm that there would be no changes.

The food was mostly gone, the airplanes were all in their hangars and the beer coolers were starting to come out for the evening.

The bid was ours and the next step, hopefully a formality, was the approval of the Knoxville Utilities Board of Commissioners. I showed up for the meeting and we were on the agenda.

"Consideration of a recommendation to accept the bid of The Sky Ranch Flying Society. for the purchase of the Cox Sky Ranch property."

The meeting moved along with some discussion on a few items, but everything on the agenda was a done deal. The backup data for our item looked good.

August 6, 1992

Knoxville Utilities Board
626 Gay Street, SW
Knoxville, Tennessee 37902

Commissioners:
The Cox Sky Ranch property, located off Alcoa Highway, was purchased by the City of Knoxville in 1975. The property was intended to be used as the site of a new waste water treatment plant to replace the old Third Creek Plant on Neyland Drive. For various reasons, the Sky Ranch site was never used for its intended purpose. In 1981, the city leased the property, for ten years, to the pilot's club. KUB obtained ownership of the property in 1987 as a part of the transfer of the Waste Water Control System to KUB.

As the lease expired on December 31, 1991, the Bureau of Water and Waste Water made a determination that it did not have a utility use for the property and accordingly, released the property to KUB's Purchasing Agent, Mr. G. H. Dalton, for sale or lease as surplus property. Mr. Dalton initiated a competitive bid process which invited proposals to buy, lease, or lease/purchase the property. The results of the process are summarized in Mr. Dalton's report to Mr. Kinnamon dated July 29, 1992, a copy of which you have been provided.

Mr. Dalton concludes his report by recommending the sale of the property to the high purchase bidder. I concur in this recommendation. Accordingly, I recommend that the Board declare the Cox Sky Ranch property surplus and approve the sale of the property to the Sky Ranch Flying Society for the high bid of $127,557.50, and that the General Manager or his designated representative(s) be authorized to execute and deliver a deed for the property, and to do any and all things necessary to consummate the sale.

Respectfully Submitted,
E. C. Hoskins
General Manager

The motion for approval sailed right through.

THE ORDINATION OF SAMUEL GREEN 1998

Big Charley, Zipper, and Big Bill were sitting in front of the hangar in the shade of the door when I arrived, so I went to the office to hunt for my coffee mug so I could join them. The answering machine had a call on it for Izzy, I jotted the number down on a sticky note and headed for the hangar. The voice sounded familiar, but the name wouldn't come up for me.

I filled my cup and had just gotten seated when Izzy came out of the parts trailer and said he was taking a break. He sat down beside me and I gave him the sticky note. He glanced at the number and said, "That's Samuel's work number. Wonder what's on his mind? I'll call him after while." I asked how Samuel was doing because we had not had a report on him for a quite a while so Izzy filled us in.

"Samuel is into two or three things, besides his ministry, depending on how you count. I'm sure you all remember when he got beat up by the berserk biker and the two dancers took him home with them. Well, it turns out that they were twins, Sally Raye and Sally Faye Farnsworth and Samuel moved in with them about three months ago.

"He has also expanded his interest in computers to include creating web sites for people and they say he is real good at it." Big Charley had to interrupt with a question, "Which one did he move in with, Izzy?" Izzy continued, "Charley that's what I'm trying to tell you, he moved in with both of them. They have a one bedroom apartment over on Red Bud Lane and the bedroom is filled up with a king-sized bed that all three of them sleep in, that is when they sleep.

"So if you count the girls as one, he has two interests, but if you count each girl, then he has three interests. The computer being the other interest. The living room is full of computers. That's where they work on the web businesses. Samuel is building me a web site to hopefully get some more business for my business here."

"What do these twins look like?" asked Charley.

Izzy continued, "I've only seen them with their clothes on Charley, but they are good looking young women, abut five-five, with great figures, and last week when I was over there to see Samuel, they were both blondes. I think that changes on a monthly basis. They have moved out of the biker bar and now they are the featured act at the Pink Pussy Cat, which is the biggest exotic bar in town."

Big Bill cut in with, "Is Samuel still interested in becoming ordained by Bishop Love?" Izzy says, "Oh yes, that's part of the reason he went into the web business, so he could raise the money for ordination. He has created a whole new division in the Bishop's operation. The Bishop now is doing big business on the web with his 'Sunday School on the Web' and 'Counseling and Prayer on the Web.'

"There are also 1-900 phone lines for those that aren't up to speed on the web yet. Samuel has learned a lot from the Bishop. This time he asked the Bishop for a fifty-fifty split up front on the take from the new operation. They settled for one fourth and three fourths, with the big end going to the Bishop. The Bishop wasn't too sure about percentages, but he could divide by four with the help of a calculator.

"Samuel set up a communications room in the church basement that houses the main church computer which handles the web site. The room also has several data stations set up for the good church people to do the Christian Counseling & Prayer, answer all the e-mail and take part in the chat rooms.

"Anyone who hits the counseling & prayer button has their choice of a man or a woman to help them through their difficult times. All of these activities require a love offering. Credit cards of all denominations are accepted.

"The whole system is monitored at the girls apartment and if there is a need for a more intense form of counseling, these folks are encouraged to select a new icon that appears on their screen which takes them to the Blue Lagoon. The Blue Lagoon is a web site in Amsterdam which has experts live or on tape for every sexual fantasy known to man.

"Lagoon does a fee split with SSS Inc.(Sally.Sam.Sally) and Samuel only splits these fees with the Sallies.

"Another option is in the works to allow the visitors to view the stage at the Pink Pussy Cat if it's open or the most recent tape if it's closed. The

Warthog will get the split on this one because he owns the Pink Pussy Cat. The big money coming in on the Pussy Cat Web though is from the icon that allows the visitor to chat live with a dancer. The dancers that work the phones and the web pages get a split on this one too. Samuel is coming over today to bring me a new computer so you all can ask him about all this stuff. I've already told you more than I know."

Izzy had gone back to work on an airplane in the hangar and the rest of us were still sitting in front of the hangar when Samuel and the Sally's came driving up in Samuel's van. They all started to unload a computer system and set it up on Izzy's desk in the back of the hangar. When that was done Sam brought the girls up and introduced them to us. Izzy had said that they were good looking and he had sold them way short. They were beautiful.

They were a delightful mix of colors from all over the globe with skin somewhere between French Vanilla and light Butterscotch. Their hair was done in long pony tails and today they were very light strawberry blondes. The white linen short shorts and mini halter tops did very little to hide their figures which have been enhanced by daily exercise at a spa and a heavy schedule of dancing at the club. They seemed to know a lot more about us than we knew about them. I guess Samuel must have been doing some talking. They were very bright and inquisitive about the stuff around the Sky Ranch.

When they left Big Charley said, "That was sure a perfect pair of twins, I couldn't find a speck of difference anywhere." Zipper cut in, "I was wondering what kind of intense analysis you were up to. You didn't take your eyes off of them the whole time they were here." Big Bill added, "The ugly index sure went way up when they left, didn't it?" I said, "Yes it did and I had some questions I wanted to ask Samuel, but I sure don't know what they were now."

It was Sunday and I was still working on two firsts, my first cup of coffee and the first section of the paper, when Big Bill called and said that I needed to crank up the Internet and go to the Pilgrim Church Web site. I did and, Lo and Behold, there was the Bishop praying live on the world wide web. The camera work and the sound quality were not the greatest in the world but it was there. I lost interest pretty quickly in the service and decided to check and see if the Pink Poodle site was up and running yet. It was and the twins, without the benefit of the shorts and halters, were dancing away. This had to be a tape because surely the Poodle had to be closed at this early hour on Sunday. I left Bill an e-mail about the Poodle site and went back to the Sunday paper.

The ordination ceremony for Samuel Green and three other candidates was scheduled as a part of the regular Sunday night service at the Pilgrim Holiness Church of Faith and Hope. The church's services had been appearing on the worldwide web for a month or so and the routine of operating the control center in the church basement was becoming old hat for Sister Sarah Semington and Deacon John Stale. They had won out over other candidates mainly because they had the time available to learn to use the equipment. Together they could control the two cameras in the church proper and also were adept at running the counseling and prayer sessions on the web site.

Sister Sarah had lost her husband about five years back and had turned to the church as the main outlet for her energies. She had very fair skin and was somewhere in her mid-forties with lots of hair and boobs to match. Her 44 double D cup bras worked overtime just to keep her contained. The big sister was a strong-willed woman who knew her rights and she had decided that John Stale was one of them.

She decided that tonight if plan "A" failed she was going to invite him over for pie and coffee, and if her new low cut blue dress got a rise out of anything else, five years of going without was quite long enough. The fire that burned inside of her needed to be extinguished and she had picked out her fireman.

Deacon John was the first black man ever elected a Deacon in the Pilgrim Church. He was a retired Navy Master Chief who had come home to Lonsdale after touring the world for twenty-five years and now operated a home and office cleaning business. His years in the Navy had taught him how to organize other people to do the labor while he sat back and collected the gravy. John made it a practice not to get in his employees pants, so that ruled out all of the young women and a large percentage of the other women that he knew. Anyway, he had decided that he wanted a substantial woman of his of own age group that he could talk to when they weren't in bed. Sister Sarah measured up to his idea of a good woman and he had plans to set the fires of romance and horizontal recreation in motion.

All of these fires together almost burned down the whole church.

Sister Sarah cut off the tape machine which had been replaying the morning service and switched to camera one just as the Bishop sounded his solo call to worship on his slide trombone and shifted into the opening hymn, "Come to Jesus Precious Lord." This evening, in honor of the ordination ceremony, the organ was supplemented by a tuba, a trumpet, an e-flat cornet, a tenor banjo, a drummer, and a baritone sax.

The barry was played by a cat that was way past blind drunk. He didn't have any idea where he was or who he was playing with, but his ear was perfect, every lick he hit all night was right on the money. The group started out following the lead of the organist who was a good musician but very straight-laced musically. The character of the music soon changed to a New Orleans style with the tiny cornet playing the part of the traditional Dixieland clarinet.

The procession reached the platform and the Bishop held up his hand for prayer, but what he got was one more solo chorus by the barry sax. He used the sweet high notes of the upper register as a perfect contrast to the raucous tones from deep down in the lower bowels of the horn, and didn't miss much in between. After the chorus was over, the trumpet player hauled the big sax man off his feet and into a chair. When he hit the chair it looked as if he were trying to swallow the whole sax mouthpiece down to the first bend, but it would not all go in his mouth even though his upper and lower plates were in his shirt pocket at the time.

The service rolled along with Sister Sarah and Deacon John swapping cameras and mikes to keep the folks at home all up to speed. When the Bishop settled into his sermon the deacon decided it was time to put his plan into motion so he turned on system three that sat to the right of the main console and set the browser for the Blue Lagoon. He soon had the screen full of a big black man giving a white gal lessons in the number of ways she could receive his attentions.

He was about to point out to Sister Sarah what was on system three when she said look what I found and pointed to system two on the left side of the main system console. She had the Pink Poodle web site up which had a tape running from the night before showing the twins well into their cowboy routine wearing little more than their big hats. The two plotters in the control room quickly figured out what the other was up to and heartily approved. The sermon would run for a long time so there would be no programmatic changes to make in the control room.

Sarah leaned over towards the Deacon so he could get a better view into the new blue dress and touched the inside of the Deacons thigh. The Deacon reached into the top of the dress and began to massage the magnificent udders, and when he placed his hand inside the bra there was an utter failure of the all of the hooks holding it together. At the same time Sarah got the Deacons zipper down and out popped the largest male organ she had ever seen.

The Bishop was an experienced spellbinder and he could tell from looking at the flock that he was losing them, but he didn't know why. He was staying with a time tested, and much used, message. When he turned around to look at one of the big monitors displaying the service as those at home were seeing it, he thought he saw a big black man screwing a white woman, but before he could get focused, the picture changed to show the front of the church with him facing the monitor.

He thought that his eyes were playing tricks on him until the picture changed again and he was looking at two naked girls with some men stuffing money in their g-strings. Two of the men in the picture were on the stage with him now waiting to be ordained. The Bishop decided to change things around by singing a hymn, so he picked up his trombone to signal the organist that he was ready for the next musical number but, when he looked over, the bench was vacant. He tried valiantly to enlist the aid of his fellow musicians but they were all dead to the world; those that weren't drunk were sound asleep. The organist had slipped out the little back door and run for the control room.

When the organist burst into the control room she saw Sister Sarah's head slowly going up and down in the Deacon's lap, but she was having the same problem the sax player did earlier, it would not all go in her mouth. Each time the good sister's head came up, her left elbow hit the switches on the console that controlled which one of the video feeds went from standby to live. The folks at home were seeing the Blue Lagoon, the Pink Pussy Cat and the church service in a randomized order for differing amounts of time depending on the motion of Sister Sarah's errant elbow.

The organist screamed causing Sister Sarah to bite down on the Deacon who kicked out with his right foot and knocked over the table holding all the equipment. Sparks started jumping everywhere and in seconds the overloaded electrical system in the old church building gave up and all the lights in the whole building went out. The smoke from the electrical fire found its way upstairs causing almost as much panic as when the steeple blew up.

The flock all got out without major injury and were gathered around the outside of the front door of the church when they started to hear music. The noise had awakened the musicians and when the trumpet player cranked off a verse to Aunt Hagar's Blues, the rest found their axes and joined in. The Bishop borrowed a flashlight from someone and went back in the church. A slide trombone joined in on the next chorus just as a van with Anchor Cleaning Service on the side rounded the corner with two people trying to sit in the same seat. There wasn't enough room for that either. A hard summer rainstorm hit suddenly and dispersed the crowd before they could compare notes on what they thought they had seen.

"Izzy how was the vacation in France?" I asked when he came into the clubhouse. Izzy replied, "I'll take three weeks in France at Uncle Sugar's expense anytime I can get it. My big bird did real well, all I had to do were some routine things that didn't take much time." "Did you hear about the big show at the church?" I asked.

"Yes, Monda was there and she said she hadn't had so much fun in years. She said that the congregation was divided into three parts. One third was totally embarrassed and revolted by what they saw but for the most part watched it anyway. Another third of the group was being turned on by all the activity and were looking around to see if someone had noticed their problem. The final group was having the most fun just watching the other two groups react to the pictures on the screen.

"J.J. Jackson, one of the older deacons, started getting a rise in his trousers and his wife grabbed him by the hand and out the door they went. Monda said that she could see that their car was moving, but not out of the parking lot.

"One of the indignant old ladies, Ms. Mary Keener, kept turning to someone next to her and saying 'well I never!', and finally a man sitting behind her shut her up by saying 'that's right Ms. Mary and that's only part of your problem.' Monda was sitting next to the side door, so when the lights went out she just slipped out as easy as pie."

"What did the Bishop do about the ordination of the new preachers since that part of the ceremony didn't take place before the fire started?" I asked. Izzy continued, "The Bishop wanted to hold up the ordination of the two preachers that were shown on tape in the church but Samuel reminded him that if the whole tape had been shown, the Bishop himself was in the next sequence trying to take one of the twins cowboy hats away from them. The Bishop relented and held a small ceremony in the church the next day and issued them their preaching papers. By the way, the Sally's were at home in the apartment when all this happened and they are going to send us a VCR tape of the whole show that went out over the web site."

DOC GOLDBURG'S ALARM SYSTEM

The phone was ringing as I entered the clubhouse and it was Billy Bob Wanger who asked me to tell Dr. Goldburg, who was to meet him, to please be patient because he was caught in traffic behind a wreck on I-75 and would be a little late. I told Billy Bob his man wasn't here yet, but that I would tell him when he arrived. I asked him if the annual inspection on his airplane had gone OK and he said that he had one jug with low compression that he was worried about, but other than that everything else had been fine.

I fixed a pot of coffee and started paying bills. Tightwad Wilson came in and commented that it seemed to him like every day was either a Friday or a Monday and every time he noticed, another whole week was gone. Time was just slipping away.

Billy Bob and Doc Goldburg arrived about the same time. It turned out they were both delayed by the same wreck on I-75. They wandered off down toward Billy Bob's hangar and I continued to pay bills. The bills were just the usual utilities and a couple of small invoices to Izzy Green for some routine maintenance on the club planes. I came out of the club-house a little while later and Billy Bob was shaking his visitors hand in the parking lot. The Doc left and Billy sat down with me on the porch.

"Did you get another job?" I asked. Billy Bob replied, "No, that's a job I finished about three months ago, or I thought that it was finished anyway. As a part of a remodel on a house across the river I installed an alarm system which Doc Goldburg claimed was malfunctioning. The alarm was going off at odd hours of the night and it always went off twice. I checked the system for bad switches, put in two new computers, and was about ready to run all new wiring when I decided I would just spend a night parked up on the hill behind his place with a night scope. Peggy Sue was at a convention in SFO with Mai Ling so I didn't have to be home anyway.

"Me and Homer noticed some movement at about 2:00 a.m. and it was Mrs. Ravitz, the Doc's mother-in-law, letting her standard poodle out for a run. When we first started looking at the problem, Doc told me that he had talked with Mrs. Ravitz and she had absolutely assured him that she never had and never would open an outside door after 10 o'clock. "Today I told him that his mother-in-law had been opening the door to let her dog go out for a run and that had been tripping the alarm system. Doc said that he believed me, but did I have a.iy proof that he could show his wife and his mother-in-law. That's when I told him that when the poodle came out I had let Homer go down and visit for a spell and he could expect to have a real interesting batch of pups from a poodle/bull mastiff mix. Homer was plumb tuckered out when he came back to the truck at daybreak.

"Doc was tickled to death about the whole thing because he said that now there would be no question that Mrs. Ravitz had let her dog out which tripped the alarm. He paid me for all the time me and the boys put in looking for a problem that wasn't there.

"What did you charge for stud service for Homer?" asked Big Charley who had joined us to hear the story. "Homer seemed to enjoy himself, so I let the stud fee slide," grinned Billy Bob.

Charley then asked, "I think I know the answer to this Billy, but was this the same night that the Russian went to jail and the Warthog was visited by a honey wagon?" "Come to think of it you're right. That was the night it happened because when I got home later in the day I found out that I had mis-set the VCR." Big Charley looked unhappy and I was sure it was because he had lost another suspect.

GORDON LADDE PASSING

Big Charley and Small Sam were sitting at the big table with their usual cup of coffee reading the copy of the newsletter that I had left on the table after stuffing the monthly epistle and invoices for the membership. The lead story was about the passing of Gordon Ladde.

THE SKY RANCH AIR MAIL
8/98
GORDON LADDE LEAVES US (dapper)
Gordon Ladde, a long time member and friend of the club and the Sky Ranch Community, has passed away. There is not room here nor would Gordon want the list of all the things that he did for the club to be listed. One of the many memories I have of Gordon is the time that he and I sat in the parking lot at the Sky Ranch when we put the final touches on the bid which bought the property from KUB.

His family tells us that he had a very nice morning with his grandchildren, had lunch with the family, sat down in his favorite chair and passed away. As we get older we discover that that is not a bad way to go.

I shall miss his sage counsel pertaining to things concerning the law, his company at dinner on Tuesday nights, and his opinions. Gordon's feeling was that "EVERYONE IS ENTITLED TO MY OPINION," and he shared them freely with anyone in range. We are all much poorer for his passing.

Small Sam looked up and asked, "How long ago was it that you wrote the story about Gordon and his new grandbaby?" I responded, "I wondered the same thing last night so I pulled the file and it was only two months back. The other story appeared in the March newsletter and here is a copy."

THE SKY RANCH AIR MAIL
3/98

DAVID LADDE GRANDBABY (dapper)

Some people will go to any lengths to be around close when their granddaughter is born, but I think Gordon Ladde has carried this idea to the extreme. Last Saturday, after laying around the house for most of the week, he talked his way into West Hospital. He claimed to have double pneumonia and sold the idea to his doctor buddy who arranged to get him to the emergency room and admitted to the hospital. Gordon's granddaughter arrived on Monday, but in the meantime the staff worked old Gordon over with needles and other indignities too numerous to mention. We don't know if the staff thought Gordon was just faking the whole thing and were trying their best to get rid of him or maybe they thought he was really sick. I guess if they thought he was too far around the bend they would have sent him up to visit Doc Kronk, the Sky Ranch shrink, who has his very own section for the strange there at West Hospital. When I talked to him on Thursday, he was ready to give the whole thing up and go home. A man can only stand so much pampering and Gordon had reached his limit. It will be good to have him back with the Knife and Fork group as soon as he is up and around again.

Small Sam said, "You know, I seem to be losing more and more friends as I go along." I added, "Yes, that's a sign of something, but luckily I've forgotten what it's a sign of."

FLAT TOP

Big Bill Henry, Small Sam, Zipper, Big Charley and I were enjoying our first cup of coffee on the porch when Big Bill said, "I bought me a houseboat yesterday." Sam asked for details and Bill continued, "It is about 35 feet, steel hull, and has a big V-8 Hemi engine in it." "Jeez Bill, I thought you were going to dance a jig when that guy pulled that last big cruiser you had out of here! You said when you sold it that you would never have another boat," jibed Big Charley.

Small Sam added, "What I remember most about that boat was all the trouble you had with the cooling system. It seemed like you spent more time with your ass sticking up out of the engine compartment than you did making the Arabs happy by cruising up and down the lake." "Who was that expert boat engine mechanic that you brought in on that job? I don't remember his name." jabbed Zipper.

Bill had done real well up to now but the reference to the expert boiled him over. He sputtered a time or two and then got started. "That no good son of a bitch called himself a professional boat mechanic and he knew less about cooling systems than the Warthog does." The reference to the Warthog came up because, while Bill was talking, the Bentley was making its usual cloud of dust as it came up the road on the other side of the island.

"I bet I know why you got the new boat," I put in. Bill had had enough and put the reason at rest with the statement, "Beulah wanted another boat."

The Warthog drove on down to his hangar and had joined us back at the clubhouse just as Zipper said, "Bill, now that you have that new ultra light you need to consider what kind of arresting gear we need to install on the roof of the houseboat so you can do carrier landings. That big Hemi should push that houseboat through the water at a pretty good speed, and the ultra light lands pretty slow, so we won't need much to stop the plane when it lands."

Big Charley jumped in with, "It's a shame that the little bird isn't a tail dragger, it would make installing a hook on it so much easier. If the arresting line gets caught in the nose gear or catches either one of the main gears you are going in the drink. How did the old-timers stop the Cubs when they landed them on top of cars back when all of the flying shows did that kind of thing?" No one had an answer for the question, but more research was promised.

Small Sam made another suggestion, "Bill, I think you should just make your bird a seaplane, add a boom pole to the boat that could put the little bird on the roof of it. Then you could cruise out to a nice cove and put it in the water and fly back for more beer when you run out. You already have the floats. All of the Vanderbilts had sea planes on their yachts, so you may as well be the first in the area to have a seaplane on your houseboat, that is if you aren't too chicken to do carrier landings."

The discussion continued concerning the various methods of trapping an ultra light aboard a houseboat and the relative merits of placing the stiff leg lifting device on the fore or aft end of the boat. The group finally ran out of options and broke up. The Warthog had seemed interested, but had not entered into the discussion which, given his mechanical abilities, probably was a good thing.

Bill and Beulah had a real nice houseboat but, as they say, everything is relative. In a few days the Warthog's new boat appeared at the dock behind the clubhouse. It was the biggest houseboat I ever saw. According to the sale flyer which was still prominently displayed on the outside of the door to the main salon the boat was described as:

STARDUST HOUSEBOAT 18' WIDE BODY, LENGTH 75',
$225,000
Aluminum hull, twin 271 hp Volvo dual prop engines, 200 gal fuel, 15KW Westerbeke generator, retractable bow, 350 gal fresh water, two 20 gal hot water heaters, 100% inverter, ice maker, microwave, dishwasher, washer, dryer, four cabins, sleeps 9, master suite king bed, double shower, bidet, flying bridge, exterior refinished Aug., many extras.

The Warthog motored up in his Bentley and was happy to show off his new indicator of opulence to the assembled underclass although it was obvious that he knew very little about his new toy. He had purchased it at the Ft. Loudon Marina the day before and the previous owner had checked him out on all the systems as they made the trip up the river from the marina to the Sky Ranch.

Big Charley asked, "Do you have to have any kind of license or papers to operate a boat like this ?" Bill answered, "No, all you have to really have is the money to buy one with, but the insurance may be a little cheaper if you have some qualifications to operate the boat."

The Warthog announced that he had an ultra light tail dragger on order and that he would be installing an arresting gear on the top of the sunshade of the houseboat in just a few days. He said that he planned to be the first in Tennessee to land an ultra light on a boat which was underway. His future plans included taking this show out on the road, or water in this case, as a feature at boat shows and fishing contests. The Warthog never lacked for big plans.

Small Sam commented after the Warthog left, "I wonder if he will put a smoke system on his new airplane?" "Goddamn, I knew you guys were kidding me when you were talking about landing on the houseboat, but it looks like the Warthog didn't. Do you think he will really try to do it?" asked Big Bill.

"Do what?" asked Tightwad Wilson who had just joined the group. "Be the first asshole to land an ultra light on a boat so he can make some money at water shows with the act," explained Bill.

T.W. sat with us on the porch of the clubhouse for a while but had very little to say and then he speculated that he could be the first local carrier pilot and do it a hell of a lot cheaper than the big time operation that the Warthog had going on.

"How cheap can you make it?" asked Big Charley egging him on.

"I can do the whole thing for less than eight grand," returned T.W.

"You mean the boat and the plane?" questioned Big Charley.

"No you thick-headed Irishman, I mean the whole show ready to go on the road for eight big bills," answered T.W.

Sarge Yenderushak, the resident bookmaker, soon was doing a lot of business on two fronts: who would land first and could Tightwad bring the operation in for eight bills.

Later in the week Tightwad Wilson came driving up the road by the runway pulling a boat trailer with a black boat on it that looked somewhat familiar. The rusty old trailer was bigger than necessary for the boat, but it worked. He backed the rig into his hangar and we all went over to see what he had found. The boat turned out to be a twenty-two foot bass fishing boat with a big block V-8 engine. The engine cover was missing but the engine appeared to have all of its parts and was covered with oil. It was, overall, a rough looking piece of gear that had been out of service for a good while.

Big Bill looked at it and said, "This is my old boat, I sold it to Cleophus and that crowd and they sunk it in the river behind the Navy Center on their first trip out. If you can get the engine running, this thing will run like a stripe-assed ape. The engine may be all right, they got the boat out pretty quick and forced all the water out of the engine with oil and pulled the accessories off and dried them out. I think they were afraid of the boat and I don't know that they ever tried to run it again."

Tightwad said that he had given $2,500 for the outfit and that Cleophus had promised him that he would refund his money if he couldn't get the engine to run. Big Charley commented, "That ain't the ugliest rig I ever saw, but it's sure in the running." T.W. returned, "The bet was that it had to work, nobody said it had to be pretty." Small Sam asked, "Have you found an ultra light yet?" T.W. said, "Not yet, the only ones I have found so far must be made out of gold because they sure want a lot of money for them."

Several hours later while I was working in the office there was a lot of noise out at the maintenance hangar and I went out to see what was going on. Tightwad had a water hose hooked up to the intake cooling hose on the boat engine and was using a battery charger connected to an old battery to turn over the engine in the boat. It would hit a pretty good lick and then die.

Luckily Willy Clyde Coyote came driving in and took charge of the operation. When he came up it was like a parting of the Red Sea. The assembled crowd just automatically deferred to his known expertise in all things mechanical. He looked the situation over and walked back to his truck and came back with a spray can of diesel starting fluid. The engine would run only when he sprayed the fluid into the carburetor.

Willy looked around and asked, "Has anyone adjusted the carburetor?" Tightwad admitted, "Yes, I turned down some of the screws on it, they use too much gas if you leave them wide open." Willy handed the spray can to Small Sam and told him, "Keep it running until I get it adjusted."

Pretty soon the big engine was running a lot better but was still missing some. Willy went back to his truck and pulled out a heavy brown tarp which he put over the engine well and then he put his head under the tarp. He then told Tightwad to put his head under the tarp and tell him what he saw. T.W. did as he was asked and when he came out from under the tarp he said it looked like a laser show going on in there.

Willy said, "I know it will go against the grain, but if you will buy a new ignition harness and probably a new set of plugs, I think most of your engine problems will be solved."

The boat was back in Tightwad's hangar the next day when I arrived at the Sky Ranch and there was a pile of used tongue and groove oak flooring beside his hangar. I stopped and claimed a chair next to T.W. and asked if he was going to floor his hangar and he told me that the flooring was for the flight deck of his boat.

He showed me some old half inch pipe with green paint on it that he was going to use to support the flight deck. The pipes were going to be attached to the boat with flanges, rise vertically, and make two 90 degree turns and return to the deck on the other side of the boat. The horizontal pipes would support the longitudinal supports for the flooring that would be the flight deck. The forwardmost support would have one pipe from the prow up vertically and two others running at an angle from the prow out the edges of the flight deck.

"How much did you give for the flooring?" I asked. "Well, Billy Bob said if I would come out to the job and help carry it out of the house he was working on, he would give it to me, and I found a bucket of rusty screws at the flea market for a two dollar bill to use to screw the flooring to the long 2"x4"s. The screws are a little short, but they should work anyhow."

I stopped to look over the project on my way home several hours later and Tightwad had already left for the day. The pipe supports were all in place. One set was mounted just forward of the transom, one set just forward of the windshield, one set in between, and the last support was at the prow.

The vertical pipes were about four feet long before they turned 90 degrees to go from side to side. There were 2"x4"s laying on the four inch side running from front to back and there were some pieces of flooring laying loose on top. The long members had j-bolts holding them at the rear and a single screw through the pipes on the rest of the cross members. If my grandfather could have looked at the project, he would have said that it was a shame that the builder couldn't afford a square or a good measuring rule to work with but, as Tightwad said, it don't have to be pretty. I really wondered if it would stay together at all.

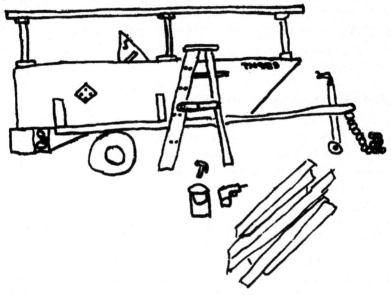

Big Charley and Tightwad took the boat out after the deck was completed and Charley said that the longer they kept the engine running the better it seemed to run. He wasn't sure that the flight deck would hold up an airplane, but it did make a good sunshade.

The Warthog was working hard at learning to fly his new ultra light. He had discovered that the most the new boat could do was about twenty miles per hour and the slowest that he could fly the ultra light was thirty. The shortest roll out on a no wind day was about ninety feet for the Warthog because the brakes on the little bird were more decorative than functional so he needed some arresting gear. He had rigged a hook attached to the tail wheel of the little bird and laid out some rope on the runway to catch. The rope was attached to some sandbags which were dragged along to stop the plane. He got so he could catch the rope most of the time.

The plan was to put the rope on the rear end of the sun deck on the houseboat and rig it so that when the plane hooked the line it lifted several bags of sand. The further the rope was pulled, the more sandbags it had to pick up.

Tightwad finally found an ultra light that he was willing to buy. It was a lot like the boat. It had been rode hard and put away wet. The engine was leaking oil all over the place and the tail surfaces were bare. According to the two sheets of paper which make up the complete pilot's and operations manual, the little bird should take off at 30 MPH, land at 30 MPH, and cruise at 50 MPH. T.W. towed the bird in on a converted boat trailer that the previous owner had cobbled together. It had wing racks for the wings and a folding ramp that you could use to push the little bird up on its trailer.

Zipper commented that if the Warthog didn't build that whole rig he must have a brother. T.W. unloaded the bird and headed out to the flea market for parts. He returned in a little while with a lawn mower and two shower curtains. He removed two wheels and the throttle cable from the mower and hung the rest of the mower on the back wall of the hangar. The wheels had to be bored out a little but they fit after a fashion. The throttle cable was used to replace the choke cable on the little engine.

T.W. then got down to the job of recovering the elevator, rudder, and horizontal stabilizer with the fabric from two yellow shower curtains with pink roses on them. Small Sam asked, "Why didn't you get blue shower curtains to match the rest of the airplane?" T.W. answered, "The ones with flowers were fifty cents cheaper."

The next day Tightwad took the little bird around the field twice and said it flew just fine. When someone asked if he was through practicing he told them that there was no reason to wear the thing out before he had a chance to make some money with it. Zipper commented that he wouldn't want to fly that bird over a dry runway let alone over water.

Saturday was to be the big day. Tightwad and the Warthog were both going to try to land on their own flattops. Willow was to pilot the big barge of a houseboat with Willow III painted across the stern and Big Charley was going to drive the bass boat for Tightwad.

The rules of engagement for the day were that the two boats would proceed up river from the Sky Ranch and reverse course at Senator Davis's dock. When the boats reached the dock the ultra lights would take off and go land on their respective flattops. Each flattop was towing a small rowboat with a video cameraman aboard to record the event. Several other club members brought their boats and were ready to enjoy a day of boating, eating and betting on the big event. We had boat trailers and coolers all over the place.

The Warthog was strutting around in a bright yellow silk flight suit with matching shoes. The Warthog had been bald as a billiard ball for years, but today he was sporting a full head of black hair. The hair piece was a real expensive one and if you didn't know him, you would have to look carefully to spot it.

Just as all the boats were getting underway Senator Davis, with his big houseboat Stargazer II, came around the bend on the south end from Little River and started up river. There were also a couple of other fast looking boats out there that didn't belong to our crew that we later found out were leased by the local TV stations.

Big Bill and Beulah had invited Small Sam and Wilma, Zipper and Genie Rae, and Shay and I to watch the festivities aboard the Yellow Canary IV. Big Charlie's wife, Minnie Bee, was at loose ends since Charley was driving Tightwad's boat, so Beulah ask her along as well. We dropped anchor between Billy Bob and Willy Clyde just as the contenders were getting started.

Big Bill asked, "Do you all have any money down on this thing?" Zipper looked up from his deck chair and said, "I don't, but if I had it would have been on none of the above." "I wish there was a category like that on the ballots. I haven't voted for a candidate in years."

Finally the race was on. The two flattops were moving off up river and the two little birds were poised at the north end of the runway ready to take off into the five mile per hour wind coming out of the south. Willow finally got the Willow III turned around and started down the river. Big Charley gunned the bass boat and headed south as well. The Sky Ranchers in their boats were spread out from the senator's dock to the Ranch but were staying out of the main channel so the flattops would have room to maneuver.

The Warthog took off first and was followed closely by Tightwad. The Warthog got the honors because his carrier was moving more slowly.

The bass boat was making very good time coming down the river so Tightwad didn't have nearly as far to go as the Warthog did. T.W. was getting lined up with his flattop when a crowd appeared on the top deck of the senator's boat which had turned around and was following along behind the Willow III.

The appearance of the people on the top of Stargazer II drew the attention of both of the leased boats and one of them cut in front of Big Charley creating a large wake. Charley had started to slow down some but was still going pretty fast when he hit the wake. The nose of the bass boat came up and the wind got under the flight deck putting a real strain on the screws holding the 2"x4"s to the pipes. When the boat went back down, the front of the flight deck parted company with the frame and started to rotate on the aft support. When the flight deck, still a single unit at this point, stood straight up, a mooring rope which was tangled up in what had been the forward support held it for just a second.

Sandy Swanson, who was videotaping from the rowboat, saw what was happening and dove over the transom. At this point the screws in the flange on the port side of the aft pipe assembly let go and the resulting stress on the short screws holding the oak flooring to the 2"x4"s was too much. The flight deck came apart in one big whoosh. It didn't look like any two pieces of wood hit the water still tied together. Tightwad made a screaming turn to the left and avoided being swatted like a bee with a giant fly swatter.

Willy Clyde, the closest boat, moved out to pick up Sandy. Big Charley, who had lost his straw hat and his sunglasses, was trying to restart the engine on the bass boat. T.W. made a circle over the wreckage and headed back to the Sky Ranch.

When Willow got down the river she saw the mess in front of her and pulled both throttles back to the stops and then reversed them to slow her boat. Her timing was terrible for the Warthog. He was on short final for the flight deck and all of a sudden he had way too much speed. He missed the arresting rope and bounced the little bird so hard on the deck that he left part of the landing gear there as he bounced back into the air.

During all the excitement, a towboat with four empty barges riding high in the water appeared from up river moving south. The Warthog's engine started to blow blue smoke and quit altogether before he could get lined up again on the Willow III. Luckily for him the barges were just where they needed to be and the little bird disappeared down into one of the open barges. It must of been more of a crash than it was a landing. The last we saw of the Warthog, yellow flight suit but sans hair, he was making his way back to the tugboat as it went out of sight around the big bend toward Lenoir City.

Billy Bob took Big Charley in tow and started out for the Sky Ranch just as a hard summer rain hit the area. There was a lot of chatter on the marine radio until Big Bill announced, "There will be a hangar party at the Sky Ranch, bring what you got and we will send out for more. Guys, let the Willow have the first shot at the dock since she is the biggest boat."

Shay picked up the mike as soon as Bill put it down and called, "Stargazer, Stargazer, this is Yellow Canary, over." Sugar Davis came back with, "Yellow Canary, this is Stargazer, how you doing Shay?" Shay returned, "Sugar, we are going to party at the hangar, why don't you come on down?" Sugar asked, "We have some extras aboard, will that be all right?" "The more the merrier," said Shay.

The radio was silent for a moment and then came back to life. "Yellow Canary, this is the tugboat Walter William II." Big Bill picked up the mike and returned to Walter William, "This is the Yellow Canary, over." "Yellow Canary, we have your pilot and his aircraft. The pilot is fine, but the aircraft is a disaster. If you can have a wrecker meet us at the Ft. Loudon Lock, he can pick the plane off before we lock down. Big Bill assured the Walter William that he would have the necessary equipment on hand at the lock. Bill looked at me and said, "Dapper, when we get in, you call One Leg Lilly and have him go down and pick up the Warthog and his airplane."

When I came out of the clubhouse after making the call to One Leg, the plane that had been in the hangar had been moved out, several folding tables set up, and some of the guys were starting to move chairs from the clubhouse to the hangar. I looked out the back window of the hangar at the Willow which was tied up next to the Sky Ranch dock.

Outboard of her, the Stargazer was in the process of putting out fenders and making fast. Something about the picture was wrong but it took me a minute to figure it out. I yelled at Big Bill to come over and take a look. He didn't see it for a moment either and then he let go with, "I'll be goddamned, how in the hell did Earthy Woman's ultra light get on the Willow?"

The little plane was sitting on the top deck just above the flying bridge where Earthy Woman and Willow were sitting drinking a coke. Small Sam walked up, took in the whole scene and said, "Two of our crack, no let me rephrase that, cracked pilots spent lots of time and money and Earthy Woman beat them both! I wonder if anyone actually saw her land on the boat?"

Senator Bobby Lee Davis tapped me on the shoulder and said, "Dapper would you and Shay come down to the boat and meet our guests before they come up to the party? I would like you all to see them before they put on their public faces. They really are nice people, except for one and he is the local in the group."

The rain had stopped before I rounded up Shay. We went down to the dock and went aboard the Stargazer. There we were introduced to Lieutenant Governor Louis Robert (Louie Bob) Gas, Speaker of the House James A. (Jimmie) Rathey, Vice Mayor Quenton Tudberry, and Rufus John (Tex) Johnston of Dallas TX. They were all easy to be around except Tudberry who was way out of his depth and was trying to compensate with bourbon.

"These folks are here to help me set up a project that we can't tell you all about yet but you will know what it is when you see it in the paper in a few days. Tex here is going to be the developer."

In East Tennessee when you are in a group like this where you don't really know anyone, you can safely talk about two subjects. Since these didn't look like Lady Vol Basketball fans, I chose Big Orange Football and we chatted amiably for while. I told them that I was sure that the folks in the hangar would be happy to have more guests and to please come on up and join the party.

On our way off the boat we noticed someone sitting up on the flying bridge and it was Lujacinda and Whizzer Whitmore. They came down to see us and Shay said, "I didn't know you all were on this boat, come on, we are going to a party." Whizzer asked, "Are you sure about this Mrs. K?" Shay took his arm and said, "Whizzer we will introduce you to the people you don't know and the ones who don't like it aren't important anyway."

Shay took Whizzer's arm and Lujacinda was on mine as we introduced them and the politicians to the various groups seated around the hangar. A lot of the guys knew and liked Whizzer but not many of them had met Lujacinda. None of them had met the Nashville politicians and couldn't of cared less. The Whitmores sat with us at a table with Small Sam and Wide Wilma. We were soon joined by big Bill and Beulah, Zipper and Genie Raye, and Big Charley and Minnie Bee.

After the group got comfortable, Small Sam said, "Whizzer I just want you to know that the comment that was made at my table after you and the politicians were introduced was, 'Whizzer has proven that he can de-

liver a Cadillac sized load of concrete and all that the politicians can deliver is a boatload of bullshit'".

Bobby Lee came over in a little while and said that he had to get the
Nashville folks out to Cherokee Aviation at Tyson so they could ride the
state jet back to Nashville and his car was on the other side of the river. I
told him that since I had not had a beer yet I could take them on over there
in 2U and he could go along if he wanted to since there was an extra seat.
He checked with them and they said fine so in a few minutes I had us on
the way over to Tyson. We landed on 5R and taxied right to the state jet
which was parked under the overhang at Cherokee. The guys got out and
headed for the jet.

When Bobby Lee got his safety belt on, I started through the process
of contacting clearance delivery, ground control, and the tower before I
was allowed to take off. Bobby Lee commented after we were in the air
and had been cleared to the Sky Ranch that the process seemed more
complicated than it needed to be. I told him it was just our friendly FAA
looking out for our best interest.

I had just gotten back to the big hangar when One Leg Lilly dropped
off the Warthog in front of the club hangar after putting what was left of
the plane in the Cleveland hangar. He parked his rig and came back to join
the party. I asked him if he had any trouble and he said, "No, but while we
were getting the little bird off the barge the Warthogs hairpiece took a hell
of a jolt. Two of the barge men were helping us and when one of them
shined a spotlight around the bottom of the barge to see if we had left any
loose parts lying around the beam hit something that looked furry.

"They must have been having some trouble with rats on the barges because the other barge man was carrying a shotgun loaded up with bird
shot. He got direct hits with both barrels of his twelve gauge, but the rat
he was shooting at turned out to be a bloodless rat. The Warthog is going
to need a new hairpiece."

"I'm a little surprised that you took the job, knowing how you and the
Warthog don't get along," I said. Leg replied, "He'll know how I feel
about him when he gets the bill."

"What got him so high up on your list anyway?" I asked. "He made
some comments a while back about Jimmy Crowe and Indian blood that
just set my teeth on edge and I ain't been able to get over it since Jimmy
died," replied Leg as he finished a hamburger.

I was fixing myself a sandwich from what was left on the table of goodies when the Warthog came up and started doing the same. He said, "You know, it hasn't been the best day I ever spent. First I bust up my airplane and have to ride all the way to Loudon Dam on a slow boat to China. Then when I get back Willow tells me that Earthy Woman has landed her ultra light on my own boat in a driving rainstorm for the first houseboat landing, and then Tudberry tells me that I just missed a chance to talk with the Speaker of the House and the Lieutenant Governor. I tell you Dapper, it just ain't been my day."

He looked like it too. His yellow silk flight suit was ripped and dirty and all that was left of his fancy head of hair was a couple of spots of glue still clinging to his bare scalp. From the looks of him, the barge that he crashed in must have been used to carry coal. I felt a little sorry for him, so I told him that the big time Dallas developer, Tex Johnston, was still here somewhere. He brightened up a little, said thanks, and hurried off to find the Texan.

As the party stretched into the night, the median age of the group in the hangar dropped by the hour. The older crowd sought shelter where it was quieter. We ended up sitting up on the top deck of the Stargazer with Sugar and Bobby Lee Davis, Genie Rae and Zipper Thomas, and Beulah and Big Bill Henry. We were joined by Lujacinda and Whizzer Whitmore in a short while.

I asked if anyone had seen Tightwad's flight deck come apart right in front of him and Whizzer responded that he was looking right at it when it just seemed to explode. He said that shape changed from a rectangle to a diamond and then was gone in an instant. Sugar added, "It came apart like a hairdo in a high wind." "Yes, Tightwad was a lucky man. If he hadn't made the turn when he did, he would have met the deck head on," added Bobby Lee.

Zipper asked, "Did anyone actually see Earthy Woman land on the Warthog's boat?" Sugar replied, "I didn't see her until she was about ready to touch down. She must have been afraid of the rain that was falling over on the landing strip and decided to land on the boat which was still in the clear at that time. She barely got stopped before the rain enveloped the whole boat."

Zipper added, "I guess if you don't know that something is very difficult to do, that makes it a lot easier. I sure would like to have that on tape to show the Warthog." Bobby Lee offered to check with the TV folks to see if they happened to catch the action.

Shay asked Beulah if she had talked to the big Texan, and she said that she did and learned that he was actually from Oneida, Tennessee, and that his uncle had worked for the Big Senator from Huntsville for years. Beulah continued that, when the Texan had mentioned the 'big senator' from Huntsville, Tudberry, who was in the group, looked like he was going to fall to his knees, face Huntsville, TN and repeat his oath to the Grand Old Party.

"Bobby Lee," I asked, "Have you had a chance to get even with the Warthog for that little piece of business with your car?" Bobby looked around a little and told us how he got his revenge, "The project that all these people were here about today involves a lot of real estate which has to be purchased and or taken if they don't want to sell and for that there has to be a Realtor to do all the work. I wrote the contract so that Bumper Bailey of Bagwell Realty, not Bumper Bailey as Bagwell Realty, will be the big dog in all of this action that will be coming up. The Warthog won't make an issue of it because he, through Bagwell, will still get good publicity but Bumper will get most of the money."

The two big engines on the boat came to life mumbling softly in the night air and Sugar looked up and said, "We have kept Whizzer up long past his bedtime and he has to work tomorrow. He needs to get us back up the river so they can pick up their car at the house."

"Does he usually operate the boat for you?" Shay asked. "Not usually. Always. He has 99 out of every 100 hours that the boat has on it. Bobby Lee and I are both helpless when it comes to running a boat this big and Whizzer seems to know where every inch of it is all the time. When we first got the boat he was going to run it until Bobby Lee got the hang of it, but it just worked out so well with Whizzer running the boat and Cindy taking care of the kitchen that we couldn't change it. We need the help, they can use the money, and we all enjoy the friendship."

The group started breaking up and Shay and I headed up the path from the dock past the hangar to the parking lot where we had the van parked. As we passed the porch of the clubhouse Quenton Tudberry was stretched out on one of the benches snoring loudly. I mentioned to Shay that I didn't mind seeing Tudberry like this, because even he couldn't steal anything in his present condition.

MYSTERY SOLVED

I had been out flying 220 for a test hop after Izzy completed a 100 hour inspection. The bird came out with no problems except there was a little more static on the radio than there should have been and I suggested that Izzy check the com antennae for a loose connection or some corrosion. Big Charley and Bill were sitting with their backs to the door working on their favorite project as I came in. After I opened the office to get the checkbook so I could pay a few bills I sat down at the other end of the table just in time to hear Bill tell Charley that there just didn't seem to be anyone left on the damn list. Everyone in the club had an alibi for the night in question.

They continued to worry that bone while I wrote checks. The next time I looked up the Warthog had come in and was standing unnoticed behind Bill and Charley. He had heard enough of the conversation to know what they were up to and interrupted them by saying, "You guys are barking up the wrong tree. The person who did it is not in the club. I've know since two days after it happened who did it."

Big Bill looked like all the air had been taken out of his sail when he asked, "Who the hell was it?" The Warthog responded, "When I went up to look at the truck, someone had taken a broom and wiped out all of the footprints that had been around the truck. Later I found prints in the woods where the flex pipe was placed to carry the stuff from the truck down to the pool. There were lots of footprints but they were all left footed."

Charley and Bill said in unison, as if it had been rehearsed for days, "I'll be goddamned, it was One Leg Lilly!" The Warthog continued, "Yes, it was Leg, and I deserved what I got. Leg was around the day I tried to make one of those funny passing comments about Jimmy Crowe's wife, that just came out very poorly. You guys are so good at the one-liners about everything and I know that I can't do them, but every now and then I just can't seem to help myself and I try another one. Someday maybe I'll learn to keep my mouth shut."

"Does One Leg know that you know?" asked Bill. "Oh yes," responded Grover, "I went to see him after I figured it out so he wouldn't have to worry about it. I told him not to say anything about it because I knew you guys were having so much fun with the mystery." Big Charley said, "I never saw a one-legged man ride a motor, but then One Leg Lilly ain't what you'd call the average one-legged man."

Everyone but Bill and I had left for the day and we were sitting on the porch of the clubhouse when I said, "Bill, the way the Warthog handled that whole thing and some of the things that he said sure does put a different slant on my opinion of him."

Bill added, "Yes, he seems to be a pretty decent guy trying to overcome his raising, and only being successful part of the time. That probably makes him just like the rest of us. We are only successful at what we want to do part of the time.

"You know Dapper, this is an interesting group around here. I wonder what they will do next to entertain us?"